THE MUSE'S TOUCH

THE WAYWARD SHADOWS BOOK 1

P. STORMCROW

For the dreamers and the fighters.
To the storytellers and the outcasts
Carry on. Carry on.

If we shadows have offended,
Think but this, and all is mended —
That you have but slumbered here
While these visions did appear.

— WILLIAM SHAKESPEAR, "A MIDSUMMER
NIGHT'S DREAM"

CHAPTER 1
Paige

The interview was almost over and Paige Summers, erotic romance writer, couldn't wait.

"So, one last question. Where does your inspiration come from? Especially for your steamier scenes. As a fan myself, I can attest to your books having vivid imagery!"

They sat on a park bench shaded by the large oak tree beside it. A pleasant spring breeze rustled the leaves above, even as faint children's laughter drifted from the playground a distance away. She hoped the camera didn't pick up that sound. The wholesome image seemed almost at odds with this interview.

Paige closed her eyes for a moment and drew air deep into her lungs. She did so enjoy being outdoors. It reminded her of last night's episode where he had laid her down on a park bench such as this.

Paige snapped her eyes back open and gave a brief smile. If she remained calm enough and didn't blush, she could pretend she was planning her response with careful consideration. Paige had expected this question all along and had crafted an answer in her mind beforehand. One does not go unprepared to an interview with one of the biggest YouTube channels (for romance book reviews), at that.

"First of all, thank you Jess, for being a fan. I'm not sure how my muse would feel if I gave all his secrets away." She laughed and waved a hand in the air, even as her interviewer's eyes grew round in excitement. "No, my inspiration doesn't come from a real person. It's more of a running joke with some of my friends. To be honest, I think it comes more from observing others and asking the what-ifs."

"What-ifs?"

"Yeah, for example. The other day, at a diner, I saw a couple having dinner with another woman and I asked myself what if they were exploring what a healthy ménage à trois relationship would look like for them?"

"Oh, my. Is that something we can expect to see in one of your future books?"

Paige winked. "Ah, that would be a spoiler, wouldn't it?"

They shared a laugh before Jess extended her hand. "Well, thank you so much for your time today and for sharing a glimpse into your writing process."

Paige accepted and offered a firm grip. "Thank you for having me. It's been an honor."

Jess nodded in acknowledgment and turned to the camera. "Paige's next book, *Heated Nights*, comes out this August. Remember to leave a comment for your chance to win a signed copy of the first in the series, *Colored Dawns*. Stay tuned as we review the hottest romances coming out this month."

The cameraman held up his fingers, using them to count down from three. Then he made a slicing motion with his hand. "And we're good."

"Thank you so much again." Jess turned with a beaming smile.

Paige shook her head. "Not at all. It was my pleasure."

"Well, I won't hold you up. You'll send me that advance copy of *Heated Nights*?"

"Definitely." Paige picked up her book bag and slung it over her shoulder. "I'll email you when the copies come in."

"Great, thank you."

Paige waved and turned to leave. She couldn't wait to get out of there. The persona she put on to drum up publicity was a far cry from her true personality. From the uncharacteristic flowy printed blouse and figure flattering pencil skirt to her charming manner, Paige performed a role. One which she assumed was part of living up to the image readers have of a romance writer. No one wanted to read erotic things from a geeky homebody.

She was eager to wash off all the makeup caked on her face and slip into her t-shirt and jeans. Then a nap. Despite the amount of sleep last night, exhaustion claimed a good part of her. Perhaps it was because of the interview.

Luckily, the park was close enough to walk home. Still, it took another twenty minutes before she closed the door to her modest basement suite and kicked off the inferno heels, nevermind that they were wedges only an inch and a half tall.

The skirt and blouse came off as soon as she made her way to the bedroom, along with the white lace bra she wore underneath. Pulling her old college t-shirt over her head, she hunted until she found her lounge shorts and tugged them on, enjoying the elastic waist.

A quick trip to her bathroom followed, and she emerged with a clean face and contacts exchanged for thick-rimmed glasses. With little ceremony, she flopped down onto her bed, too inviting to resist, and closed her eyes.

"Hello, my little sparrow."

The silken voice caressed her, and goosebumps rose along her bare arms. This was his nickname for her. The first time he came to her in her dreams, she was sitting in a tree full of all kinds of birds. With her light brown hair, tanned skin, and darker acorn eyes, he had told her she reminded him of a little bird herself.

"Shade." Paige breathed his name out like a sigh as she spun around on one heel. It was what he had asked her to call him. *A shade of your dream, shaped by your desires.*

Her feet found the solid ground beneath, but it was beyond what her eyes could discern, covered by a blanket of fog and cloud, raw material for them to mold to their will. Already in his presence, the area surrounding them was morphing into their familiar bedroom. While she was just learning to control her dreams, he seemed to do so with ease. *Makes sense with him being a dream creature.* Or so she reasoned since his explanations were never straight answers.

A bed, covered with deep red silken sheets, dominated the space, posts rising on all four sides to support a rectangular frame on top, all made of dark wood. A soft rug lay at its foot and on the other side, a fireplace flickered. Large French doors lined one wall leading to a balcony that spanned the length of the room, but she could never quite hold in her memory what the view beyond was. Nothing else mattered but the two of them in this space.

He crossed the distance between them, long fingers reaching out to caress her face. Unable to resist, she leaned into his touch to savor the heat he left in their wake. *Oh, the things he does to me with the simplest of gestures.*

Dark chuckles drew her gaze upwards. His amber eyes glowed in the darkness. Despite having fallen asleep in the afternoon, it always seemed to be nighttime here. Not that she visited during the day often.

Come to think of it...

Confusion knitted her brows together. "You don't normally show up in my cat naps."

The straightforwardness of her statement evoked another snicker from him. "You're the one that called for me."

"I did? I was worn out from the interview. Maybe it's

because they asked me where my inspiration was coming from..." Trailing off, she frowned, struggling to remember her train of thought before she'd fallen asleep. "I'm sorry. There's not much time. I may have set my alarm for half an hour."

Her dream lover leaned forward and pressed a feather-light kiss on Paige's forehead. "My poor sparrow, no need to worry. We are here; that's all that matters."

His lips, full of sensuality, curved upwards in an impish grin. "Though, now I am curious. How did you answer that question?"

A particular spot on the floor caught Paige's interest, and she stared at it with newfound intensity. When the silence of Shade's anticipation grew too much for her to bear, she heaved a sigh. "... I said something about not wanting to give away my muse's secret," she muttered beneath her breath.

Shade's laughter came on the heels of Paige's answer and melted her heart, so she pouted to maintain the appearance of being peeved at him for asking.

Two fingers lifted Paige's chin to Shade, and he brushed his lips against the corner of her mouth. "Well come then, let this muse do his job, to inspire his creator, in what little time we have."

Paige should have been too tired for sex. After he had wrung orgasm after orgasm from her last night, she had lain exhausted in his arms. She knew that wonderful ache that only comes from being sated despite being in a dream. But today, rather than remembering the echoes of those aches, her body warmed at the suggestion and sent a shot of heat straight to her core. Her panties grew damp and Paige hoped that, back in reality, she was not laying on her hard-to-wash duvet cover.

Shade led her to the bed and sat down on its edge, pulling her close. "Your scent is so wonderful." He nuzzled his nose along her neck, while he busied his hands by lifting her t-shirt. The warmth of his palm against her heated skin made her body tremble with delight, and her lips parted in a soft moan.

"That's it, my little bird. Let me hear your pleasure." Shade skipped his hands upward, over Paige's flat belly, caressing, giving her light scratches until he was tracing the curves of her breasts with the tips of his fingers.

"Please, Shade." Paige wasn't sure if she wanted to pull away or for him to continue his teasing. Such sweet torture, drawing out the anticipation. *But if that alarm goes off…*

"Patience—" he tugged her shirt upwards inch by inch, then helped her out of it— "only leads to greater pleasure." Shade's hands returned to trail down Paige's sides, his lips pressing against her neck, parting to taste her with his roving tongue.

"You should know this." There was a note of admonishment that made Paige flush and duck her head.

Without another word, Shade spun Paige around and pulled her into his lap. She grew aware of his hardness against her rear and could not help but squirm to rub herself against him. With a small groan and a pass of his hand over her, he dissolved her shorts and panties. Or perhaps she dreamed them away. She wasn't sure and at that moment, didn't care.

"Spread your legs, my sparrow, then hold still," Shade cooed and resumed his lips' administration along Paige's neck, while his breath sent shivers down her spine with every spoken word.

"Please, I have to go soon," she gasped.

"Well then, we better make use of what little we have." He brushed his lips against her skin. "Don't force me to repeat myself." His tone grew more stern, and Paige obeyed without question, her legs parting to straddle him, exposing just how wet she had become.

"Now my sweet, we can begin."

CHAPTER 2

There was something about Paige Summers that he couldn't put his finger on. Her call to him was a siren's song that demanded a response. Never had Davin Murphy, or "Shade", as she had named him, felt any dreamer's summon so keenly.

So when Paige's thoughts of him, from the waking world, carried to the dreamscape as she fell asleep, Davin asked Katelyn, the only employee he had on duty, to monitor the bookstore while he hurried to his small modest back office. It took less than a minute for him to lock the door then compose himself to slip into the trance needed to reach Paige in the intimate realm, a space where they shared a home tucked somewhere between their subconscious minds.

And now Paige was here, where she belonged: in his lap, wet, ready, and more than willing.

"Shade." This time, she said his name with a whimper of need.

Davin felt his pants tighten, but refused to give himself the satisfaction just yet. Instead, Davin scraped a nail up along her inner thigh, enjoying the way Paige struggled to follow his commands. *My little sparrow has a submissive streak in her.*

Davin trailed his hand higher until it hovered above her dripping sex. The scent was intoxicating and for a moment, it tempted him to abandon all control and throw Paige onto the bed and devour her. Instead, he slipped his forefinger down her mound, tracing along her slit, reveling in the way she quivered at his touch.

Paige shifted, forgetting to hold still as her hips rose to increase the pressure of his finger on her slit. With a chuckle at such a delightful reaction, Davin conceded, parting her folds to tease her entrance. The rumble of frustration he felt vibrating from her chest was even sweeter music to his ears.

Davin stroked upward and as he found her little nub of pleasure; he trailed his other hand upwards to cup one breast, testing its weight though he already knew every inch of her body. As he kneaded with increasing pressure, he circled his fingers around the sensitive flesh surrounding her clit, poking past its hood, now straining for attention.

A steady stream of moans spilled from Paige's lips as her hips rocked steadily against his hand. With a wicked grin, Davin summoned tendrils of invisible rope to bind her down, limiting her movements further. Paige groaned, body trembling, so close to the edge. Just a little more-- and then Davin stopped. *Denying both of us for a moment, will make this feast that much richer.*

Paige's head whipped around; eyes wide with disbelief as she tried to escape her bonds. Davin had learned that, when driven far enough, Paige would overcome her shyness and attack him like a wild woman. But this freedom was always followed by guilt, as if the physical aggressiveness was a crime and no amount of coaxing would change her feelings. So, Davin would restrain her when he played and teased. He didn't want to leave any negative emotions for her.

"Shade!" Her tone was a mix of need and exasperation. Later, he might punish her for pleading. That would be fun, too.

"Yes, little bird?" Davin batted his lashes at Paige but could not hide the shit-eating grin on his face, especially when he saw she half wanted to strangle him. "Is there something you need?"

"You." Paige hissed. She changed tactics and ground herself against him, squirming with what limited movements her invisible restraints allowed. Her rear rubbing against his crotch only made his cock harder, straining against his jeans.

Vixen. Davin groaned and nipped Paige's neck, with a growl of warning deep in his throat. "Be still," he snapped, his tone brokering no more misbehavior, and she froze in his lap, only a slight tremor betraying how difficult her body found the order.

Davin's pants vanished. The tendrils released Paige, now that she was obeying, and without another word, he gripped her hips, lifting just enough to guide her onto him. With one swift stroke, he impaled her to the hilt. He needed this.

"Yes, please, please Shade," Paige whispered as she settled, rocking herself again. This time he permitted it, though he kept a hand on her hip. The other snaked across her lap to seek her clit.

Deft fingers found the treasure. Davin shifted to take hold of the sweet bundle of nerves and began pinching without mercy as she rode him. "That's it, my sparrow, use me. Make yourself come."

Davin's control, developed through the ages, was his only saving grace as Paige exploded on him, her body arching, head falling back on his shoulder as her lips parted in a wordless scream. Intense pleasure rolled through her as she crested, her inner muscles holding him so tightly he could only manage small thrusts deep inside her.

Davin drank in every bit of Paige's ecstasy, the energy

filling him in indescribable ways. The euphoria she produced warmed the demon in him.

Paige's orgasms were never a short thing. In his experience, most women's lasted just a few seconds before they grew oversensitive and wanted nothing more of their lover's touch. Not with Paige. Davin could prolong a single orgasm for minutes on end, and her natural endurance made it such that he could play with her for hours and feast on the succession of climaxes.

Paige was the only one who satisfied him like this. Davin had tried to find others. Dependency for a demon was death, but he was already resigning himself to that.

None of it mattered at the moment though, as Davin played Paige's body and listened as her moans became gasps of breaths and her muscles loosened.

"My turn." Davin held her hips with both hands now, intent on bringing her over the edge again, this time with his cock alone.

And then Paige disappeared, leaving him with a throbbing hard member, still glistening with her juices.

Davin groaned and rubbed his face. *Damn that alarm.*

It was an unexpected afternoon snack, yet, despite the full belly, Davin still grumbled in frustration as he emerged from the trance. His mind entertained the thought of unzipping his pants and finishing himself off, but somehow, it didn't feel... proper. This was his place of work and his employee was just outside, after all. Maybe even a customer.

An incubus concerned about propriety. Damn, perhaps Finn and the others from my brood are right, and I'm going native.

Davin rose from his office chair with a sigh and adjusted himself as best he could. A knock on the door startled him and he cleared his throat. "Just a sec."

"A Mr. Turpin's here to see you!" Katelyn called out. His preternatural hearing picked up her footsteps as she walked away.

Right. Davin made his way around the desk to the opposite side of the room, where he unlocked the glass case that held rare editions of books, no longer in print. There was no money in running bookstores anymore, but this modest shop he ran lent him credibility for his other business. Davin's true profit came from finding, and obtaining, rarities for collectors; of which, half of his transactions were conducted online. Along with the decent semi-obscure book sales from the internet , he didn't often have to dip into his reserves t. And it was a sizable sum. Saving for hundreds of years had given him a nice nest egg.

From the cabinet, he retrieved a thin volume. HP Lovecraft's *The Whispers of Yig*. Many knew of his *Call of Cthulhu* but few were aware of the last book the author wrote. It was only half-finished and someone had turned it into a single edition after they found the incomplete manuscript buried in a drawer. That someone may have been him.

Now, work kept his mind off unfinished business. By the time he left his office, he had softened enough that the bulge in his pants was no longer obvious.

"Ah, Mr. Turpin, I presume?"

A wizened old man turned, his hand rubbing the handle of his cane back and forth. "Mr. Murphy?"

The skeptical tone was familiar. Davin's youthful appearance often surprised customers, who came expecting another elderly, or at least a younger person with glasses and a bow tie. Davin knew he projected a bad boy/model image. All incubi play into certain stereotypes, and he was no different.

"Yes, thank you for coming out this way," Davin replied and with both hands, offered the book to the man who reached out with shaky hands.

"Dear Lord above," the man mumbled with reverence in his voice. Given the subject of the novel in the discussion,

Davin wasn't sure if the exclamation was appropriate, but he held his tongue.

"Thank you," Mr. Turpin whispered, then cleared his throat. "Thank you again, Mr. Murphy." He set his cane aside and opened the briefcase left on the bookstore's counter. With light hands, he placed the book within, then withdrew an envelope from his jacket. "As agreed."

Davin accepted it and peered inside at the thick stack of hundred-dollar bills, then nodded even as Mr. Turpin snapped his briefcase shut. "Pleasure doing business. If there's anything else you're interested in, please don't be afraid to call."

"Of course." The old man waved, then picking up his cane, and turned to make his way out of the shop. Davin opened the door for his customer as he said a final goodbye.

The door closed with a tinkling of a bell.

"I don't know why you even have this store. Our sales make only a fraction of what you get with these collectors, and it barely covers its own rent," Katelyn muttered.

"Ah, but that's the fun part of all of this." Davin threw his arms out wide and winked, then turned and waved the envelope at her. "I'm heading to the bank to deposit this. Call me if something comes up."

"Yeah, yeah, boss."

Davin drew in a breath of fresh air as he stepped outside, in better cheer than he ought to be, especially after being cock-blocked by an alarm. But at least he had an extra meal today.

The bank was not far but halfway there, his mobile rang, humming to a violin version of "The Boys are Back in Town".

"Finn."

"Hey bro. What're you up to?"

"Just closed a find. On my way to the bank."

"You and your money. I don't get it. It's not like you need it."

"Ah, but the work is fun. Got to keep things interesting after all these years." Davin chuckled at the age-old argument. Before the bookstore, it was a restaurant (a century back).

"Sure, Dav. Whatever you say. Anyway, speaking of fun, Dante and I are heading over to check out that new bar on Fourth tonight. You in?"

Davin hesitated. It had the potential to cut into his "sparrow" time.

"Dav, come on. Don't tell me you still prefer to feed by prancing through bored housewives' wet dreams. After so long, wouldn't you crave a real taste?"

His brows knitted together in a frown. "Finn, you know I don't feed that way anymore."

"Are you still hung up on Anna? Let it go."

"Finn." His voice deepened with a warning - then he sighed. "Is it a hunt then?"

"Hmm. If the place is hot enough."

"Fine, I'll wingman you guys but don't expect me to join in."

"Thanks, man, you're the best."

"Yeah, yeah. And hey, I don't prance."

Finn laughed from the other end. "See ya at eight tonight."

With that, they both hung up. Davin stared at his phone and shook his head. It was almost unheard of for a brood of higher-level demons, such as the incubi, to be on friendly terms, much less behave as a pack. They hadn't begun like this. But modernization bringing concepts such as feminism and the #MeToo movement was making the hunt harder. They had to evolve to adapt. No longer could they steal into a house and have their way with a human. No, they had to be more creative as hunters and encourage their prey to invite them into their beds. Not that it took more effort, and Davin had never liked, nor subscribed, to the old ways. Seduction was too much fun.

Finn had started it, calling all their brothers and sisters and so, including himself, they were six strong. At first, they were wary, but through the millennia, they had learned to trust and lean on each other. Although none of them knew what had happened to their mother, they were still the best family a demon could hope for.

Though sometimes that meant obligations. Davin huffed a sigh. It was going to be a long, and frustrating night.

CHAPTER 3
Paige

*H**e surged within her, and she cried out in the pleasure at their joining. They soon settled into a steady rhythm and their hips moved together as one. She tightened her grip, fingers interlaced with his above her head as her body strained to pull him in deeper still.*

Paige pushed her glasses back up along the ridge of her nose before she returned to her computer, her fingers flying across the keyboard. Channeling her frustration from the interrupted dream to her writing was pure therapy, even if it meant she would make her poor characters suffer more.

A sudden knock on the door jolted her out of her flow. With a semi-coherent mumble of irritation, Paige pushed her chair back and plodded across the laminate pine floors.

"Paige, I know you're in there!"

If it was anyone else, Paige would have tried to hide and pretend no one was home. But recognizing the voice of her best friend since tenth grade, Ainsley, she opened the door.

With energetic steps and a bounce of golden curls, Ainsley swept into her suite. Paige had always held an admiration for the way Ainsley took up space despite her diminutive form; her presence was truly larger than life. Standing beside Ainsley, even though she was taller, Paige felt meek and awkward by comparison. She had to admit, she modeled much of her author persona after her best friend.

"So, how did the interview go?" Ainsley tossed her handbag on the couch and plopped down next to it, eyes flashing with excitement. Paige had to smile. Her guest was often the first to ask about progress or to cheer her on, and she was also a damn good beta reader.

"It went well, I think. Jess asked for an advance copy of *Heated Nights*, to review, and said she was a fan."

Ainsley squealed and clapped her hands together. "That's awesome! See? All that preparation was worth it!"

Paige nodded and pulled her computer chair over to sit. "Definitely. Thank you." Ainsley, who also was a public relations professional, had insisted they roleplay to practice. Without her, Paige wasn't sure if she would have answered each question so smoothly.

"Well then, we need to go out and celebrate!"

She swallowed hard. Ainsley's idea of celebration often ended with hangovers the next day. "Ains, it was just an interview…"

"With only one of the biggest YouTube channels of your industry! Think: millions will hear about your work."

Rather than becoming excited, Paige paled. Her mind replayed the conversation, nitpicking over whether she said anything regrettable.

"Paige. Paige! Snap out of it!" Ainsley waved a hand in front of her face. "See? You've proven my point. Sitting here by yourself in the basement, dwelling, will not do you much good. There's a new bar on Fourth. Come check it out with me and live a little."

Ainsley was not someone people said "no" to. Or at least

Paige found that to be the case. With a sigh, she nodded her assent. "Okay, you win. Let me take a shower."

"You go do that. I'll raid your closet and get your outfit ready." Ainsley tapped a finger on her lips in thought. "I think for tonight, we want something that doesn't scream trying hard, but not your usual. Didn't we buy you that nice backless black top the last time we were at the mall?"

"What's wrong with my t-shirt and jeans?"

Ainsley leveled her a stare and answered by herding her to the bathroom. "Go."

BY THE TIME they arrived at the bar, Paige was wondering if Ainsley had an ulterior motive. Paige had to admit they looked good. Her best friend was in a pair of waist-high shorts and a rose-pink crop top that showed off her flat tummy, paired with stilettos that gave her at least another two inches. In contrast, Ainsley had dressed Paige in ripped tight jeans that reached just above her ankles, and topped with that drapey dark thing that exposed most of her back. It framed the larger black and white tattoo between her shoulders: a tree of life with birds flying away. That image was likely what inspired the dream where she had met Shade all those years ago.

Ainsley hadn't dressed them up for casual drinks, but to attract. Paige had drawn the line with "helping" at makeup.

Outside of the club, half the city seemed to share their idea as they waited in a line that circled most of the block. At least Paige could see the door from where she was, but it didn't help that she was back in those wedges again. Paige crossed her arms, her mind wandering to the memory of Shade's hands on her. So much for her plans to go to bed early and dream him into existence once more so he would finish what he started.

"Maybe we should just head to another club." They had been waiting for half an hour, and Paige kept casting longing glances away from the building. Even if they got in now, she did not relish how jam packed it would be inside.

A fresh wave of murmurs and whispers rippled through the crowd.

"Over there." Ainsley elbowed Paige, and she followed her friend's gaze. Three gorgeous guys strolled down the street, their pace slow and casual. The shortest of them had an almost cherubic face with a textured crop of light blond hair ending in frosted tips. His grin, and wink to the ladies that met his eyes, however, spoke of a naughty innocence.

Behind him walked two others. The guy closer to the side of the line was lean and tall. With short gelled back nut-brown locks, sunglasses and hands jammed into his pocket, he looked off to the other side, paying no heed to the fawning girls, a complete contrast to his friend's flirtatious manner.

As he moved out of the way, Paige glimpsed the third. Her heart stopped. The mop of dark hair, the almost too pretty face. That hint of the all-around bad boy aura clothed in black jeans and a matching button-down shirt.

Shade.

There was that smirk on his lips as he turned to the ladies and only then did Paige realize his eyes were steel blue, not the glowing amber of her muse's. She exhaled. *Not Shade.*

Their gaze met. Paige could have sworn that his grin faltered for just a quick second, but if hard-pressed, she would admit she couldn't be sure.

"You okay?" Ainsley stepped closer to Paige and whispered, placing one hand on her shoulder.

"Yeah…" It was the only answer she had to give. How could she explain that her muse, the source of all her inspiration, in particular the erotic parts, just took flesh and form before her? *Nopes, not happening.* Still, her gaze followed the trio as they breezed past the rest of the line and with a quick conversation with the bouncers, were allowed entrance.

What. The. Hell.

"Must be some VIP, but I don't recognize them." Ainsley had taken her phone out and her thumbs were hammering at the screen. Paige peered over her shoulder. Her friend was typing up notes and searching for anything that would inform her who they were.

"Ains, that's bugging you, isn't it?"

Paige could tell Ainsley was reluctant to put her device away, but she did anyway.

"Of course. It's my job to know who the movers and shakers of the town are. Three guys that can just talk their way into a brand-new club can't be nobodies." She groaned in frustration. "I don't think they were paying to get in, either. I didn't see anyone slip bills to the bouncers."

Now it was Paige's turn to pat Ainsley on the shoulder. Part of her wanted to know who those men were, too. Okay, she wanted to find out who that one particular guy was that looked so much like her dream lover. Had she seen him somewhere before and had modeled Shade after him in her subconscious? Was he someone she knew in the past? This was driving her nuts. Paige contemplated asking Shade when she saw him next, but that would be silly. How would a guy she invented be aware of something she did not?

"Finally!" Ainsley grabbed Paige's hand as the line moved. As they shuffled through, they both breathed a sigh of relief when the bouncers let them through and relatched the velvet-covered chain behind them. *Velvet-covered chain.* Paige eyed it, wondering if she could work that into her story.

"Come on!" Now that they were in, Ainsley was all action. Soon they had paid for cover and made their way to the bar. The music was hot, and club-goers packed the place, but crowds parted for Ainsley all the same as they squeezed through. In her mind, Paige thanked her friend's superpower as they stood with their first drink of the night in their hands - a rum and Coke for her best friend and a lemon sour cocktail for herself.

Her eyes scanned the room, seeking that male trio, only to travel upwards as if pulled by something. There they sat, at a table on the second-floor lounge. Ready for the bachelors was an ice bucket with a bottle of wine, and in front of it, were three glasses waiting to be filled. A few girls sat with them, one leaning over to whisper to the Shade-look-alike. Paige felt an unreasonable shot of jealousy and had to shake her head.

"Damn. Mystery aside, they're hot." Ainsley sipped her drink.

"I don't know..." Realizing she was grinding her teeth, Paige forced her jaw loose and took a healthy swallow of her drink.

"Hey, doesn't that black-haired guy look a bit like Tobias from your books?"

Paige flushed at that and busied herself by lifting the glass to her lips again. At this rate, she was going to down the entire thing in less than a minute.

"Slow down girl," Ainsley murmured but finished her own drink in one big gulp. "Come on, let's go dancing."

Ainsley garnered attention as soon as they hit the floor. Who could resist her vivacious friend who, despite her smaller form, seemed to have legs that went on for miles? Paige herself, however, was content to just let loose, allowing the beat of the music to wash over her as she swayed her hips.

Someone stepped up from behind and the heat of his body radiated against her back. He was close, so close. And then she felt it, hands on her hips. Paige's head whipped backward, with the full intention of telling the guy off, but the words died in her throat.

It was the near white-haired one from the trio - and meeting her eyes, gave her the most charming smile, a mix of delight and mischief. When she didn't sock him right away, he leaned forward to whisper in her ear.

"Whoops, caught."

Paige could not help but laugh. The laughter, however, died off when the Shade-look-alike approached, hovering over both of them, lips set in a tight line.

"Hands off, Finn."

CHAPTER 4
Davin

*W*hat *is she doing here?* Davin struggled to maintain a neutral expression as he watched Paige make her way to the dance floor. When their eyes had met for that brief instant outside the club, he almost faltered in his steps, and it took all his years of acting to keep up appearances. But his brother, Dante, had noticed and turned with a glance towards him, one brow lifted in question, just above his sunglasses. In return, Davin had responded with a barely perceptible shrug.

The rest of the night felt forced. Instead of enjoying the company of the surrounding females, Davin gritted his teeth and managed to not shove away a girl leaning on him. For some, these women with their glittering dresses and careful makeup were the epitome of beauty and desire. Yet, his mind only circled around his "sparrow", now so close and within reach. He wanted nothing to do with anyone else, no matter how attractive.

Finn lounged, flashing a charming grin here or whispering in one of the woman's ear there, but Dante had fallen into complete silence. With more ladies than any of them could pay attention to at once, many of them chatted amongst themselves. It grated on his nerves, like magpies that wouldn't shut up.

Davin knew his brothers could not help themselves. Incubi secreted a sort of pheromone that drew prey to them, heightening attraction and arousal. Over time, their kind had gained the ability to leash the natural phenomena to blend with humanity. For the three of them in particular, it also kept the hunt more interesting.

Still, it took a low-level conscious effort, and it was never a hundred percent. It meant that the ones looking for hookups in the first place lost all their inhibitions, such that they had no qualms about throwing themselves at the men, doing whatever they could to vie for attention. A tinge of guilt prickled at Davin's soul. It made the idea of bringing any of these women to his bed even less palatable, because he would be taking advantage of their vulnerability

"I'm heading down. The blonde one with her friend there." Dante spoke in a low voice, leaning in to make himself heard to Finn.

"Those two dancing? Sure, I'll go with you." Finn grinned and Davin's interest was piqued. It wasn't often Dante made a move on his own.

His blood, however, ran cold as he followed their gaze. They were all staring down towards Paige and the woman she was with. Ainsley, or Ains. He remembered his sparrow talking about her friend.

No! Davin screamed on the inside, but held himself back, as he racked his brain for an excuse. Then it was too late. His brothers made their way down and approached the pair, leaving him alone to fend off the women who were now pouting, realizing that they only had one left to fight over. It was part of a wingman's job - being the sacrificial lamb.

Blood roared in his ears as he watched Finn sidle up to

Paige. *Mine. Mine. Mine.* His brothers will respect his claim. He just had to make it clear. Appearances didn't matter anymore.

"Excuse me," he muttered, and this time, shoved the woman for real. With preternatural speed, he wove his way through the crowd, only slowing as he approached.

"Hands off, Finn." There was an unmistakable primitive growl in his voice.

Finn pouted, but the glint in his eye spoke of a readiness to challenge his stake. Despite his temper, Davin wouldn't blame him. For all intents and purposes, Finn had first dibs on the prey. And just because Davin had fed on her before, didn't mean she wasn't fair game for others. The only long-term claim incubi would recognize was "mate" status.

Shit, why am I acting like she is my mate?

Before any of them spoke another word, Ainsley stepped up to them and tugged at Paige's arm to draw her attention. "Come on, let's take a break and grab a drink." Her eyes were sparkling as she gestured to Dante standing behind her. "He's buying."

The men both stood their ground, now glaring at each other. From the corner of his eye, he noticed Paige swallow hard, then eyeing Ainsley, as if trying to figure out how to get past them to safety. *Is she afraid of me?* Something in him wilted, but it was Finn that backed off first, with a shrug.

His brother turned to the blonde and winked. "And if it'd please milady, I'll buy the round after." That said, Finn followed Dante and Ainsley, tossing a last look at Davin.

Inside, Davin groaned. That expression promised a reckoning later. Chances were good, that it would turn into the grilling equivalent of a fifth-degree trial.

"Sorry about my brother," Davin muttered, a hand rubbing the back of his head as he swept his gaze across the floor. Anything to avoid her staring, though he knew his colored contacts helped disguise his eyes. But the likelihood of her recognizing him was still high. *What would she suspect? What is going through her mind?*

Did she like what she saw now that he stood before her flesh and blood?

Shit.

"It's okay. I would have spoken up if he went further." A glance showed Paige was also avoiding looking at him. Was she being shy? It was not an uncommon reaction for less aggressive women. Even so, how did they end up as if they were two awkward teenagers at a high school dance? This was unbecoming of an incubus.

"Davin, Davin Murphy." He stuck his hand out. Best to do away with introductions before he forgot and let it slip he knew her name.

"Paige Summers," she replied, reaching to shake it.

She felt warm. Her cheeks flushed, reminding Davin of how he had drawn out that same blush just earlier this afternoon. Unable to resist, he bowed down a little, even as he raised her hand to him, brushing his lips against the back of it. Her taste was as he remembered from their dallies in the dreams and yet, more, at the same time. Her sweetness in the dreamscape paled compared to reality.

Davin needed to go before he lost hold of himself. This was getting dangerous. For both of them.

When he sensed only a stillness from Paige in return, he looked up at last. She was breathless, eyes glazing over. Davin redoubled his efforts and reined in his essence. *Fuck. How can this girl make it so easy for my control to slip? Even as dream lovers, it's only been a meusly two-and-a-half years.*

"Come on, let's go before your friend gets worried." Davin released her hand and placed it on the small of her back to guide her.

"Okay." Paige followed, almost docile in her behavior. Davin had planned to leave as soon as he returned her to Ainsley, but now he was uncertain. In this state, she was too susceptible to suggestions of any kind. Anybody could take advantage of her.

When they caught up, his brothers glanced at Paige, then turned to him in alarm. Rather than shirk away, Davin moved his body to shield his charge as if his stance would ward off any unwanted attention towards her. They would pepper him with questions anyway, so why bother with pretenses?

"Paige?" Davin heard the concern in Ainsley's words and scolded himself once again. He was too old to be that careless.

"Are you okay?" He kept his hand on her back, rubbing slow circles to ground her.

Paige cleared her throat and nodded. "I think so." Her eyes stared at the bar, then she squinted as if trying to regain her focus. His effects would fade soon, but not fast enough for him.

"Um, no." Paige shook her head. "I'm a little woozy."

"Maybe we should go home." Ainsley moved closer.

Home! Going home was a capital idea. It would get her away from him and she wouldn't be so vulnerable. Davin was reluctant to cede territory but recognized her friend was best for Paige right now.

"Yes, if you aren't feeling well, head home and rest." Davin softened his voice, putting in just enough power to push the suggestion into both girls' minds. He disliked using his ability to influence human thoughts in normal circumstances, but at this moment, he would use every tool at his disposal to keep her safe.

"Yeah, okay."

"Let me help you get a cab."

"Come on, Paige." Ainsley kept a hand on her pal's arm.

Davin turned to his brothers. Finn was pouting again, but Dante was, as usual, hard to read. "I'll help the girls on their way." Without waiting for protests, Davin herded them towards the door.

"Sorry to be a spoilsport," Paige muttered as Davin cleared a path for them through the crowd.

"It's fine. We can come back another day."

"Okay."

As the cab whisked Ainsley and Paige away, Davin remained to watch until he could no longer see the vehicle. Pushing his hair from his face, he sighed. Perhaps now would be a good time to head home himself. The hunt couldn't have gone worse. Thanks to him.

"Davin."

No such luck.

"We should talk." Whatever retort Davin had, died in his throat. Something moved in Dante's eyes, something that said he owed them an explanation.

"Fine, but not here."

And that was how the three of them ended up in Davin's penthouse apartment, overlooking the city skyline.

"Okay Dav, what the hell was that?"

Finn exploded as soon as they stepped into his home. "I thought you weren't interested in feeding this way."

"Finn, calm down." Dante placed a hand on the shorter incubus' shoulder and gripped none too lightly. Of the three of them, Dante had the most physical strength and was the better fighter. Combined with his level-headedness, he had become the brood's de facto peacekeeper.

Davin stared out the window towards the network of city lights shining below them, his back facing his brothers for fear of the judgment he was about to see on their faces. Try as he might, though, he could still glimpse their reflections on the glass. "Paige Summers. Age 28. Erotic romance novel writer. Quit her lucrative job at a large accounting firm to make a serious go of her writing four years ago today. She hit it big two years ago."

Finn paled. "What?"

With another heavy sigh, Davin turned. "I've been visiting

her dreams for a while now. She thinks I'm someone she conjured up to be her muse." He braced himself.

Both Dante and Finn stared at him, eyes round, mouths hanging open. *Great, they are in shock.*

"You've been feeding on the same human all this time?" Dante was the first to recover enough to speak.

"It's different in the dreamscape." It sounded like a feeble explanation even to his own ears. *Time to fess up.* "There are others. But yes. I've been with her for over two years." He didn't want to call it feeding because it wasn't just "feeding". She wasn't prey.

"What is she to you? A pet?"

"No," Davin snapped back. "She's human, with brains and smarts, just like us. Paige's not some livestock." He wanted to smack Finn but refrained. *What is she to me?*

"Are you…" Dante started.

"No!"

"Dav, it never ends well to bond with a human. Remember Anna?"

"Shut the fuck up about Anna. Paige is nothing like her!" Davin thundered. His eyes glowed despite the contacts, and his apartment shook as his powers unfurled.

"Davin." Dante stepped towards him, raising himself to full height. "Calm. Yourself."

It took minutes before the glow faded. The temporary rise of his magic left his breathing shallow.

"You know we're worried about you. This is what having a family means. We ask each other the hard questions so we can keep each other safe." Dante's low voice rolled through him.

"Dav, I'm sorry." Finn stepped up from behind. Gone was the mischievous boy persona, replaced by genuine concern. Sometimes Davin forgot he was the youngest of them all. "I just don't want to see you hurt by another human again."

"I know." Davin rubbed his face. "I never expected to

meet Paige in person. Tonight took me by surprise. I'm sorry."

Dante patted his back as soon as he closed the distance between them. "I think some space from this Paige may be a good idea until you figure things out. Go feed on some others you visit for a while."

He hated to admit it, but Dante was right. He did not relish meeting up with Paige right now. What if she started questioning him as Shade?

"Yeah, okay," Davin agreed and gave his brothers a weak smile.

Nonetheless, he would miss her.

CHAPTER 5
Paige

He didn't come to her.

Paige opened her eyes but left her arm over her face. In the darkness of her room, all she heard was the comforting tick tock of an old wall clock she had bought in a garage sale.

Why couldn't she wish him back into existence?

With a soft groan, she shifted to her side and reached beside her bed until she found her phone. She squinted as the light came on. Five o'clock. It was way too early in the morning.

Disappointment sat like a lump in the pit of her stomach as she tossed and turned, but by now, sleep eluded her. She had been looking forward to seeing Shade. It wasn't even the sex. After meeting his double in real life, all she wanted was a cuddle and comfort to wash away the haze of confusion that clouded her mind.

He didn't come to her every night. So this may have been a lapse. *That must be it*. Paige sat up and slapped her own cheeks with both hands. *No use dwelling*. The extra hours would be useful to do some upkeep, reply to emails, and write a new blog post for that book tour.

Paige paused as she slid off the side of her bed. Something was off. Her skin crawled. Her eyes darted back and forth around her bedroom, trying to pick out anything that seemed out of place. The shadows formed odd shapes across her furniture, but everything else appeared as it should be. So why did unease chill her blood? With agonizing slow movements, afraid to draw some unseen attention to herself, she bent her knees until she reached under her bed. A minor sense of relief helped her breathe a little easier when her hand grasped the wooden baseball bat.

With it cocked and ready, she began exploring her room. Swept. Cleared. Next. All those action movies she binged the other night were helping.

Paige emerged and jumped at a dull thud that rattled her door. Another one. It sounded like a body slamming against the thick planks, over and over. The wood creaked in protest.

She wished she had a back door. Or even windows big enough through which to escape. *Nopes, no such luck.* The only other exit available led to her landlady above, and being upstairs was too exposed. Another thud, then another, this time in quicker successions. At this rate, the door would not hold. She dove back into her bedroom and grabbed her phone, readying a call to 911. And then came a loud whine. *There is no way a human throat made that sound. A large animal? In the middle of a city? Wait, should I be calling wildlife control instead?*

The noise stopped suddenly. Silence resumed. Hands still shaking, Paige clutched the bat, the makeshift weapon looking even more ridiculous at what she may be up against. But it was better than nothing. She pocketed her phone, then ventured out. One step, then another.

Something made her look up at the half window that showed above ground. A glimpse, that was all it took. Paige pressed herself flat against the wall underneath the glass with haste, her hand lifting to cover her mouth lest the screams of terror that threatened to spill out, did.

Malevolent red orbs peered through the glass before the creature lifted its head to show a grotesque maw dripping with spit, and fangs protruding past lips that stretched to points in a permanent macabre smile. It snarled like a dog, but it was nothing like any canine Paige had ever seen.

Paige squeezed her eyes shut, clutching the bat to her chest, willing herself to be still, to be invisible. Her mind blanked from the terror. There was no deity she'd pray to, the atheist she was, but oh how she wished Shade was real and was here to protect her.

"Please, please, please," she mouthed without a sound, wishing the creature to leave. It panted. Paige heard it heaving through the window. And then, with a chuff, it padded off.

Paige stood, rooted to her spot for a good fifteen minutes more, listening for any sign of movement. Forcing herself to step away from the wall, she glanced around again. Nothing. Instead, the first notes of a bird song that heralded the dawn. Only then did she find the strength to loosen her fingers to let go of the bat. It dropped to the rug beneath her feet with a heavy thump.

She winced at the sound, then swept her gaze across the room, anxiety peaking. No scary dog returned. As rays of the early sun shone through the window, Paige slumped on the couch and sighed. Maybe she was dreaming? Oh, how she hoped that's what it was. More like a nightmare, though, or a maybe a hallucination? Her mind sped to rationalize as she sat, still in a stupor. With a hesitant touch, she reached up to test the temperature on her forehead. No fever, but perhaps she had eaten or drank something funny. She remembered not feeling well the previous evening. *Yes, that must be it.* With everything explained in a tidy little box, she focused more on her breathing. In. Out. In. Out. Her shoulders, achy from holding tension all night, eased at last.

As the morning progressed and the immediacy of the imagined attack lessened, she became functional again.

It was too nice a day to spend it indoors. As fingerlings of sunlight reached across her suite, the earlier horrors faded. By the time she emerged from her shower, Paige was once more ready to tackle the world. With a nod of determination to put the night behind her, she got dressed, packed her laptop in her backpack and readied on her quest outdoors for coffee and breakfast.

The first steps out of her apartment stole Paige's breath. She stood, frozen in fear, her heart racing as if it wanted to crawl out of her throat. The lawn was a mess, deep track marks having ripped the grass to shreds. The flowerbeds tended by her landlady upstairs with living care, lay dead and tattered. But, worse- they weren't just destroyed. They seemed to have wilted overnight. Paige took one step back as she hyperventilated, stumbling over a displaced rock from the flowerbed. Her hand reached out to brace against the frame and her head turned as it landed, unexpectedly, on rough splintered wood.

From this view, Paige could see that something had rendered large diagonal marks into the entryway, as if some creature was trying to claw its way into her suite. A bear? No, the scratches were grouped in threes rather than fours and sank much deeper than she thought possible. But, what other kind of animal would venture this far into the city? Paige's mind could rationalize a lot of things but confronted with undeniable proof; she had to concede that something unnatural happened in the wee hours of the morning.

She should be gibbering in terror. Instead, she stepped back into her unit with a kind of numbness settling in and closed the door, ensuring all the locks were in place. The creature had tried to get in but wasn't able to, so it stood to reason that home was the safest place. *Perfectly reasonable explanation.* Her trembling hands were the only indication of an impending nervous breakdown.

A sudden knock, this time on the back door that led upstairs. Paige's heart jumped to her throat.

"Paige? Paige, dear. It's Lillian."

She scrambled to unlatch the lock.

"Oh, thank heavens you're up and okay."

Her landlady stood before her, silver hair poking out of the loose bun, a wide apron over a flowery dress. Large and portly, Lillian was the image of everyone's favorite grandmother and in some ways she behaved that way. When she saw Paige, her eyes lit up as they always did.

"Lillian," Paige started, turning sideways to gesture towards outside.

"Oh, I know, dreadful thing, isn't it! I'll call the city today to report it. Must be some poor animal, half-starving with madness. Never mind that. Fancy struck me this morning for pancakes, and I made too many. Would you care to share some with me?"

The upstairs still felt too exposed, and Paige wasn't sure she had the appetite to eat, but her stomach rumbled right on cue, proving her wrong.

Lillian laughed. "Very good then, come along."

Breakfast helped settled some nerves, enough that Paige was a semi-functioning adult for the rest of the day. But by night, the worry returned in full force. Paige tossed and turned in her bed. Every time she closed her eyes, all she saw were the glowing red eyes and grotesque grin as if they were mocking her, daring her to sleep. Paige gave up, changed back into her jeans and t-shirt in case she had to make a run for it and ended up sitting on her couch, baseball bat in hand, remaining vigilant in her watch for the creature's return.

Paige remained in this mode for three days and nights. Unwilling to leave the house during the day, unable to sleep at night, by the fourth cycle, her eyes were bloodshot and the thought of another attack frayed her nerves to the point of startling at every little noise. She had placated Ainsley with false cheer over text messages, unwilling to drag her friend into danger, but otherwise, she was unsure of next steps. This pattern could not continue.

Paige conducted research, and was still reading up on folklore and superstition, trying to track down any description of what she may have seen when, exhausted to the bone, when she finally nodded off, slumped in her office chair.

She was in some kind of maze but instead of trimmed tamed hedges, brambles forced her path with every twist and turn. Hesitant at first, Paige remained rooted to her spot until she picked up a snarl, reminiscent of last night. It set her feet to a mad scramble as she sprinted down this way and that. Anything to escape from whatever was making that sound. There were no choices, no junctions for her to pause and consider, so she ran where it led her. At least the noises faded further away as she sped through. She must be moving in the right direction.

And then she stopped. Dead end. This time in her dreams, Paige froze as her sick subconscious treated her to a full view of the creature. Midnight-dirty, matted, fur covered its emaciated body, which was the size of -at least- three times larger than an adult Saint Bernard. It had four legs, a tail and pointed ears like a dog, but that was where the resemblance ended. Fortunately, with its back turned away, it spared Paige the sight of its grotesque face. Unfortunately, the monster was gorging on something, something so far gone, that there was no saving its life.

This was a dream. Paige tried to exert her will, to shape her surroundings as Shade had taught her. Nothing. Okay, she would deal with this. She couldn't die in this nightmare. The reasoning gave her enough courage to move her feet. If she backed away ever so slowly...

Like something straight out of a horror movie, the body the monster was still devouring moved. A head turned, vacant eyes opening to stare at her.

Paige's mouth opened in a wordless scream. Her. The beast was eating _her_.

Caution and any other semblance of logical thought fled from Paige's mind. She spun around to run and smacked straight into a powerful chest. When she found her voice once more, she screamed. As arms surrounded her, restraining her, she flailed, fists pounding against an immovable wall.

"Paige. Paige!" The words, spoken by a male, broke through her terror and she stared up in shock.

Shade. Oh, thank God.

CHAPTER 6
Davin

$\mathcal{D}$avin had tried so hard to stay away, knowing nothing good could come out of his prolonged dallying with Paige. The more time he spent with her, the more their affection for each other would grow. For him, it had already gone too far, even knowing there was no future for them. So, the only logical step was to cut off all contact, never mind that every other woman, he tried to be with, paled in comparison. Ghosting as an option, sat uneasily with Davin but at least he wasn't dooming Paige to fall for an immortal demon for real.

Davin imagined this was what amputation felt like. A phantom pain haunted him, pangs that would only remind him of her absence. *No, I have better control than this.* It was for the best. Davin kept trying to convince himself of that.

Four days later, in the middle of Davin shelving a new shipment of books, the distress call came. Even in waking, he heard Paige, sensed the sheer terror in the way her mind screamed for him through the dreamscape. Without hesitation, he stepped into the realm she created, only to stare in shock at the scene unfolding before them.

Before the inugami could react, Davin wrapped his arms around Paige and took them away, back to the familiar, and safe, walls of their bedroom. Minutes passed as Paige kept her face buried against his chest. Davin's preternatural hearing picked up her heart's drumming as adrenaline continued to course through her veins, even in the dream state. Davin extended his control to prepare the bedroom by lighting the fireplace with his thoughts.

"Shade?"

He looked down at his little sparrow, relieved to have her in his arms once more even when he knew how wrong this was. Just until she calmed down, he promised himself.

Paige's heartbeat began to return to normal. As color returned to her face, Davin felt her lean back and so he loosened his hold. Davin watched as she ventured a glance around her surroundings.

"Little sparrow." One hand rose to cup her cheek, the pad of his thumb stroking her cheekbone. With each pass of his finger, he tapped into his power to influence her mind, just a small push to instill calm to help her deal. Slowly, Davin sensed her fears receding as he tried to dull the horrors she had just witnessed. Paige's eyes fluttered shut. She looked exhausted. *Has she slept at all these past few nights?*

Davin's own mind, however, was still reeling from what the scene, with so many questions crowding for answers. Like, *what the hell was an inugami doing in her dreams? That was no figment of her imagination. I sensed the malevolence of the monster as it had come to the dreamscape to terrorize and break her mind.*

"Paige, look at me."

Her eyes snapped open, surprised at his serious tone. *Good, I have her attention.*

"Paige, this is important." He kept his voice inflections

even, and was soft-spoken, so that he could keep up pretenses, and make Paige think the creature was just another thing she had conjured up, in the same way her mind had created him. If Paige realized any of it was real, her mind may break all the same and he would just be finishing the inugami's job for it. "Tell me, where have you seen a dog like that before?"

Paige's body gave a great shudder and Davin's stomach sank. Had he overstepped? Would she wonder why he asked? He'd cross that bridge when he got to it.

Paige tilted her head with a quizzical look but her explanation came, all the same, each sentence spoken with reluctance. "The other night. I first heard something outside. It sounded like it was trying to take down the door, and when it couldn't, it started circling the house. I saw it through a window, just the eyes and its fangs." Paige swallowed hard and paused, taking a moment to steady herself.

Despite wanting to know everything right away, Davin waited, calling on what little patience he had.

"Afterwards, I thought I was just hallucinating. I mean, that night had already been crazy enough as it was. I met someone who looked just like you but, after I started feeling off, for no particular reason, and went home early-- so hey, why not a nightmare dog, right?" Her self-deprecating laugh was shaky.

Davin frowned, but was reluctant to interrupt.

Paige winced. "Except when I went outside, I saw the damage. Someone- no, I mean something, had shredded Lillian's garden to pieces. Lillian thinks it's some wild animal, mad with hunger but what I saw..." Her words trailed off.

Davin pulled on a little more power to resettle Paige before she broke into panic again.

So, it had happened the same night he sent her home. There were few moments in his long life that he hated himself for, as much as he did right now. The inugami had failed on a physical attack and was trying a mental one. Paige was in danger. *Why? Has my association with her drawn unwanted attention?*

"Shade? You're scaring me. Say something."

Davin pulled his wandering mind back to focus on the moment. Unable to help himself, he drew his hands to rub both of her arms in an attempt to soothe. "Paige, I need you to trust me."

"Okay."

"Tell me where you live."

Confusion settled in Paige's features. Davin hated himself even more as he pushed her mind further, compelling her to obey without question. He had lasted so long without manipulating a human's mind but now he was making a conscious decision to break every rule he ever held himself to, in order to protect this woman.

"2302 Railway Drive." The answer came slow, and he sensed her resistance pushing back at his influence. Hell, she was strong. Davin spared a moment of admiration for her.

"Good girl." He wanted to pull her into a kiss but held himself back. "I want you to stay there, okay? I'll come to you soon."

"Shade, what do you mean?" Panic edged in her voice, but this time, he refrained from touching her mind. Any more and she could become addicted to the euphoria he creates and lose her wits. And Davin knew well, they would need theirs for what may be coming.

"Fifteen minutes. I'll be there in fifteen." Desperation thickened his voice as he hoped she could hold out till then. And then he had to go.

"Oh my God, Davin. Are you okay?"

He woke to Kathryn hovering over him with concern. It

must have appeared to her as if he had fainted. In his haste to rescue Paige, he had sat down on the floor, next to the bookshelf he was working on, and slumped over as he stepped into the dreamscape. It was no wonder she was freaking out.

"I'm fine." In one swift motion, he rose and waved her off. "I need you to close the shop. You know where the spare keys are. Just slip them back under the door after you're done. I need to go."

He left no explanation despite the shocked look on Kathryn's face. It didn't matter.

Paige lived further away than he liked. If he pushed hard, he could make it there on foot in the short time he promised. But Davin knew he had to conserve his energy; he had to be prepared in case a fight was at hand. He made his way home in record time and within a few minutes, he was roaring down the street with his one-true-love, his sleek, black '63 Corvette Stingray.

The house sat at the end of a cul-de-sac, the front lawn still smelling of soil freshly turned. What surprised him as he got out of his car and approached was the warding he sensed surrounding the innocent-looking two-floored building. It presented only minor discomfort for an incubus but now he understood why the inugami had trouble with its first attack.

Still, it took all his willpower to stand in front of Paige's door. He understood the significance of what he was about to do. After this, he would leave for real, would never see her again, would never sup again on the feast she produced.

Her safety mattered more than what he stood to lose.

The door opened a crack, then wider. Paige stood in front of him, skin pale, hair sticking out this way and that, eyes rimmed with red. She was a wreck, yet she was beautiful.

"Shade?" Confusion marred her face just as in her dreams. "Davin?"

Right, still wearing colored contact lenses.

A door from behind Paige flung open and a large woman entered, brandishing a dagger. *No, an athame.* "Demon!"

Shit.

A low snarl of warning sounded from behind and he half turned. The inugami was back, taking advantage of the cusp of in-between's when day turned to night and their powers peaked. But what it didn't expect was the appearance of a significantly stronger demon. Him.

Davin's face shifted, and he growled back with enough power to make the inugami bow his head and whine. But Davin knew it was a temporary respite. Soon, the monster's hunger for its prey would drive it beyond any self-preservation instinct.

"Paige, we have to go. I promise I'll explain everything." He extended his hand towards her, palm up.

He saw Paige hesitate and glance back at Lillian, who took another step forward, although she herself was shaking like a leaf.

"Please, Sparrow."

Her eyes widened, and he knew he was right in using his name for her.

"But Lillian…"

"It's after you. It'll leave if you're not here."

"Come away from that demon," Lillian called out, offering her own hand to Paige.

"Davin. My name is Davin Murphy and I own a bookshop on 255 Dun Street. There, now you know. Please, you know your wards can't hold out against that thing for long. Let me take her somewhere safe. I can offer better protection. I promise you she will come to no harm while she's under my protection."

Maybe it was the agony on his face, or perhaps it was the recklessness in which he shared his human identity with Lillian, despite her recognizing what he was, but something in her face softened. She lowered her hands and nodded.

"Come on, Paige."

The grotesque dog still hung its head though it maintained a low growl, glaring at them both. As Paige crossed the threshold of the house, placing her hand in Davin's, the inugami leaped.

Davin cursed under his breath, his arm rising to shield them. The creature's fangs sank into his flesh. "Fucking mutt," he cursed with a wince, and despite the dog's size, swung his arm, flinging the inugami away. It slammed into the brick facade of the house with a sickening crack.

"Let's go," Davin urged, and ushered Paige into his car, even as blood wept from his wound. As soon as she was in, he grabbed a spare shirt from the backseat, wrapped his arm, and got in, driving away before the dog could recover.

"Davin. Shade."

It was as if she was tasting both names on her tongue. *What would it be like to hear her scream my actual name in the throes of passion?* Davin growled at himself for such thoughts.

"Where are we going?" It sounded like she was recovering from the shock she must have been experiencing.

"My place. It's better warded. Then we can talk and figure out the next steps."

"You're Shade."

Davin gritted his teeth. "Yes."

"I didn't make you up."

"Yes."

"We've been…"

"Yes."

"That was a demon."

Okay, conceivably, she was still dazed.

"The dog? Sorta. Yes."

"Lillian called you a demon, too."

Damn that witch. "Yes."

"Oh."

Silence filled the car. "Demons are real."

Davin didn't bother to answer but stole a glance at Paige. Yeah, definitely shaken to the core. The last statement, said in a hushed whisper, sounded like a woman trying to convince herself she was not crazy.

"Sparrow..." He extended a hand to touch the back of hers only for her to pull away, her whole body recoiling from him, as much as the seatbelt allowed.

"Don't touch me."

He withdrew his hand, placing it back on the steering wheel.

A heavy pause hung in the air before Paige spoke again. "Don't call me that, either."

He told himself he didn't love her. She wasn't mate material. So why was his heart breaking all the same?

CHAPTER 7
Paige

$\mathcal{U}$ ntil an hour ago, Paige's world was rational. Maybe it had gotten scarier, but was still explainable by rules of science. And now the coincidental look-a-like was telling her he was the same guy as her muse. Oh, God- the things they had done in her dreams.

Paige felt her face redden and sank deeper into her seat.

But that was only a part of her whole confusion. Hit with a series of sucker punches, she wasn't sure which was the worst. In the thick silence that settled in the car, her brain took stock of the situation and made a list.

One: Demons existed. They are real.

Two: Such a creature just attacked her and according to Davin, was targeting her.

Three: Davin is a demon, too.

Four: Davin claims to be Shade. Given his use of her nickname, a private matter she had never spoken to anyone about, she had no choice but to believe him. Okay, fact revision. Davin _is_ Shade.

Five: That meant Davin, as Shade, had led her on, letting

her sink into self-delusion. For what purpose? Just to have dream sex? What other lies had he told her?

It wasn't until he pulled the car into an underground garage of one of the most luxurious apartment buildings in town that she registered that she was riding in a Corvette.

Six: Davin was damn rich.

Of all the additional facts Paige had to process, the last seemed the least relevant. She filed that away for now and returned to the other items on the list. Anger was the first emotion she could name. She was embarrassed for being played. A healthy shot of fear was lurking somewhere in the background. She clung to the seething rage roiling inside her, finding strength in it.

"We're here."

Jolted out of her inner monologue, Paige looked up to see Davin opening her car door. Next he was offering s his hand. She stared at it, then up to his face, schooling her features into a mask of distaste.

WITH A SIGH, Davin took a step backward and withdrew his hand, smoothing his hair back with it instead. It was a gesture so reminiscent of Shade that for a second, Paige's heart softened. But the memory of how she had begged for his touch resurfaced, so she gritted her teeth and got out of the car herself.

It wasn't until Paige stood in the parking lot, arms wrapped around herself, that Paige realized how foolish this was. She was following a complete stranger - *no, worse, someone that lied to her - to his own home.* Her mind had been so focused on wanting answers, she had allowed him to lull her into a false sense of security with his familiar face. *Stupid.* "Hold on. What's the address here?"

"566 Smithe Street. My unit is 4044." There was no hesitation.

Paige dug her phone out of her pocket and typed a brief text to Ainsley.

I'm okay. I can't explain right now, but I am at Davin Murphy's place at 4044 Smithe Street. He's the dark-haired guy we met at the club the other day. I will check in again in 30 mins.

She brandished the device up at him. "Ains knows where I am. If I don't call her in thirty minutes, she will notify the cops." It wasn't enough, but it was the best she could do in these circumstances.

Davin only nodded, though his face fell further. He looked so much like a kicked puppy that a part of her wanted to forgive him. *No. Nuh-uh.* She steeled her will.

"This way." He reached out as if to take her hand, but paused and jammed it into his pocket before turning and walking away. *Good, he got the message and is respecting my space.*

She followed.

4044 turned out to be the penthouse. It was hard to believe some independent bookshop owner could afford this kind of opulence between the over-the-top car and this ridiculous apartment. Not unless he had more than one lifetime to amass wealth. It added more credibility to his impossible story.

"Please. Sit." Letting them in, he gestured towards the long sectional before moving to the open concept kitchen, bustling about. The gallery itself was almost as large as her entire suite.

"No, thanks." The couch was too far away from the door.

There was a weariness as he returned, a mug of steaming hot tea in hand, which he held up to her. "Please spa... Paige."

She stared at the light liquid before other things clicked in her mind and she snapped her head back. "Did you drug me the other night?"

"What? Hell, no! It's not like what you think."

Warning bells sounded in her mind as a sick feeling

settled in the pit of his stomach. *Not what I think? What the hell does that mean?*

Paige had to remind herself that the horrified expression on his face might be an act, even if it was an Oscar-winning performance. If he was indeed a demon, she shouldn't judge by human standards.

"You don't trust me." It was more of a statement than a question.

"Not for a minute. Can you blame me?"

"No." Davin winced. "The other night was an accident. My kind releases a sort of pheromone that puts others in a suggestible state. It happens naturally, but we've learned to keep it leashed. Seeing you in person was a shock and my control slipped. I'm sorry."

Sorry, my ass.

"I have an idea. Wait here. Please." There was that look of desperation again.

Something else nagged at Paige. Davin hadn't taken advantage of her back there. He had pushed for her to go home and didn't visit her in her dreams afterwards. Even now, he could have made her groggy and docile. Instead, she was sure she had clarity of mind, and if he had used his powers, she would not be feeling her fury so keenly. That was the only reason she nodded in agreement.

Davin set the mug on the counter and retreated deeper into the apartment. Left to her own devices, Paige studied his home in more detail.

The kitchen stood to the right of the entryway and opened up to a large living room. Windows lined the other side, a view of the city spread beneath. Further away was a fireplace and beyond that, the space led to a long hall where Davin had disappeared. Clean, modern lines. Not what she expected to find in a demon's home. Not that she'd ever given it much thought

Her gaze came back to the mug at the table. The tea called to her, its subtle aroma inviting. Was this her poison apple?

"Paige."

Davin returned, cradling a large velvet box in his arms. With slow care, he set it down on the counter and opened it. From there, he produced a long dagger, almost spartan in its design, and sheathed in a simple scabbard. He handed it to Paige with a solemn expression.

"This is a pure iron weapon, made back in the 1920s before everything got radiated and tainted. It's something all of us are vulnerable to. Now you can hurt me, as insurance."

Paige took it and unsheathed the sword. She'd like to think she looked badass, but her butterfingers almost dropped the leather scabbard. "Okay. But iron works on fae, not demons." She raised a brow at him.

In response, Davin stepped closer and without warning, wrapped his grip over the tip of the blade. The smell of burning flesh permeated the air, and he hissed at the pain, withdrawing his hand in haste and holding it up for Paige's inspection. The skin around Davin's palm and fingers swelled with angry red blisters.

"I promise you, iron burns. You *can* hurt me."

It took several minutes for Paige to recover enough to remember her anger. Her first instinct was to run up and try to treat his injury, to berate him for hurting himself to prove a point. *Dumb male.* Instead, she set her chin and kept the sword up, pointing straight at his throat. Paige knew she was being a cold bitch. But, it was that or give in to the impulse to forgive him. She'd take the bitch.

Davin backed up, giving her space, and raised his hands in surrender.

"Fine, let's go have a seat and have a little conversation." Paige waved the tip of the blade in that general direction.

They settled there, Davin with his back towards the door, and she perched on the edge of the coffee table, facing him, dagger still at his throat as she tried to channel Lara Croft. "Okay, talk."

Paige watched in fascination as his chest rose and fell with a deep breath. Did creatures like him need to breathe or was it to emulate humans? He studied her closely. "The beast or me first?"

"Tough question, but there was a straightforward answer. "You."

"Some call us demons, some fae. We are shadows of humankind, born of your fantasies."

Paige shook her head. "Cut the poetic bullshit. Give me the facts."

"I am!" Davin groaned in frustration. "We have many names. As much as our own lore explains, we existed before humanity, but people's imagination gave us shape, gave us our history and background. We all became distinct races of demons, fae, whatever you want to call it. I don't know, it's not clear."

"Okay, fast forward then. What are *you*?"

"An incubus."

Paige sickened.

"I never fed on you directly! I use dreams to sustain myself, just taking what I need. I could never put you in that kind of danger."

"Oh? And what kind of 'danger' would I be in if you did lunch on me for real?" *Homework reading topic: incubus.*

"You could become weak, die if I drain too much." Davin swallowed hard. "At the very least, prolonged exposure would get you addicted to me." His expression hardened. "But I've made an active choice to *not* do that. It's what I am, it's not who I am. This is why I only feed in dreams."

Bile rose in the back of Piage's throat and the tip of her dagger dipped down before she brought it up once more, elbow braced against her knee for support. "And you do this to other women?"

"Reach them through the dreamscape? Yeah." Abject misery resumed on Davin's face and he hung his head as low as the blade allowed. It fascinated a part of her with how he oscillated between accepting, and defending himself against her accusations.

"Give me one reason not to end you right now."

He looked up, eyes hardening. "You can. But I'm your best shot at survival."

The recent memory of Davin flinging the demonic dog aside with ease rose in her mind. *Well, damn it, there was that.*

Later, Paige would cry this out. But at this moment, she allowed anger to drive the conversation and stayed in the realm of pragmatism. She wanted to ask Davin if the last two years meant anything at all, or if she was just an easy meal. They never said the L-word to each other, but the depth of affection was there. What about the other women? Did he have a nickname for each of them? How many?

Paige shook her head clear and gripped the hilt harder even as her arm tired. "How do I know this is not part of your plan somehow? Hook me into being your victim."

"You don't. And I understand that nothing I say, or do,, right now can prove it." Davin grew quieter. "It's a leap of faith for you. But I..." He paused, and she saw the hesitation in how his hands trembled, then curled into fists to stop the shaking. "If you can find it in yourself to give me one last chance, to trust me just this one last time, I will promise you that the only way whoever is behind this could get to you is over my dead body. I won't let anyone hurt you."

The emotion in Davin's voice moved her. Paige felt as if she was standing on the edge of a precipice of something so much bigger than her, staring down into a pit of unknowns. But if she didn't jump, she would never find out what was down there. She wanted to know. At last, she lowered the blade. "Why?"

"Because." Davin offered her a weak smile. "Because you're not like other women. You're... special."

Bullshit. "Oh, please," she muttered. The skepticism must have shown in her expression.

"I avoid visiting anyone else more than once in their dream."

"What?" Paige's eyes widened.

"I never give them my name. Most of the time, they can hardly see me."

Her traitorous heart leaped at his words. What girl wouldn't wish that she was special? Her novels used this trope often enough. "I don't trust you. You've given me no reason to believe you."

"I know." Davin rubbed his face. "I didn't tell you because I'd think you would forgive me. I told you because I didn't want you to assume I didn't care. Yes, I see the disgust you have for me right now." Bitterness thickened his voice. "You don't have to absolve me. I just need you safe and alive. Please, let me protect you."

"So I can be what? Your long-term meal ticket?"

"No, damn it, Paige." Davin exploded, rising to his full height in one swift movement. "So that I don't lose you. You! Not as prey, not even as my lover. Just you. As you."

Paige struggled to remain calm in the face of his outburst. "English, Davin."

He slumped back in his seat. "I can't bear the thought of you no longer roaming this earth. I can stay away after all this over, but I need to know you are alive and well."

Understanding of him eluded her, and she couldn't wrap her head around why Davin felt the way he did. But he seemed genuine enough, and he wasn't pushing for more than she wanted to give.

"You're crazy."

"Yeah, I guess." As if drained, he half-closed his eyes even as his shoulders rose in a shrug. Could she take the risk? With that demonic dog out there, could she afford not to? Paige sighed and set the sword down.

"I suppose I am, too. Fine. No more lies. And I'm not forgiving you, but I'll stay. So you better prove that you're worth this one last chance. Deal?"

Davin nodded, his shoulders sagging in relief. "Deal."

CHAPTER 8
Paige

Paige left the long dagger on the coffee table and shifted to plop down on the couch, though she took care to keep a healthy distance between them. She wasn't sure she was ready for the feelings Davin may stir with his touch. Instead, she rested her head against the plush back and rolled to rest one cheek against the fabric to observe him.

"You're still injured."

Davin unwound the shirt around his arm and lifted it to show her. The flesh was pink and puffy, but the wound had already healed over with patches of lighter skin. "See? Almost good as new."

No human could heal that fast. Every time the skeptic in her tried to voice concerns of a scam, some fresh evidence would prove everything to be real.

Paige's gaze followed Davin's movements down to his hand where angry blisters still covered the area. Her brows knitted, and she frowned. "That one isn't getting better."

He studied it and shrugged. "It'll heal. Just takes longer since it's from the iron."

"That was dumb." Inside, Paige noted how mean she sounded and wished she could take back those words.

A chuckle drew her attention, her eyes rounding in surprise. Davin gave her an impish grin. "It made you stay and hear me out. I'd say it was worth it."

Paige's face grew hot, and she cleared her throat, forcing herself to look away from him. "Idiot." A slight pause helped her decide on next steps. "Do you have a first aid kid?"

"Ah, no," he rubbed the back of his head with his uninjured hand. "I don't bring humans over and you can see it's not something incubi need."

Great. She set her hands on her hips, surveyed the apartment and walked over to the kitchen, returning with a roll of paper towels.

"Give it." Paige waved at him and he extended his injury to her.

With several napkins torn off, she wrapped his hand in a makeshift bandage. It would have to suffice until they could get some gauze. Paige's gaze lifted upwards but darted back down. In the brief glimpse, she had caught Davin staring at her with a mingling of intensity and tenderness. It was a familiar look, one he sometimes gave her as Shade in the middle of a session, that moment before he would ramp up their pleasure, full of wonder and possessiveness that would melt her core.

Paige cleared her throat. "Let me call Ains, then you can tell me about the dog." Calling it that seemed an insult to dogs.

"Okay."

She walked closer to the large windows and turned her back towards Davin, aware of the way his eyes followed her. *Damn that demon, he is probably hungry, as in, incubus-hungry.*

Paige refused to believe she was special to some long-living entity. Too cliche.

"Oh my God, Paige. Are you okay? What's going on?"

No, no, she wasn't okay. She entertained the idea of lying to Ains. But then she would be no better than Davin if she did that.

"I'm okay. I'm alive. Listen, I wish I could explain in person but I can't, so please just hear me out, okay?"

Her friend inhaled, and she pictured in her mind Ainsley's firm nod.

"Yes, yes, I can do that."

"This will sound crazy." An idea popped into her head. Hadn't Davin called her landlady a witch? "But Lillian should be able to verify at least some of what I am telling you. I'd call her next."

"Paige. You are a lot of things, but crazy would be pretty low on the list. So stop dancing around and tell me."

"Okay." *Here goes.* "You know how we always joke that I have a muse in my dreams and he gives me all the ideas? It's... the truth. Except it turns out it's not my imagination. Tobias, or Davin, is an actual person, well sort of." Paige swallowed hard. "He's not human."

"Paige." The incubus growl from behind was approaching. "Telling others was never part of the deal."

She shot him a pointed look. It wasn't as if she could take back the words, and if he suggested mind-wiping, she'd deck him, demon or not.

"What? Are you okay?"

"Yeah. Davin's whining that I told you." She smirked at him with a challenge and he growled again. A small part of Paige recognized that she was riling him up to hear that sexy sound.

"Anyway, it's why he looks like Tobias from my books. Because I based him on my supposed muse."

"Okay."

Paige wasn't sure how "fine" Ainsley was, but she had to plunge ahead. "Some creature attacked me. Davin showed up and fought it off. Lillian can tell you more about those attacks, but right now, it's safer to stay with Davin. So... you're caught up."

"Okay." Ainsley sounded faint over the phone.

"Ains. I'm sorry."

The apology seemed to jolt her friend out of it. Ainsley "tch-ed" on the other end of the line. "You've got nothing to apologize for. My grandmama had the knack herself, always told me she was fae-touched."

"What, you never mentioned it before!"

"Well, it's crazy-sounding, right?"

Paige gave a small laugh, the first one she'd had in days. It felt good.

"In all seriousness, how much do you trust this Davin?"

Wasn't that the million-dollar question? She turned to see the incubus still watching her and sighed. "Not a lot, but I know he's my best chance at survival."

"That's not very reassuring."

"He gave me an old, but sharp, pointy iron sword that burns fae."

"Okay, more reassuring."

Paige grinned and remembered why she adored Ainsley. "I'll keep you posted, okay?"

"You better. Be careful. Don't go falling for this stranger, no matter how good he is in bed."

Crap. "How did you...?"

"I've read all your books, remember? If he does half the things Tobias does, he's likely some sex god between the sheets."

Page blushed even as Davin raised a brow at her.

"I'm hanging up now."

Ainsley's laughter on the other end warmed her heart.

"Okay, okay. But truly, stay safe, and take care of yourself. I want my best friend back in one piece."

"Promise. You, too."

They hung up and Paige spun around on her heels. "Ever heard of privacy?"

Davin scowled. "You were talking about me." He brightened "You know, it's true. You make Tobias sound like a 'god between the sheets."

Paige's jaw dropped, and she wasn't sure if her cheeks grew redder. "How?"

He tapped his ear. "Most supernatural beings have heightened senses."

Another thing to remember. She had much to learn. Mortified and speechless, she turned away to buy herself some space to find composure.

"There's nothing embarrassing about your writing. You're a wonderful author."

The glass held his reflection such that she saw his smile grow sheepish.

"You know, I have signed first editions of your books."

She spun around, incredulous. "What?"

It was Davin's turn to blush, and he studied his shoes. "I always order and stock copy of them in the store, and I send one of my staff over to your book signings. You honor me with your writing."

It was getting harder by the minute to stay mad at Davin. But it didn't mean he had earned her trust back just yet. They needed safer ground. "Tell me about the dog."

Right on cue, Paige's stomach rumbled, and she wrapped her arms around her midsection in concern.

"How long has it been since you last ate?" He took a step closer and this time, Paige refrained from backing up.

"I... don't remember."

Davin looked thoughtful, a frown tugging his lips

downwards, and he drew nearer, enough to venture to place a tentative hand on her shoulder.

Paige let him and found his touch more reassuring than arousing, as she had feared. "New deal. You let me cook you something and I can tell you all about the inugami in the meantime."

"Okay." He was already herding her towards the kitchen. It was so easy to lapse back into the almost dominant/submissive dynamic they always had in her dreams. Paige had enjoyed how much Shade took care of her, how she didn't have to think about deciding with him. But this was different. She had to keep reminding herself.

As Davin pulled one of the high stools from the kitchen island, Paige took a seat. "The inugami," she repeated, struggling to exert some control over the conversation to show she would not submit to him.

Davin was already moving into the gallery proper, studying the fridge to figure out what he had on hand. "Right. Dog god in Japanese, I think. But they're created in a pretty gruesome way by someone with enough juice to power the ritual."

"How?"

He looked around with unease. "Are you sure you want to know?"

Paige rolled her eyes and crossed her arms, resting them on the counter. "Didn't I witness it gorge itself on my guts only an hour ago?" When she saw Davin turn away, she grumbled. "I'm no wilting princess."

Davin muttered something intelligible under his breath and returned to face her. "Fine, but don't blame me if you get nightmares about it."

"Don't you control that?" She shot back.

In return, he winced. "No Paige, I don't control your dreams." As if unwilling to discuss that topic further, he paused and caught her gaze. "The inugami is created by keeping a live dog chained up in sight, but out of reach of food, starving it to the point of desperation, before cutting off its head."

Paige shuddered in horror, eyes growing round. "That's... that's..."

"Barbaric? Yeah, I know."

"Poor thing." She recalled the ravenous hunger she saw.

"Paige, you can't pity the thing. It's beyond that now and if you go all bleeding heart on the inugami, it will kill you."

"I get that," she snapped, but she glanced at the weapon lying on the coffee table. "I guess the best we can do is to put the creature out of its misery."

"Not yet."

With his back towards her, Paige couldn't tell his expression, but she unfolded her arms to place both hands on the counter. "What?"

There was a pause in his movements as Davin cooked over the stove. But not even the delicious smells wafting in the air could deter her demand for a reason. "Why?"

"Creating an inugami is one thing. To exert enough control to set it on a specific prey? That takes both skill and a certain level of power. We need to figure out who is behind this before they send something worse."

There was a creature worse than that monster? What kind of world had she gotten sucked into? *No, if I stop to analyze too deeply, I'm going to run for the hills screaming. Eyes on the prize.* "Okay, what next?"

"Next," Davin began and brought over a plate of bacon, eggs, and toast.

Paige salivated at the sight but restrained herself from pigging out right away. Instead, she picked up the fork and took a bite.

"You eat and rest. I will go out, try to pick up the thing's trail and track down who's holding its leash."

Paige paused mid bite. "Nuh-uh. I'm not sitting this out.

It's after me. Someone or something supernatural has a beef with me and I want to know why."

"Paige…"

"Besides, if whoever it is made me the target, then put me out there as bait and you won't even have to track the thing."

"No!"

When Davin shifted to loom over the counter, it was almost as if he grew in size. "I am not putting you in harm's way. You're staying here where it's safe."

She set down the fork and stood up. Against his full height, she felt diminutive, but hell if she would let him put her in a damsel-in-distress role. "And I'm saying I'm going. Either I go alone or you can come with me."

They glared at each other at an impasse as minutes ticked by. Paige crowed inside when Davin caved and spoke first, his back still stiff.

"Fine, then instead you will learn to defend yourself before we make any other moves." He nodded towards the iron dagger.

"Fine." Paige huffed and sat down again. Without prompting, she began shoveling food into her mouth, staring at it and ignoring him.

Davin watched her eat, something in his eyes softening. With a tender smile, he reached out and hooked one brown curl back around her ear. "Paige, you are the most frustrating woman I've ever met in all my years on this earth."

She swallowed and looked up, with a comeback readied on her lips. But words died as her gaze caught his. She studied his eyes, looking for traces of a lie in the affection and tenderness Davin seemed to hold for her. One could fall for him. In her mind, she kicked herself. Paige needed distance.

"What's the actual eye color?"

It was enough to break up whatever that tension building up was. Davin rubbed the back of his head as his lips formed a sheepish smile. "I'm wearing contacts. The color you saw me with as Shade is the real one. I just thought blue might blend in more with humans."

Paige wondered why fitting in was so important. Lillian had seemed satisfied when Davin had given her his true identity as collateral. She filed it away as a question to ask another time.

"I like the amber better," she muttered, then cursed herself. Her and her big mouth. Paige returned to shoveling food in instead of her foot.

Davin grinned at that. She thought he would comment, but he changed the subject. "Don't worry about cleaning up. I'll go prep a guest room. You must be exhausted. Turn in early and get some sleep."

Paige couldn't argue with that. Weariness seemed to seep into her bones.

As Davin paused by her side, he reached out to caress her hair, fingers dancing like the touch of a butterfly. "I will stand guard and keep you safe in your dreams tonight." And with that, before she could reply, he walked away.

CHAPTER 9
Davin

*F*uck.

Davin stared at his bandaged hand, still pulsing with pain, and knew even without unwrapping it, that his wound wasn't healing. *Serves me right for being a showoff.*

But she was here. Paige, in his apartment, flesh and blood. The demon in him clamored to go to her, to feel her naked body under his hands as he touched and teased every inch. To lick and taste all of her before diving into the sweet nectar between her legs. To listen to her moans and cries fill the air in the sweetest symphony of all ages. To plunge into her molten core at last, to feel her tightness wrap around his cock, to move and drive her to heights of pleasures beyond what she could imagine, over and over while he fed...

Davin groaned. This cold shower was not working. It also didn't help that his injured hand was his dominant one. *Fuck me, I am a damn fool.*

Before she had retired for the night, Paige had muttered something about the lack of pajamas to sleep in. Davin had jumped to provide her with the necessities - a charger for her phone, a new toothbrush, towels, and a large clean t-shirt for her. The latter had proven to be a mistake. The very thought of her wearing his clothing, his scent imprinting on her, had sent the incubus into overdrive and was the very reason he was standing here gritting his teeth through this freezing shower.

As Davin shut off the water, he pressed his forehead against the cold tile and tried to turn his mind towards the attack instead. Was it a fan she had crossed? Why now? She hadn't published her most recent book yet, so there were no changes. Was it one of her blog posts? No, he had read all of them faithfully and nothing in them would garner such hatred. She was an old hat at that game. The interview she just did? No, that wasn't released yet.

Davin wracked his brain and groaned. He needed a drink. Despite alcohol having little effect on a demon's system, the soothing burn sometimes helped him clear his head. He grabbed a large towel, wrapped it around his waist, threw one more over his shoulders and padded outside.

As Davin passed by the door to her room, the last in the hall before it opened up into the kitchen and living space, faint sounds of fighting caught his attention. His oh-so-creative mind provided him with another image — Paige curled up in bed, watching a movie on her phone, the tip of her tongue sticking out, a habit she had when she focused on something. A habit he found both endearing and sexy.

He needed that drink.

Davin was downing his second glass of scotch, neat, when he heard the slight creak of the hinges. A squeak made him turn around, glimpsing a pair of long pale legs poking through his shirt before the door slammed closed. His lips moved into a smirk and he set the liquor down to make his way to the room. As he cleared his throat, Davin rapped his knuckles on the wood.

"You okay in there, Paige?"

A rustle on the other side "I'm fine!"

Was that a smidgen of fluster he picked up in her tone? His grin spread wider.

"Are you sure? Did you need something?" He could not keep the teasing out of his voice.

"Yeah, put some goddamn clothes on."

Davin struggled to not chuckle but failed. "It's nothing you haven't seen before, Paige."

"Doesn't mean I want to see it now!"

So, his body affected her. At least, she still found him attractive. "Okay, okay. My apologies, I'm not used to sharing my place with someone. I'll head to my room."

The sound of the guest room door creaking open echoed like faint music to Davin's ears. The little sparrow was curious. He smiled to himself as he toweled off and dressed. For the rest of the night, he sequestered himself in his large bedroom, allowing Paige to have free rein of his home with no more embarrassment.

Later, once Davin settled in and stepped into her dream, he raised a brow. This was a far cry from what he was expecting. He found himself in a gym of sorts, polished wooden floors gleaming with crisp white lines. But rather than nets or basketball hoops, a variety of weaponry lined the walls. And in the middle was Paige, stance wide but knees still straight so that her center of gravity remained high. She was holding a long dagger and was attempting to lunge into a strike without falling off balance.

Davin leaned against the wall, lips quirked in half-amusement, half-admiration. Clothed in a black sports bra and tight yoga pants, Paige's outfit left little to the imagination. Memories of her body pressed against him resurfaced and his member stirred in his trousers.

Damn the libido.

Before his incubus started demanding more action again, Davin coughed.

Startled, Paige jumped and lost the grip on her dagger. It fell with a clatter that echoed across the room.

"Are we starting practice early? I was going to give you the night off."

Paige's cheeks flushed as she glanced sideways at the blade she'd dropped and shrugged. "I must have fallen asleep to the YouTube videos."

Davin took a step, and then another, closing the distance between them before he bent down to pick up the weapon, his gaze never leaving hers.

"And what were you watching?" His features morphed into a mask of innocence spoiled only by a slight grin. In his head, he pieced together what she was attempting. The sounds of fighting he'd caught earlier, coupled with her comment about videos, meant she was likely doing her homework before his promised lesson tomorrow.

"Stuff," she replied again, affecting the most nonchalant expression she could manage.

But Davin recognized that caginess in the way she shuffled her feet, her gaze darting this way and that.

"What are you doing here?" It was a nice, if futile, attempt at deflection.

Davin's smile softened. "I promised I would guard your dreams, Paige, in case the inugami returned. I meant that. Nothing else, I promise. But since you set this up..." He offered the weapon to her, hilt up, blade down. "Let me show you?"

Paige hesitated, staring at the dagger before taking it, her fingers skimming over the back of his hand. Davin's heart skipped a beat, and he wondered at what it was about this woman that made him respond like he was a teenager with his first girl, all those thousand years ago.

"Let's start with the stance. Show me."

As Paige guessed at how to stand, Davin beamed with pride. Already she had learned from her earlier mistakes . This time she bent her knees and found a better distance between her feet. Paige had good instincts.

"Stay on the balls of your feet. You should feel balanced but remain light-footed."

Davin kept his touch gentle as he positioned, and corrected, the finer points of a readying pose. The delicate contact quieted the incubus but set his memories free. How many times had she allowed him to position her for different purposes, obeying his hands without question? Even now, she responded so well.

Hell, she is beautiful. Davin drew in a breath as he circled her, studying the stance she held steady. Every bit the fighter he knew hid beneath the shy exterior of a geeky writer. When he came to stand behind Paige, he gave her a little shove with no warning. Her feet remained planted on the ground. *Good.*

Davin stepped up, closing the distance between them so that he could feel the heat of her body, her scent filling his head. With gentle care, he touched her shoulder. "May I?"

When she nodded her assent, he skimmed his hand down along her arm, taking hold. The pain of his injured hand shot through but he ignored it, grateful that with Paige facing ahead, she would not see the wince. "Now if you want to attack, let's start with a simple strike."

The nearness of her almost undid him, her heat calling to his every instinct. Davin guided her limb into a forward thrust, their arms moving in unison, hers braced against his. "Remember this movement. Remember how it feels."

"Shade." There was a breathlessness to her voice, a kind of whimper of want, so familiar that he hardened. With a start, he realized his other hand was on her hip.

"Oh, shit." Davin jumped back, putting as much space between them as possible. "I'm so, so sorry," he muttered, eyes looking down in shame. Paige was trusting him to keep control and here he was, his subconscious seducing her when he knew she wanted nothing to do with him.

A look of pity passed over Paige, surprising him. "You can't help it, can you?" There was a softness in her words as if, for the first time, she comprehended his nature in whole.

Davin gritted his teeth and his fingers curled into fists. "No, it's my baser instinct, but we've evolved from that. I'm better than that. I'm not some out-of-control young buck. Being an incubus… this is what I am, but not *who* I am." The last he repeated more to himself, a mantra he played often in his mind in moments of weakness.

"I know."

Davin's head whipped back at the two little words that he never thought would come out of her mouth, his body stiffening with wariness.

With a sigh, Paige crossed the floor of the gym as she spoke. "I can't be certain if your celibacy thing is true or not, but I have realized that you've had plenty of chances to manipulate me into sex tonight, and before that. You didn't. The fact is, I'm still angry at you for gaslighting me all this time." She lifted the sword and placed it in its spot on the wall. "I also don't know if I trust you right now. Heck, I am not buying this whole supernatural business just yet, but I'm going to choose to believe, both in what you are telling me and your intentions, even if I come off an idiot for it." She turned and gave him the first genuine smile he had seen since he told her he was both Davin and Shade.

"Thank you." Her leap of faith shook him. "I promise I'll do everything in my power to live up to that trust."

"Good. I'll hold you to that."

Davin cleared his throat. "We'll go to visit my brother tomorrow. He owns a dojo and can teach you better than me." He could see Dante's disapproving face already, but it would be safer for Paige.

"Is that the tall one from the other night?"

Not much escaped the observant eye of the writer in her. Davin nodded. "His name is Dante."

"He's like you?"

"Yeah, but we'll go to his human business. The dojo will be full of students and other people, all mortal. He is older and is better at some things." It galled him to admit it, but he understood Paige's need for reassurance.

"Okay."

The dream shifted back to the bedroom they shared. Davin blinked in surprise, for it was not his doing.

"Hm, I'm getting the hang of this."

Indeed, she was.

"Can you whip up some books for me on yours, and other kinds, of fae?"

Davin chuckled. He remembered her mentioning that even for a romance novel, research was key. A bookcase shimmered into existence, filled with his memories and knowledge of the subject. "You read, and I'll stand guard."

"Mmkay."

Davin's nature, and hunger, might desire Paige's body, but the smile she gave him in return was one that warmed his simple heart.

CHAPTER 10
Davin

"Why can't you just buy new clothes?" Davin pushed his hair back in frustration.

"Because it's not only that! I don't even have my wallet with me. My underthings! My laptop! I need to keep writing, you know. I've got deadlines." Paige snapped.

Davin's interest piqued at the mention of underthings. Heading to her place didn't seem like such a bad idea anymore, despite having to face the witch that was her landlady.

"So, tell me again, why are we knocking on your landlady's door instead of going straight down to your unit downstairs?" The renewed wards made his skin itch as they stood on the house's landing.

"In case you don't remember, again, her name's Lillian, and it's because you didn't even give me time to get my keys. Besides, I want to make sure she's okay."

Davin knew he'd be lucky if she didn't hex him. Perhaps he should have waited in the car, but his more primitive instincts had urged him to stick to Paige's side. *In case the inugami attacks again. Yeah, that it is why.*

"Oh, my dear." As Lillian opened the door, she wasted no time in enveloping Paige in a smothering hug. "Thank the powers that be you're okay."

Paige hugged back and clung to the older woman like a lifeline. A shot of envy coursed through Davin. Would she ever embrace him with that same level of trust again? He averted his eyes, letting her have a private moment with the woman whom he was learning was her surrogate mother.

"You."

The one word made him snap his head back up. "Hello Lillian," he greeted, caution making him a man of few words.

Lillian nodded. "Demon."

"This is Davin," Paige introduced, shifting out of her embrace to angle and include him in the conversation.

"I remember his name," the witch sniffed.

"Is that Paige?" A familiar voice called out from inside and the door opened a little wider to reveal a relieved Ainsley.

"Oh, my God." Another round of hugging. Davin looked away, taking the chance to search for any fresh signs of the inugami. He was right, it hadn't been back with Paige gone.

"Come in. Come in." Lillian ushered both girls into the house before throwing a backwards glance at Davin. "I suppose you, too."

The itchiness lessened, and he followed the three in, closing the door behind him. Davin scanned the airy interior. Thick rugs and old, but well cared for, furniture filled the place with little to show what Lillian truly was, except for small, subtle, signs. Herbs strung above for drying - he recognized sage, thistle, and pennyroyal to name a few. He noticed salt lining the sills and holly tied to the top of the window and entranceway frames. It wouldn't surprise him to find out Paige wasn't aware she rented from a hedge witch.

"Davin, come on."

"We should get going. We need to catch Dante before his classes start."

"A few minutes, okay?"

Davin sighed and followed his charge to the dining table, where Lillian had already brought out two more mugs and a plate of fresh scones. *Fine.*

Before sitting down, Paige dropped the messenger bag Davin had lent her onto the table. It landed with a heavy thud.

"What are you carrying? Rocks?" Ainsley asked. Her gaze traveled from the bag up to Davin. He had noticed her curious glances.

In response, Paige withdrew the long iron dagger, and Davin watched with satisfaction as Lillian's eyes grew round.

"For protection." Paige ran her fingers along the scabbard. She was growing a rather unhealthy attachment to the blade, and Davin wasn't sure how he felt about it.

As he took his seat at the dining table, he remained silent, wary of a power of some sort he sensed from all three women. There was something moving here that he didn't quite understand, but even the incubus in him had quieted in their presence. It reminded him of when his sisters got together, but this was a very different energy from what the succubi held.

"Lillian caught me up over the phone last night and I came over this morning with these." Ainsley pulled over a large binder. "This is your file. Every interview and blog post, any fan mail you received that sounded stalker-ish or off base. I also have here a list of any other authors that you've interacted with that may have jealousy issues with your success."

Davin sat up. This friend of Paige's was useful.

"Wait, wait, wait." Paige held up both her hands.

Lillian passed a dish of scones and a mug of tea towards

Paige and gave her a reassuring smile. "I did some research as well. The inugami is not a natural creature. Someone with power created it. Like the demon said yesterday, before he whisked you away, they targeted you, which means they very much want you dead."

"And I can't think of anyone in your personal life that's that big of an enemy. Unless there's something you haven't told me before?"

Paige shook her head, her expression like a deer caught in the headlights.

"Eat your scone, dear." Lillian patted Paige on her back. "Here, have some cream and jam with it." A brief pause later, she placed a mug in front of Davin as well but made no offer on the food. It was apparent that he didn't deserve a pastry yet.

Only when Paige took a bite, did the white-haired witch ease herself into one of the remaining chairs.

"May I see that?" Davin nodded at the binder.

Ainsley waited until her friend gave her permission, with a quick bob of her head, before pushing the thing toward Davin.

"Ainsley Knight." She offered a handshake, and Davin noted the professional cool tone. He was in the doghouse with all her friends. *Great.*

"Davin Murphy." He gave the proffered hand a shake then let go, turning his attention to the treasure trove of information on Paige as an author.

"You can come home, dear. I've strengthened the wards."

Davin's head snapped up, but he withheld a verbal denial. His initial instinct was to sweep Paige up in his arms and take her away, but that was unreasonable and not a good way to regain her trust. If he wanted it, Davin needed to first, accept Paige's decisions. And he knew her stubborn streak. If Davin answered for her, she was going to stay here just to spite him.

"Wards," Paige echoed with a blink of her eyes and took another bite of her scone.

Ainsley and Lillian exchanged a look before Lillian gave a soft sigh. "Yes, dear. I may not be as powerful as that demon you've got there, but I am a witch and I know my protection spells. Now that I'm aware of what I'm warding against, I can keep you safe."

Perhaps Lillian is right, but what about the next thing they send? Davin kept his thoughts to himself.

"I understand."

Davin could almost see Paige's mind working overtime to process this additional information. After a pause, she shook her head, much to Davin's relief.

"I came to get some of my stuff. I'd feel better if we go on the offense. Ains, if you can keep researching with Lillian, Davin and I will try another tactic and lure them out." Paige gave them what he presumed, a supposed reassuring smile. It turned into more of a grimace. "Who knows, if we're lucky, I'll be back home tonight or tomorrow."

"Are you sure about this, dear?"

"Paige, that sounds dangerous."

What am I, invisible? Davin straightened his spine, making himself taller. *Do they underestimate my ability to protect her that much?*

"It'll be okay. The inugami is no match for Davin, right?"

His heart swelled with pride. It didn't matter what these other females' opinions were. Paige thought he was damn fine as her protector. *Wait, no, she is not mine.*

"I will keep her safe."

"I need to go downstairs and grab everything." Paige nodded and rose from her seat, ending any other protests.

Before he could say anything, Ainsley also stood up. "Let me help you pack."

Paige flashed her friend a quick smile, then leaned over to

give Lillian a light peck on her cheek. "I'll be okay, I promise." Grabbing her messenger bag, she was off with Ainsley in tow.

Davin blinked, awkward silence thickening the air. The sound of a clock ticked somewhere, counting the seconds that went by. His gaze strayed on the binder. He could study it, though he doubted he could focus with Lillian's eyes boring into him.

"What're your intentions with Paige?"

And here comes the grilling.

With a heavy sigh, Davin closed the book, folded his arms on the table and stared straight at Lillian, unafraid to meet her eyes. "To keep her safe."

"For what purpose?"

His answer this time was more composed than the incoherent babble he gave to Paige last night. "For her well-being. Contrary to popular belief, we're not all evil selfish monsters. We come in all shapes, sizes and nature, no different from humans. I only want her to be okay. And after this, if she wants, I'll disappear from her life."

Lillian studied him. "Why her?"

Why her for what? He wasn't sure what Lillian was asking but ventured a guess. "We have been together for over two years in her dreams. I've come to know her, to enjoy her company. She's funny, brilliant, and as charming as she's beautiful." Okay, he hadn't meant to say the last bit and now he hesitated.

"You care for her." Lillian's voice grew soft.

Davin exhaled and his gaze fell. "Yes, I care for her." It was the first time he'd admitted his feelings to anyone.

"It'll be hard, for a demon with long life and a mortal human."

Davin winced and wished everyone would stop telling him that, or variations of. "I don't intend for there to be an 'us'. I just need her unharmed."

When he felt Lillian's hand, warm and gentle on his arm,

he looked up in surprise. It was the last thing he expected from the witch that seemed to hate him on sight.

"If you mean what you say, then it's not only her body you want to keep whole. The heart can be more fragile than anything physical."

Davin snorted. "She hates my guts for lying to her, letting her pretend I wasn't real all this time."

"I had a lover once, who decided keeping his violent history from me was the best thing he could have done for us. But the past has a way of catching up, and when it did, I was so angry. It wasn't his choice to make alone. But when the rage faded, I understood he did it out of love and out of what he hoped would keep me safe." Lillian smiled and gave Davin's arm a gentle squeeze. "Paige will come to the same conclusion sooner or later. Like you said, she's a smart girl."

"Maybe the anger is better for her." Davin wasn't sure why he was confiding in Lillian when he couldn't even bring himself to admit anything to his own brothers. But her motherly mannerisms were effective at inspiring confidence.

"Resentment and grudges are never healthy, dear boy. Don't mix up the two. Once you both have a clearer head, you can decide, together, if the hardships would be worth trying." There was a sadness in Lillian's eyes, and Davin wondered at what history made her words sound so bittersweet. Was the lover she described fae?

The shadows disappeared as if they were never there in the first place, and Lillian's smile brightened her face again. "The girls will be awhile. Have a scone while you wait. I'll be in the garden if you need me."

He watched as Lillian walked away. Davin shook his head as he helped himself to one pastry and some jam. He must have passed a test of some sort, though damn if he knew what it was. But that would not stop him from enjoying homemade baked goods, even if his emotions still swirled in confusion.

It was another fifteen minutes before Paige popped back upstairs with a full backpack slung over her shoulder. Ainsley followed, fanning herself.

"Okay, ready to go."

Davin eyed the heavy bag, wondering how much, and what, she packed. Did she have the same pretty underthings she wore in her dreams? He cleared his throat and held out his hand.

"Please, let me."

Paige stared at him and after a moment handed her stuff to him. Ainsley walked them to the door.

"Say 'hi' to Dante for me. I'll text you if anything comes up."

"Thanks, Ains, you're the best. Tell Lillian I said 'bye'?"

"Will do. Be careful."

"You, too."

Then they were off.

CHAPTER 11
Paige

A nondescript store in a mixed-use building was the last thing Paige expected as they pulled up and parked by the curb.

"Here?"

Davin grinned and nodded, circling around to open the door for her. As she emerged, she studied the place just off the main street. Well lit, she could make out the thick mats on one side while hardwood floors lined the other. They were still early enough that few were in yet, but the large window left little privacy.

"Come on." He motioned for her to follow, and shifting the messenger bag on her shoulder, she fell into step behind him until they were both inside. They found Dante half-hidden in the equipment closet, hauling out a full bin of shinais. Paige did a double-take. Dante's clothes, the dogi, the crisp, white, clean uniform of many martial arts schools, combined with the deep blue hakama, a pair of wide-legged skirt-like trousers that reached the ankle, appeared at odds with his coloring.

"Davin?" Dante lifted his brow in mild surprise until his brother stepped away and Paige came face to face with him. Confusion and shock made his almond-shaped eyes grow round.

"Paige?"

She nodded with a shy smile, unsure why she felt self-conscious around Dante in a way she didn't feel with Davin. Maybe it was in knowing what he was, without the history of him having done her wrong. Still, if he was anything like Davin, Dante was someone to be wary of.

Davin touched his arm. "Can we speak in private with you?"

"My office is in the back." Dante set down the bin and yelled. "Kaito, finish setting up for the kendo class here."

A younger boy, who could be no older than sixteen, popped up. "Hai sensei."

"Dante spent a century in Japan. Picked up a lot of their mannerisms."

A what? Paige remembered from her reading that fae had long lives or were even immortal. But just how old were these brothers? *Yeesh.*

"Come along." Dante's curt commands cut through her musings.

They followed and crammed into a small but tidy office. As Paige closed the door behind her, she had to breathe as claustrophobia threatened to overwhelm her. Between the two incubi and her, the room felt like it was shrinking.

"Paige?" In the blink of an eye, Davin was at her side, hand on her elbow with a light touch.

Paige shut her eyes, focusing on that warmth before opening them again. "I'm okay."

Dante watched the exchange in silence, but when they both turned to him, his hands were at his hips, one brow raised.

"An inugami has been attacking Paige."

"What?"

Great, how many times can I shock this incubus today?

Paige cleared her throat. "We were hoping to use me as bait to lure it out and find its master. But Davin insisted that I earn to protect myself first." With that, she shifted her messenger bag and withdrew from it, the long dagger. "Would you have time to teach me some stuff?"

Dante had flinched at the sight of the iron sword, but it was so subtle it would have been easy to miss had she not had a habit of observing people. His gaze traveled from her to Davin, to her, then back to his brother.

"So she knows."

Davin heaved the heaviest of sighs. "Yeah, she knows."

"Ava will not be happy about that."

Who the hell was Ava and why did she care? Paige's eyes darted between the two, struggling to comprehend both the conversation and the subtle undercurrents at play.

"I'll cross that bridge when I get there," Davin replied. "Now, can you train her?"

Paige stood still as Dante studied her, but she recognized the assessment for potential rather than as a meal. This was no crass checking out but the cool appraisal of a candidate student, and it was something she could appreciate.

"I can give her some basics, but nobody gets good at fighting overnight and it'll take time for those skills to become muscle memory."

"Damn." Davin's face soured, but she shrugged.

"Better than nothing. When do we start?"

"Now. I don't have a class to teach until two, so we have a few hours. There is one starting here in a few though, so we'll have to use the smaller sparring room in the back."

She nodded. "All right, got a place I can go change?"

"Out and to your left."

Five minutes later, Paige found both Dante and Davin barefooted, laying out thin foam mats while sounds of students chattering and filtering in, letting her know that the other classes were starting soon. The knowledge that there were other humans close by reassured her. This is what Davin had meant, and his consideration touched her.

"Your best chance is that blade, but before we move on to weaponry, you need to learn some basic moves. I'll show you with Dav first."

Dav. His brothers call him Dav. Paige made a mental note.

"All motion stems from the hip. Punch Dav."

On cue, Davin threw a jab at Dante in slow motion. Dante swung his hips back, his foot following while his big toe dragged along the ground for balance.

"This is the foundation of all movements in martial arts. Keep going, Dav."

They mesmerized her with the rhythm they established, one side then the other. Each of Davin's strikes was smooth and graceful, his muscles straining in precision while Dante glided back and forth. Their pace increased, gradually at first, then more until it was obvious Davin was trying to catch Dante with a punch. Faster and faster until her human eyes could no longer follow.

Without warning, Dante changed and dove in while grabbing Davin's arm, throwing Davin off-balance. For a brief second, Davin was suspended in the air, upside down, then his body slammed into the mat with a loud smack that shook the walls. Paige winced and suppressed the urge to rush to his side.

Dante straightened and turned to look down at Davin, who had rolled to lay flat on his back.

"Since you are so eager, we can go over break falls next."

"Ruthless," Davin muttered, and Paige had to stifle a giggle.

They continued for another two hours, taking occasional breaks. Dante and Davin would demonstrate, then Paige would perform the technique on Davin with corrections from

Dante. But with his brother in the room, the tension that had formed between them in her dream last night did not reappear. In the last half hour, they moved on to weapons and it surprised Paige that she found it easier than expected, as if whatever blade she held were extensions of her arm.

Paige stood bent over, hands braced against her thighs as she caught her breath. Feeling eyes on her, she looked up to find Dante studying her.

"Are you sure you have had no training before?"

She shook her head, still too winded to speak.

"I rarely meet anyone who's such a natural. If you keep at it, you can go far."

Davin turned to Dante, shock on his face. "A compliment from you? About someone's fighting?"

"Compliments are in order where they're deserved. You and Finn are lazy and she has more talent and instincts in her pinkie than the two of you combined." Dante leveled a stare at Davin as he spoke.

"Ouch," Davin pressed a hand on his heart, affecting the most wounded expression.

Dante rubbed his forehead as if in pain. "Go get us some lunch."

It looked for a moment like Davin was about to protest, but he snapped his mouth shut. Instead, he glanced at Paige.

"I'll be fine here. I can use some food."

"All right."

Silence resettled. Paige wracked her brain to break the awkwardness and brightened at an idea. "So… my friend, Ainsley said 'hi'."

Was that a faint tinge of pink under the tanned skin? She refrained from smirking. For a pack of incubi, these guys sure got embarrassed easily. Sneaking a peek, she caught Dante studying a spot on the floor as if it was the most interesting sight.

"Dante?"

He cleared his throat, coughing into the crook of his arm. "Ah, when you have a chance, please say 'hi' back."

Despite all that was happening, Paige couldn't help but grin. "No problem."

"So," Dante straightened and tugged at his hakama. "What happened to Dav's hand?"

Now it was her turn to be flustered. Her eyes fell on the messenger bag leaning against one wall. "The idiot wanted to prove iron would hurt him. I don't know why the wound hasn't healed yet." Frustration crept into her voice.

"It's because he hasn't fed."

Paige blinked at him in surprise.

Dante shrugged. "It takes a long time to heal from that kind of injury. It could take months for even a minor scrape, but feeding helps speed up the body's healing process."

Feeding. As in... sex? Paige shifted her weight from foot to foot and snuck a peek at Dante, wondering if he held her responsible for his brother's injury, but there was nothing on his impassive face. It was Davin's fault for being so reckless. Despite that, logic didn't stop guilt from stabbing her heart.

"Paige, if you want to continue to train, I am willing to take you on as a student. We teach a variety of styles here and you can choose classes that fit your interest and schedule."

"Oh."

"Oh?"

Hesitation made her stutter her next words. "I thought you would ask about me and Davin."

Again, Dante shrugged. "A human woman hurt Davin a few decades ago, but he insisted you're different. I trust my brother to have learned his lesson and make his decisions more wisely."

"Is that why he only feeds in dreams?"

Dante nodded once.

Kaito poked his head through the door. "Sensei? There's someone outside looking to register."

At Dante's nod of acknowledgement, Kaito disappeared.

"Go change, Paige. We should call it. Think about my offer." With that he walked out, leaving Paige alone in the room.

She was emerging when Davin returned, holding paper bags up. "I gave Dante his lunch already, but looks like he's going to be too busy to join us Let's eat."

They ate in the backroom, chatting in quiet voices. It was an opportunity for Paige to ask questions, some about the readings from last night, other more personal ones. As they chatted, she grew more at ease.

"We can head home and drop off your stuff."

THE MAD DOG was waiting for them in the parking lot, slinking out from the shadows with a low growl as they got out of the car. Paige gasped as Davin imposed himself between them even as her hand dropped towards her messenger bag. This monster seemed thrice the size of what it was last time. Also, the timbre of its sound was off and as the inugami stalked closer, a shudder passed through her. There was a new craze to its eyes and drool fell in large globs from its open mouth. Something glinted from within.

"Paige, get in the car."

"No, I'm not..."

"Now!"

The creature launched itself towards them. Ready this time, Davin caught it by the throat, but the weight of it caused him to fall backwards. She jumped back, but it was close enough to reveal its fangs. *Shit, some metal coated them. Iron?* It must have gone rabid, driven by the pain someone inflicted on it.

The monster-dog was much stronger than before. Davin brought up his other hand to hold it at bay, but now it used its entire weight to press down on him. With Davin's injury, he wasn't at full strength like yesterday. Paige froze - unable to move

"What... the fuck..."

And then it sank its fangs into his neck, and Davin let out a blood-curdling scream of pain.

It was enough to spur Paige into action. With one swift movement, she drew the iron dagger from her bag and from its scabbard. With the inugami occupied with its current prey, she rushed at it, plunging the blade straight into its throat.

The thing whimpered and collapsed on top of Davin before its body disintegrated. Soon, nothing but a thin coat of ashes covered Davin.

"Davin? Davin!" Paige fell to her knees beside him. Blood was everywhere, but what was worse were the blisters forming on his neck. But unlike the other wound, black lines spidered outwards. She recognized the image from a book she'd read last night. *Iron poisoning.*

"Oh good, you're okay. I... didn't want to scare you... with my full form." He reached up to brush his knuckles by her cheek, then fell to the floor beside him.

Shit, he is becoming delusional. Paige ripped off the t-shirt she was wearing and used it to stop the bleeding.

"Stay with me, Davin, stay with me." His eyes closed.

He was dying.

CHAPTER 12
Paige

"No, no, no, no, no. Don't you fucking dare," Paige slapped his face and when Davin stirred, barely conscious, she took his hand to hold her t-shirt to his neck. "Keep pressure." Her heart pounded, but a calm settled like a numbing blanket over her. *First the weapon. I can't leave it laying here.*

Paige shuffled to retrieve the blade, shoved it back in the messenger bag and slung it over her shoulder.

With what strength she could summon from her adrenaline, she wrapped Davin's arm over her neck and used her entire body to hoist him off the ground. He staggered, leaning on her, and she half-dragged him to the elevator.

They were lucky that they didn't run into anyone. Paige wasn't sure how she could explain any of this. She dug around in his pocket for his keys and just got them inside the apartment and to the guest room bed before her strength gave out.

His blood on her hands, she stared at Davin's still form, panting from the excursion. Paige dropped the bag off to one side and with slow care, leaned over and peeled back the soaked t-shirt. The wound wasn't closing and the black lines were spidering out further. Davin's eyes remained shut, the only sign of life now, his labored breathing. Paige cringed.

What did Dante say? Davin had to feed to heal from iron. How? Was he already too far gone?

Damn it.

"Fine!" Paige stripped off her remaining clothes until she was naked. It wasn't as if he was conscious enough to see, anyway. "Fine. This is just sex. I write sex all the time. This means nothing. I'm still mad at you!" She was shouting at him now, but he remained on the bed like a dead fish.

Paige sighed and sank to her knees beside him and brushed his hair away from his face. "I haven't forgiven you yet, but that doesn't mean I want you to die. Please let this work." And with that, she pressed her lips against his.

It felt almost as if she were kissing a corpse. "Davin. Shade. Come back." She kissed him again and her shoulders dropped in relief when he moved his mouth against her, hesitant at first, then more hungrily. He raised one hand, tangling his fingers in her hair, pulling her closer to deepen the kiss until her lips felt bruised. Something flowed out of her.

With a gasp, Davin yanked her away, eyes glowing despite his contacts. "Paige, no."

She shifted to stroke his cheek, thumb tracing the contours of his face. "It's okay, Davin. Take what you need. You can't protect me if you're dead."

His body trembled against her touch, but with a groan that spoke of every restraint breaking, he tugged her back towards him. Their lips met once more, his uninjured hand cupping her neck then trailing down along her shoulders, down to her sides, before moving forward to cup one of her breasts. He broke their kiss, eyes darkening as his thumb traced circles around the areola, drawing a small moan from her.

"Come up here, little bird." His voice grew hoarse with need.

It was so easy to fall back to their old dynamics. Paige moved to obey, straddling his midsection. The fabric of his clothes rubbed against her thighs. His fingers traced the lines of her body, leaving her skin burning from his touch even as heat pooled at her core.

Davin pushed at her, gentle but insistent, guiding her to bend down towards him. They kissed again, except this time, he moved his hands to cup both her breasts, thumbs rubbing over her nipples, teasing them to stiffness. He drank in her moans as she squirmed above him, her growing wetness dampening his clothes. And in the process, something else left her body, though lost in this moment, she could not describe what.

Davin fell back onto the bed and watched as she wiggled and grinded down against him, struggling to undo the buttons of his shirt. He alternated between kneading her breasts and taking hold of those nipples, hard as diamonds, rolling them between his fingers until they ached so wonderfully.

"More" Paige gasped when he pinched them, sending a shot of pure lust straight to her groin. It was as if there were nerves connected from them to her core, but it wasn't enough. The need to feel some part of him against her below, skin to skin, grew more and more urgent until it was the only thought that encompassed her mind. Paige slid further down. Feeling his hardened member straining against his pants, she grounded her wet slit on him hard before lifting herself to undo the button and zipper.

An almost feral growl rumbled at the base of Davin's throat and he took hold of her hands, holding them in a vice-like grip. "No, Sparrow."

Her lips parted with a whimper of protest and on purpose, she lifted herself and rolled her hips to entice.

"Brat." Something in his eyes grew darker and naked hunger sharpened his features. That was the only warning she got. In one swift, inhuman motion, he sat up, held her close to him, and flipped her onto her back.

"You are not in control." His grip transferred to her wrists and before she could protest, he dove for her breasts, licking and nibbling on her most erogenous zones until she trembled with the nearness of her first climax.

Davin released her wrist and snuck his hand down until he slid his fingers through her slickness to part her folds. Her entire body tightened with anticipation. Small whispers of "please" turned into gasps as, with infinite slowness, he dragged his fingertips upwards.

And then he touched her clit.

That was all it took, that single touch. Paige screamed as she exploded, coming undone as he pushed her over the edge, flicking with lazy motions and tugging at the most sensitive bundle of nerves.

Davin's eyes glowed as he drank in her orgasm and, unsure if it was her imagination, she thought she saw turquoise light, shimmering like a thread, joining them.

Her hips fell back to the bed as she panted, struggling for breath. Davin was watching her and shook his head. "Not yet, my sparrow."

Not yet?

Davin took hold of her limbs, fingers digging in hard and, she found her legs thrown over his shoulders as he moved in between. He shifted his grip and held her hips before lowering his lips to her nether ones. There was no gentleness, no lead-up. Instead, he dove in and began devouring her like a starving man who hadn't eaten in days. And she was his feast, in more ways than one.

Already sensitive from her first climax, Paige screamed

out as his tongue lashed cruelly against her clit. Within seconds, she came again, every nerve coming alive as he drew out her orgasm until he reduced her to nothing but a quivering mess.

Still, Davin continued. Paige reached down, tugging at his curls, but she didn't know if she was trying to pull him away or to hold him closer. Something tugged at her hands, and it was as if silken ropes bound her, keeping each of them held against the bed. She had very little presence of mind to register the odd phenomenon as he kept hold of her hips. "Please... I can't."

Davin eased off to lick and tease more now, giving her a small reprieve as his talented tongue slid amongst her folds, the flat of it lapping against the abundance of juices flowing. He drank her in and just as she caught her breath, his lips closed on her clit, sucking it hard like he was trying to draw a pit out of a cherry. A finger pushed inside, crooking to find and press against the soft place within that was her g-spot.

Paige arched her back, hips bucking as she parted her lips in a wordless scream, senses overloading until her vision darkened, until all she saw were stars. Another torrent of wetness flooded his mouth, but he drank it all down as he feasted on her orgasm. Her entire world narrowed to the almost painful pleasure, as he pushed her body beyond its capabilities. In this singular moment in time, her awareness consisted only of his lips and hands on her, and of the ecstasy that was spinning out of control, until she was reduced to a mindless creature. A distant part of her understood reason for fear. This was why an incubus was so dangerous, but she was past the point of concern.

At last, Davin relented, easing off as her body fell back on the bed, her breathing turning into ragged sobs. He clambered up, stroking her face, her hair, his soothing voice washing over her. "Oh Paige, Paige, my little sparrow. You are such a feast."

Davin let her rest, pressing small kisses all over until she calmed enough that she could breathe more evenly. Paige hadn't realized she had closed her eyes, but when she opened them again, the first thing she saw was Davin's tender smile. "Let me get you some water."

She whimpered and clung to him, needing his warmth against her body. He chuckled and laid back down beside her, running his fingers through her hair. When her vision focused, she noticed his wounds had closed and his coloring had returned. But black continued to ring the peeling blisters.

"You still have iron in you," she croaked out, her voice almost unrecognizable in its scratchiness.

"I'll live Paige, thanks to you." He pressed another kiss on her temple, but she shook her head.

"I'm not risking it. I don't want you so weakened."

"Paige, I..."

"Take me. Take more." She didn't beg. This wasn't about pleasure. Her eyes cleared and hardened.

Davin stared at Paige while seconds, then minutes ticked by before he kissed her lips. "I'll go slow," he whispered as he shifted to hover over her once more. With little effort, he tugged his pants down and kicked them off before he lined his cock against her cum-soaked opening. His eyes met hers as he rubbed his length against her.

They never stopped looking at each other as he entered her, inch by agonizing inch. The familiarity of him inside her, as her body stretched to accommodate him, almost made her cry but, this was also more. Everything was more. His heat, the thickness of him parting her, the warmth of him around her. This was heaven.

Davin kept pushing more and more of himself into her. Her eyes grew round as he hit her cervix and bottomed out. How could someone fill her so perfectly? She moaned and rolled her hips up in slow motion, experimenting with this new fullness. In return, she heard him groan.

"You'll be the end of me, Paige." His hand trailed down her side, scratching the skin, producing the most delicious shivers. "Let me. I don't want to lose control."

She nodded and struggled to remain still as he withdrew until he held only the tip of himself inside her, then sank back down. He set a slow, almost languid pace, driving her mad with a newfound lust. Her hips thrusted with him, following the rhythm they now shared.

"Paige, Paige, Paige," he whispered with reverence against her skin as if her name was all he knew. Her hands rose to grip his arms, caressing his lovely muscles as he strained to keep himself up.

"More, Davin, please," she pleaded with him and he granted her wish, increasing their pace, thrusting harder inside her. As his cock moved, rubbing at places no one had ever touched before, her stomach tightened, familiar tingles of what's coming dancing over her nerves. "I can't... hold..." she stammered.

"Come for me, my sparrow." He lowered his lips to her breast, engulfing and suckling her nipple.

Paige's entire body convulsed in sheer bliss as she came on his cock, her pussy tightening to keep him inside. She heard a long, low, moan from Davin as, with a last thrust, he spilled his seed within her. Blue shimmered around both of them and a remote part of Paige wondered how much she was hallucinating in her orgasm but little mattered as she jerked and spasmed beneath him, until she collapsed onto the bed.

"Dear gods above and below," he muttered, falling on top of her, though he braced himself to not crush her. They lay there, both trying to catch their breath before he withdrew. Paige felt a gush of wetness flow from between her legs, but she couldn't bring herself to care. Instead, her eyes searched for remaining signs of the wound and a deep satisfaction filled her as she found him healed.

"Shit, are you okay? Talk to me, Paige." The edge of panic in Davin's voice brought her wandering thoughts back. He placed two fingers on her neck, checking her pulse, though he trembled too much for any accurate assessment. Fear twisted his features as he tried to discern her consciousness, and it was only then she realized he was scared to death.

Paige nodded. When the worry did not recede from his expression, she cleared her throat. It took several attempts to find her voice.

"I'm fine. Exhausted, but fine."

Davin let out a slow exhale. "You sure? I didn't drain too much from you?" He swallowed, his face still pale. "You need food. Sugar." He tried to rise.

"Later, please." Paige grabbed his hand. "I only want you right now."

Davin studied her before nodding. "Okay, but let's go sleep on clean sheets."

Paige was about to protest when he rose from the bed and scooped her up, carrying her bridal style to the other room. He laid her down, then crawled in, gathering her in his arms. "Rest. I'll stand guard. Here and in your dreams."

That was all she needed. Paige closed her eyes and let the exhaustion take her away.

CHAPTER 13
Paige

Her sleep was dreamless, and she didn't stir until early the next morning. Bleary-eyed, Paige languished in bed, too lethargic to do more than watch dust motes dance in the rays of the sun filtering through the window.

"Good, you're awake." Davin entered the room with a tray ladened with food — heaps of French toast, bacon, eggs, sausage, bread, plus more variety of fruits than she could discern. It was enough to feed five people. Her stomach rumbled.

Davin set the platter down on one side of the bed and turned to pour from a carafe that he must have brought in while she was still sleeping. The proffered orange juice looked tantalizing enough for her to sit up and grasp it.

She rubbed her groggy eyes with her other free hand and lifted the glass to her lips. "How long was I out?" Fresh and so sweet. Not the store stuff she bought.

Davin glanced at his watch. "About fifteen or sixteen hours." He sat down next to her, careful to keep a distance.

"It's normal. Your body needed time to replenish your reserves."

Fear whispered to her. Sleeping for that much time after a lusty bout of sex wasn't natural. Neither was how drained she was. The absolute lack of energy made every movement harder, as if weights tied down each of her limbs. In contrast, Davin was a picture of health, cheeks rosy, wounds, including the one on his hand, were completely healed as if he'd not been injured. Paige checked herself. At least she didn't seem to crave his touch. *Oh goodie, my bar is so low that as long as I haven't turned into a nymphomaniac, then it's still an okay day.*

"How are you feeling?" There was a new wariness in his eyes.

Perhaps it was the way Davin looked at her, so careful and hesitant. Or the food heaping over the tray. Maybe it was the distance he kept between them. But something in her softened. He couldn't help what he was. And if ever he would have lost control, it would have been the previous day. Instead, here she was, still alive. He hadn't drained her to death.

"Exhausted." Paige mustered a weak smile. "Like I just trained with Dante for twelve hours straight."

"Food and a soak in the bath might make you feel better." His eyes didn't meet hers.

"Hey. It's okay. Yesterday was my choice."

"I know, but it wasn't much of one. I should go, let you eat in peace." He turned as if to head for the door, his body hunched over.

He reminded her of a small child ready for a scolding.

"Davin." She reached out and grabbed his wrist, giving it a gentle tug back towards her. "I'm angry at you for lying, not for who, or what, you are."

"What I am is not good for you."

Her heart ached at the sadness in his voice. That was true,

but regardless, she gave him a gentle squeeze. "Have you told me the complete truth?"

"That I am a long-lived incubus demon that has to feed on sex to live? Yeah, I can't think of anything else." The self-deprecating chuckle that followed had Page shaking her head.

"Then whether you're good to me is not for you to decide." That was all she could give him as reassurance for now. The rich aromas of bacon beckoned, and she turned to investigate, grabbing a piece and munching on it.

The slack-jaw combined with the stare of amazement he wore amused her but busy with food, she didn't dignify it with a retort. Instead, her body craved fuel, and she submitted to its demands, eating with gusto. In between gulps, she gestured to the tray. "I can't finish all this by myself, you know. Would be a waste." She kept her eyes on Davin until he reached for a piece of bread.

When he relaxed, Paige returned to the food herself. By silent agreement, neither of them discussed further what happened last night, chalking it up to a one-time necessity. Or that's what she told herself.

Davin finished much faster than she did, and she was still placing a bite of French toast in her mouth when he rose from the bed. "Let me draw you a bath. I'll put a warming spell on it so no rush, okay?" He didn't wait for her reply when he walked towards the ensuite bathroom, and only then did she realize this was *his* bedroom.

Paige's gaze roamed, studying the space. It was sparse, devoid of most personal touches save for a low bookshelf, upon which sat a small reading lamp. A large armchair stood beside it, a throw draped over its back. As she munched on her last bite, she slid off the bed with shaky legs and made her way over to observe his selection of books.

There they were, her own books standing in a neat row along the top shelf. Every single thing she wrote was there, including the collection of short stories that hadn't sold well and had been out of print for quite some time. He wasn't lying. Paige blushed. This somehow seemed personal, even intimate.

Paige made her way to the bathroom, gasping at the luxury that greeted her eyes. A clawfoot tub stood in the middle of the pristine white tiles against the backdrop of a floor to ceiling window. If not for the unobstructed view with no other buildings reaching this height, she would have serious issues about being naked here. To the right, a two-sink vanity dominated the wall, while to her left was a large shower stall, big enough for three, with more jets than she thought possible.

"Yeesh, so that's how the one percent lives," she muttered to herself as she stripped. Might as well enjoy it while she could. Treat it as a splurge on a spa trip or something. She sank into the tub and exhaled. Oh, bliss.

A cushion lined the edge behind her and she rested her neck, letting her head fall back. Her muscles relaxed, and she closed her eyes again until she began dozing again. The water never cooled but stayed warm as the minutes ticked away until Paige lost all track of time.

A phone ringing roused her, but she continued to rest. It was none of her business. Then she heard voices, and none too soft. Even with the door closed, she made out every word.

"What the hell happened?"

"Finn, calm down."

"Calm down? You were near death! We all sensed it!"

Another voice spoke, lower and barely audible, such that she couldn't quite make out what they said.

Shit. Paige shot up, water spilling out from the bathtub. No matter. Barefoot, she looked around and grabbed the first piece of clothing she could find, a fluffy robe. It would have to do for now. She quickly wring out her hair before she emerged from the bathroom.

She cracked the door open to glimpse what was going on, but given the bedroom was the last room at the end of a long hall, it was hard to make out anything. So on tiptoes, she crept out.

Dante and another man she recognized from the club, who must be Finn, stood with their backs to her. Finn spoke with large exaggerated arm movements even as Davin held up both hands.

"I'm fine. See?"

"You fed." Dante was quick to point that out. How did he know?

When Davin tilted his head in puzzlement, Dante gestured towards his hand.

"That wound healed."

Oh, that's how he knew.

"Yes, I did." Davin set his chin and stiffened, everything in his pose challenging his brothers to disapprove.

Paige summoned her courage with a deep breath and stepped out into view. "It was consensual." Her hands on her hips, lips pursed, she looked at the brothers, also daring them to say another word as they turned to face her.

"Paige..." Davin hurried to her side and imposed himself between them.

"Her?" Finn sounded almost hysterical.

"The inugami?" Dante asked. Understanding dawned on him.

A weary sigh escaped Davin's lips and his posture relaxed. "Yeah. Its owner juiced it up and set it waiting for us in the garage after we came back from your place. Paige—" he nodded towards her — "killed it while it was trying to end me and she got me up here."

"That would explain why we thought you were at death's door, then you were fine." Dante stated as if everything had been explained while Finn crossed his arms across his chest with a humph. *Is the white-haired incubus pouting?* She ignored him and turned to Dante.

"Felt?" She had not learned this in her reading.

"Because we all share the same mother, we can somewhat sense each other. Just enough to know if one of our own is about to move on," Dante answered.

It was a closer call than she imagined.

"The only reason we didn't come storming up here right away was because we all felt Davin was fine in the next five to ten minutes. Wait, why are we explaining this to the human?" Finn looked between Dante and Davin. "And what inugami?"

"An inugami was after Paige. We're still not sure why. And she knows about everything, anyway."

Dismay marred Finn's otherwise beautiful features. "The others are gathering. Explain all this to Ava once she gets in town."

"Ava?"

"Avaline, our oldest sister."

"Oh." Paige paled and leaned against the wall for support. It was the second time she heard the name, and this Ava person sounded as scary as before.

"Paige?" In an instant, Davin was at her side, one hand on her elbow. "You okay?"

"Just a little wobbly, I guess."

"Let me help you to bed. You need more rest."

"Davin, I slept for sixteen hours already." She knew it came out whiny, but she was tired of resting.

"Now." The hardened expression on Davin's face broke no argument and with a huff, Paige allowed him herd her to the guest room, regardless of the others. The new clean sheets were soothing to her skin as she stripped off the robe, and try as she might to stay awake, she slipped back into slumber.

When she woke next, silence had resumed in the apartment. She spied her large pack in the corner. Davin must have gone downstairs to retrieve it while she passed out. Grateful to have her stuff again, she rummaged for fresh clothes and pulled on proper ones this time. She crept out of the bedroom to see him poring over a book. At the sound of her footsteps, he closed the book and set it aside.

"How are you feeling?"

"Stop asking me that." She smiled to take the sting out of her words.

He leveled her a look of admonishment.

Paige attempted to ignore it. "What about the others?"

He rose from his chair. "Don't worry about them. We bicker like the siblings we are, but they'll come around. They're my brothers. Let me handle them."

For once, she dropped the question. She didn't want to touch his family dynamics with a ten feet pole. Her gaze traveled to the tome on the table. "What are you reading?"

"Divination," Davin admitted. "But to be honest, I can't make heads or tails of it. Now that we've lost the connection to whoever made the inugami, it'll be harder to figure out who was behind all this."

So, they can attack again. Maybe with something even nastier. Paige shivered.

"Dante suggested we visit an oracle."

Why oracles existed would surprise her still, she had no idea. "Sure, oracle, why not?"

He chuckled. "I need to check on the bookstore, then we'll go. You up for it?"

"Yes! Stop babying me." she rolled her eyes.

"I can't help it!" Davin laughed a little, sending slivers of warmth traveling across her skin. "You saved my life. The least I can do is worry about you and spoil you a bit." His face lit up as his lips quirked upwards with that cheeky smile, looking much more like himself.

Good. Paige didn't want him guilt-ridden and walking on

eggshells around her. Still, Paige raised a brow then shook her head, refusing to let Davin know how relieved she was.

"Fine. I'll take the spoiling. But stop worrying. I'm okay now. Come on. I want to see this bookstore of yours."

"Okay, okay. Let's go."

CHAPTER 14
Davin

"**B**oss man!" Calvin waved with a cheerful grin from behind the counter as they arrived at the bookstore. Another head poked out from above, between two shelves.

"Oh, thank God." Kathryn stepped down from the ladder and hurried.

"Hey, guys. Kathryn, I thought you were off today." Davin kept the door open until Paige entered. Inside, he reveled the way her eyes widened and her lips parted in wonder. Ah, they were very kissable lips, even more so in reality. His incubus stirred but made no demands, still sated from yesterday.

Neither of his workers answered. Instead, they both turned towards Paige behind him, who, oblivious to the staring, wandered, fingers trailing along the shelves. Davin understood. He had never brought anyone to his shop before, and his staff were under the impression he was a confirmed bachelor.

And then recognition lit up Kathryn's eyes. "Oh, my God. Are you Paige Summers?"

The sparrow meeped and blushed. "Um... yes?"

It was an adorable sound, and Davin tried his best not to grin. As Paige didn't seem to require any introduction, he took a step away, grateful that her status as an author trumped any demand for him to explain why she was his guest.

"I can't believe it. I am such a fan of your work." By now, Kathryn had made her way over. "I watched your interview just this morning."

"Oh." Paige's cheeks remained pink, and Davin had to turn towards Calvin to hide the smile he could no longer hold back.

"Pass me the logbook." He opened the sales log and pretended to study it while monitoring the exchange from the corner of his eye.

"I'm glad you enjoyed the books," Paige managed a reply beyond one-word exclamations at last.

"So I've been dying to know. Were you really joking about the muse thing? Or is there someone...?"

Okay, that was enough. "Kathryn, how was yesterday?"

"Hmm? Oh? It was fine."

It was a very distracted answer and Davin, withholding a sigh, tried again. "Any customers asking for me?"

"What? Er...no boss."

In the background, Calvin smirked while Paige swept her gaze around as if looking for a way out.

Davin watched his little author and chuckled. He found it interesting how take-charge Paige could be one minute then mild and meek the next, depending on the situation.

"Oh, my God." Kathryn gasped and her hands flew over her mouth. "Tobias does look like the boss."

Calvin broke into a full cackle.

Okay, that was enough. Davin moved behind Paige and placed a hand on the small of her back. "I'll have to take a couple of days off. If anyone asks for me, tell them to shoot me a text. Otherwise, you guys have the shift schedule. Anything else comes up, call me. Kathryn, go home. I'm not paying you extra."

Without waiting for a reply, Davin ushered them out of the store, only slumping in relief once they got back into his car.

"Maybe I should give Tobias a haircut and a dye job," Paige muttered under her breath.

"What? No, don't you dare!" He turned to face her.

At Davin's horrified expression, Paige giggled, and soon, they were both laughing at the absurdity of the situation. Her laughter, like warm sunshine, washed over him and eased his remaining tension. She was still here. She hadn't run for the hills.

It was almost cliche as their eyes met. Somewhere in between the life and death situations they had been in the past forty-eight hours and the small moments of intimacy, something shifted. Davin was the first to lean across, a hand tucking a stray strand of hair that had fallen to cover her warm autumn-colored eyes. When Paige leaned into his touch, he switched to cupping her face.

This was not good for either of them.

Davin stopped caring as he tilted his head towards her and delighted when Paige closed the distance. The moment their lips met, every voice of caution or reason silenced. There was only her, her fragrance, the softness of her mouth, the small intakes of breath.

When they parted, Davin moved his thumb along her lower lip, tracing the memory of them. The possibility of never tasting them again scared him. And that fear unnerved him even more.

"Paige."

His phone rang.

As Davin cursed the damn timing, he eased back from Paige to dig for the device. The name on the caller ID drew a groan from him as Paige peered at his screen with curiosity. Filled with both reluctance and wariness, Davin hit the button and put the thing to his ear.

"If you are coming over, then move it. You're going to be late." The deep voice over the line held a peevish tone. The caller hung up, not waiting for Davin's answer.

"Oracles." Davin heaved a sigh. They needed to talk, but now was not the right time. "We better go. Never good to keep them hanging."

Paige laughed and patted his arm. The sound soothed his nerves, and Davin wondered how he ever thought he could live without hearing it again.

Crap. I've got it bad.

"Tell me about this oracle?" Paige asked as he drove them out towards the suburbs. "Wait, let me guess. An older woman, silver-haired, hippie dress. Oh and... big gemstone jewelry."

Davin smirked. "Aren't you describing Lillian?"

"Well." Paige's mouth opened then closed it. "Not intentionally. I suppose I was playing more into the typical stereotypes."

"You're going to be in for a rude surprise then."

"What do you mean?"

Davin shook his head and for the rest of the trip, remained tight-lipped. When Paige tried to tempt him into a game of twenty questions, he only laughed as her guesses grew more and more wild.

The one-storied house they pulled up to was like any other on the street. Davin smiled at the dubious expression on Paige's face, held out his hand for her as they approached and gave it a reassuring squeeze.

The door opened before they could knock and a woman very fitting of Paige's description appeared. About to point out she was right in the first place, the woman interrupted Paige's utterance by calling out over her shoulder. "Seth, your customers are here."

She swung the door wider and beamed at them. "Please, come in. Seth is down in the basement. Take the stairs in the back and knock on the gate- then head on in."

Familiar with this song and dance, Davin gave a polite smile of greeting. "Thanks." Leading a still-stunned Paige through the house and down, they paused at another entrance, this one with a homemade "keep out" sign, completed with hand-drawn skull and crossbones.

A surly man, only twenty years old, opened the way and let them in. He sported bondage pants and a black shirt with an anarchist symbol on it. With bangs, died too dark to be natural, falling over his eyes, the emo goth stared at the two of them.

Davin wasn't sure he liked the fact that Seth's jaws were hanging open. If he was expecting them, why was he so surprised?

"We came for a reading," Davin prompted.

"Fine." Seth stepped out of the way to allow them to enter the dim room that turned out to be his bedroom, crossed with his gaming space. Every console of the latest generation strung across the floor all hooked up to a giant tv screen hanging from one wall. Game discs laid in piles and they followed Seth's lead in navigating between the stacks until they reached a table, the only space devoid of clutter.

"Sit."

They both eased themselves into plastic folding chairs. It wasn't much, but Seth was as real as they came. And he had not steered anyone wrong yet, for the right price.

"Can't say a lot about this human here if you want a reading for your pet. She's ordinary as fuck."

"Hey!" Paige protested, rising from her seat.

Davin placed a hand on her arm, applying just enough

pressure to urge her to sit back down. He knew Seth's rudeness would come out, having witnessed it from the one other time he had been here, but this was downright belligerent, even for him. "Seth, this is Paige and someone means her harm. We need to find out who."

"Okay, it's your money to waste." Seth sighed and rolled his eyes, then extended his hand. Davin reached into his pocket, pulling out his wallet, then placed several large bills in the Oracle's palm. Seth pocketed them and returned to the same motion.

"More once we have our intel."

"Fine." Seth gave a theatric huff. How, after living thousands of years, did an Oracle still affect such a sullen teenager attitude was beyond Davin's imagination.

Davin turned to check on Paige and found her fists clenched; her jaws locked as she gritted her teeth. She was spitting mad. Davin reached under the table to give one of her knees a gentle squeeze. He felt her relax next to him.

"Hands, human."

"I have a name, you know. It's Paige and you can use it."

"Sure, whatever." Seth motioned for her again and she gave in with a short exhale, placing both of her hands in his.

With more care than he had shown so far, Seth turned them palm up and tilted his head back. As he cupped them, Seth's eyes rolled backward, his entire body trembling. Sweat beaded his brow the longer he remained in a trance until, without warning, he broke contact, shrinking away as if Paige were burning him.

"Jesus fucking Christ," Seth muttered.

Davin rose from his chair and moved to stand beside Paige, wrapping an arm over her shoulders. He looked down at her then followed her gaze to stare at the shaken Oracle who was busy coughing and clearing his throat.

"Well, she has a stalker."

Yeah, no shit.

"Female, can't tell too much more. Strong you-don't-see-me spells around her so you're looking at a heavy-weight witch." Seth shrugged, still rubbing his hands. "Tomorrow. Keep that sword close and stay by water."

"Dagger," Paige corrected.

"Whatever. Pay up."

A chill ran down Davin's spine, but he reached for his wallet. Future telling was a tricky business, and he knew this was as good as it was going to get.

Some screeching guttural voice startled them all and the Oracle cursed again. It was only seconds later that Davin realized it was a mobile ringtone.

"Just leave the money on the table." Without seeing them out, Seth disappeared into the back of the room, separated by a beaded curtain.

"Okay, you're right. That was a rude awakening." Paige rose from her seat and turned to go, but Davin placed a finger on his lips, asking for silence.

It was hard to pick up the whispered words, and he closed his eyes to concentrate.

"Yeah, she was here a sec ago. Got some nasty witch on her tail."

"Hey take it easy, I only gave them what they asked for, no more."

Another pause.

"She's with the incubus named Davin. I think her awakening will be soon. No, neither of them has any idea yet."

"Chill. I tiptoed. If she wakes up, it's not going to me that triggered it. Free tip: if I were you, I'd get my ass in town like now."

"I don't know, okay? Look, I'm done. Held my end of the deal, blah blah blah. I expect my money in my account."

His first instinct was to barge in and demand answers. Davin's fingers curled into fists, but he reined in his temper.

Upstairs was a damn powerful witch, and to start something on her home turf was stupid. Paige could get hurt even as a bystander.

"Let's go." Davin grabbed Paige's hand, his face pale.

They remained quiet until they returned to the car.

"What was that?"

"I'm not sure." Each word came out slow. "Seth was talking to someone about you and me. But I don't think it was whoever is after us." He slammed his hands on the steering wheel.

"Damn it. I hate being so in the dark."

"Hey, we'll figure it out?" Paige gave him a wane smile and reached out to take his hand, giving it a light squeeze.

"Yeah." He better. Soon.

CHAPTER 15

Paige

"So, we know whoever sent the inugami will turn up sometime tomorrow." Paige paced back and forth, stopping from time to time only to check on Davin sitting on the couch, stoic.

"You're going to wear a hole down on my floors, Paige." There was a hint of grumble in Davin's throat.

The waiting didn't sit well with either of them, and not for the first time since they left, Paige wished they pushed for more with Seth. But being so new to the supernatural world, she took her cues from Davin. The thought startled her. Was she relearning to trust him? Or was it because she had no choice?

She paused again and turned to face Davin in full, noting the drawn lines on his forehead, the way he sat on the edge of the couch, arms braced against his knees, fingers steepled against his lips. That mouth. The tender kiss they shared in the car rose from her mind and she shook her head. Instead, she focused on his worried expression. Davin didn't look half as concerned about the inugami.

"What is it?"

"I don't like this. Seth may have given us information about our original problem, but we have no idea who he was talking to on the phone." Something about the wariness in Davin's voice told her he was holding back.

"Davin?" She moved closer and kneeled down before him, so they were at eye-level. He promised to not withhold anything from her anymore, even if he was reluctant to share. She needed him to keep that promise. When he spoke again, she almost sighed in relief. She could trust him. No more lies, no more hiding.

"Seth mentioned something about an awakening, I'm pretty sure regarding you."

What? Paige blinked once, then twice. *None of that made sense.* "An awakening refers to when the powers in one of you start showing, right?"

"Exactly."

Their faces mirrored each other in their confusion. But like in the car, the mood shifted. Caught once more in his gaze, her heart raced until she could hear the pulsing in her ears. They had not spoken of the kiss since, but it hovered in the back of her mind. She couldn't deny the attraction between them, the desire she had for him that had nothing to do with him as an incubus and everything to do with his intimate knowledge of her mind and body.

"Paige." The hoarse whisper betrayed Davin's own desires. "You shouldn't be kneeling before me."

She didn't want to. The last thing she wanted was to submit to him. Sex to save his life was logical, sane - he was her ticket to survival, or so she told herself. This- this was something different. She swept her tongue across her lower lip, trying to wet her dry mouth.

"Paige, you have ten seconds to run back to your room."

It was a stark reminder. Davin wasn't a man who could control himself. He was an incubus, a demon with urges. The logical part of Paige screamed for her to flee, to get to a safe place, slam the door shut and if need be, work out her frustrations through her writing. But her body remained rooted to the spot. As his amber orbs glazed over, she bowed her head in submission.

That was all the permission he needed.

Davin brushed his fingers across her face, the feathery touches that sent shivers down her spine. They traced the contours of her jaw, only to tilt her chin up. "Look at me, little bird."

When Paige's eyes lifted to meet his, Davin spoke again. "You understand what this means."

There was a new savageness in those golden eyes, gleaming with power. This was the incubus talking. Some part of her knew they were the same, but the duality of his nature could not be more prominent than it was now.

Flee. Flee. This is insane. He could kill you.

Just once, she wanted to toss caution in the wind. To sample the forbidden fruit.

"Yes."

Davin surged forward. The hand that was so gentle with its touch before, snaked up to brush against the back of her neck, then grabbed a fistful of her hair. With a light tug, Davin pulled Paige's head backward, and as her lips parted, he pressed against hers, his tongue plunging in to duel with hers. When she made a small whimper, stunned by his ferocity, he swallowed the sound whole.

Davin's free hand drifted downwards, following the contours of her neck, knuckles brushing past her collarbone until he reached her breast. Cupping her flesh, he molded and kneaded, drawing moans of sweet torture. When he pulled back, his teeth nipped and tugged at her lower lip.

Sex with him, even dream sex, had always been amazing, but never like this. He had gone feral. She was playing with fire.

"Stand up."

Her body, detached from her mind, moved to obey. Was he controlling her? No, Paige was certain she had her free will. It was something else in her responding, a more primal instinct.

He rose with her, the nearness of him an inferno of heat. Davin spun her around until her back pressed against him, hands running up and down her body. His breath tickled her neck, his teeth scraping against her skin. A warning and a threat.

She held still for him as one hand slipped under her shirt, the other undoing the button and zipper of her pants. He took his time, tracing infuriating random patterns across her stomach, inching closer up to the other aching nipple, each second agonizing. But something else was happening. Every part of her came alive with heightened sensitivity as his scent, sandalwood mixed with a hint of citrus, intensified. Was this what he meant by pheromones?

It was an aphrodisiac.

"Davin." His name was a whimper of longing.

His hands ceased their movements, muscles taut with barely controlled restraint. Even now, despite all the instincts telling him otherwise, he was holding back, giving her a chance to withdraw consent. It was what made her decide.

"More, please."

A dark chuckle in her ear sent a delicious shot of pure lust to her core. Moments later, he followed the burning path, tracing the heat to slip under her panties, fingers slipping between her folds. He gripped her breast, just tight enough to be on the edge of pleasure and pain.

"You're mine, Paige."

He scraped a nail against her clit and pinched her nipple. The sudden over-stimulation drove her to double over, every muscle clenching as he followed her position, leaning on top of her, pressed against her back. He did not relent. There was no build-up. He slammed two fingers into her dripping pussy, the heel of his palm continued to grind against that nub of sensitivity. His length pushed up her ass, straining against his pants. He alternated between her nipples, pinching and rolling them. There was no tenderness and yet, she could not help the ceaseless moans that spilled from her lips as he finger-fucked her ruthlessly, bent over like animals in heat. She registered that his own breathing remained controlled.

She was, by nature, sensitive, but this was beyond what even her body was used to. When he bit down hard on her neck, Paige exploded in a quivering mess, screaming out her orgasm. Locked under him, she could only sag against him as, he relented at last, easing the pressure on her overstimulated clit.

Limp as a noodle, she scarcely registered him stripping her, then pushing her back to lie on the coffee table. Invisible bonds tied each of her limbs to a corresponding leg of the furniture, holding her spread-eagled for him.

The cold air nipped at her achy body and yet she still craved him inside. She licked her lips while he removed his clothes as well, and slid over her prone form. The practical side of Paige hoped the table would hold, but then there was no more room to think as his lips returned to travel across her body.

Davin began at her ear, the tip of his tongue tracing along the ridge in contrast to the earlier ferocity. He licked and suckled every inch of her downwards until he had her trembling with need again. And then he withdrew, staring at her with glittering eyes.

"What a delicious feast before me. You want it, don't you, little one?" A hand dropped between her legs and traced upwards. "Maybe I should leave you here wanting. It makes the meal even more delectable after."

The thought horrified her and she stared up at him in

shock. She strained against her bonds, but while they didn't hurt her, there was no give, either.

He parted her labia, and she groaned in embarrassment when her juices dropped downwards.

"Ah, I'll have to have a taste later." He held his finger up and licked, his tongue sliding with sensual grace around his digits. If she could escape, she would jump him, demon or no.

He must have read her mind as his lips curved into an almost cruel smirk.

This is what it means to tangle with the incubus, this wicked vicious pleasure. Will it always be like this? Do I care?

"What do you think, little bird?" He leaned down; face so close she felt his words brush by her skin. One hand rose to pet her before his fingers tangled in her hair. "Should I leave you tied up until the lust consumes you? Or do you want me to fuck you into oblivion?"

This was madness. And oh, how she wanted to embrace it.

"Please, fuck me." She didn't recognize the desperation in the whisper.

His laughter of delight filled her in ways she hadn't expected. And then he surged into her in one powerful thrust, burying himself to the hilt. Her hips struggled to meet his, but another invisible bond tied her midsection to the table, restricting her further. Held tight against the hard surface, she became a passive receptacle for his passion.

He started nice and slow, brows now drawn in concentration as he withdrew until only the tip remained, then thrust forward. With legs spread wide as she was, he felt massive, stretching her beyond what she remembered. And then as he pulled back and pushed in, a groan of pleasure causing her inner walls to spasm around his cock. Again. And again. The pace increased until he set a harsh rhythm, pounding into her relentlessly.

She saw it then, amidst the haze of lust and ecstasy, her

shimmering with blue, him absorbing it into himself. She closed her eyes, lightheaded and dizzy.

"Look at me," Davin barked, and she snapped them back open at the command. "My face is the only thing you should see when you come."

The words drove her to higher heights and when his fingers found her clit, she crested and fell over the edge. Euphoria clouded her mind, her world narrowing to only him and his cock thrusting inside her, now with a renewed urgency until, with a roar, he too came, within her.

His pace slowed until he was rocking against her, every movement forcing another moan, another gasp to escape. And that was when she realized.

He was still hard.

A part of her began to panic. He was going to break her. She couldn't handle one more like that, her nerves too overloaded from the new intensity of these orgasms. She was too weak to pull against her bonds, but she whimpered.

"Shh, it's okay, my pet. It's all right. I will take care of you." He petted her, disentangling his fingers from her hair as he ceased his movement within her. As her panic receded, he kissed her, her forehead, her brows, her nose, then a light peck on her lips.

"Do you trust me?" There was a quiver in his voice and all the bonds tying her to the table dissipated.

"I do." It came out as a croak.

He smiled for an instant, looking very much like the normal Davin. As he leaned back and withdrew from her, he scooped her up and carried her bridal style to his bedroom.

"Sleep?" Lethargy was settling in.

"Perhaps." His smirk, however, said otherwise.

CHAPTER 16
Paige

The cool sheets soothed her fevered skin as Paige laid on her side, curled up. Her body shivered at every minute movement of air, so hypersensitive from the aphrodisiac that was part of Davin's nature. She made a small mewling sound, her eyes half-closed as she panted for breath.

"Here, drink this, pet." Her lips parted to take hold of the straw, cold sweet liquid coursing down her throat. *Gatorade.*

"That's enough." Davin set the glass aside and brushed her hair back.

Paige trembled at his touch. Her body ached and yet she still craved him. *Oh God, am I addicted already?* The idea should horrify her, but a pleasant numbness blanketed her mind.

Davin climbed into bed with Paige and shifted until he was spooning her from behind, an arm wrapped around her midsection, pinning her to him. "It'll fade in a short while," he murmured in her ear. *Had he read her thoughts again? How?*

Paige's limbs were weak from the exertion, but that did not stop her from rubbing her legs together, their combined fluids dripping from her still, slickening her thighs. His cock, hard and throbbing, resting between her butt cheeks, and she couldn't suppress the whimper of desire that emerged.

"Careful my sparrow. You're not ready for me yet - so soon. Don't tempt the beast. I would not have you ruined."

With more willpower than she ever thought possible, Paige stilled her squirming and closed her eyes, attempting to find sleep. But the arousal that laid smoldering would not let her succumb to the darkness.

Unsure how much time had passed, Paige tensed when his hand dipped lower. With a soft moan, her legs parted for him.

"Good girl." Davin caressed her ear with his lips as he spoke, then trailed down, nibbling every exposed part of her neck. Her insides ached, but there was no pain as a digit entered her.

When she didn't seem to flinch from his touch, he added another finger, pumping in and out at a more casual pace. Her arousal increased but refused to peak as he continued his administrations.

"So wet and ready."

Whereas the last round was fierce, this time, he took it slow building up layer after layer of pleasure that pushed her closer but never over the edge. His languid movements drove her mad with lust as her hips began moving more erratically, seeking the relief that only he could provide. When he withdrew, she let out a whine and her hands flew to her own clit, ready to finish herself off.

"Bad pet." He squatted her hand away, then took hold of her wrist, drawing it behind her back. "Here, your only pleasure is what I choose to give you."

What had she done? Submitting to a fictional dream man was one thing. Submitting to a sex demon in real life? But it was such sweet surrender.

His body pressed close, trapping her arm between them.

His own hand moved downwards, leaving a streak of red as he scraped his nails against her skin. The hint of pain only made her inner muscles clench, already missing him, any part of him, inside her. The hand slid forward and lifted her leg up.

"How much do you want this, little bird?"

She knew he wanted an answer and wouldn't proceed further without one. The tip of his cock circled her entrance, teasing, prodding, but never pushing into her. Her clit burned for his touch. Words. She wrote words, but she never spoke them out loud before. They came with halting pauses in a hoarse whisper as he drove her mad with need. "I want this. I want you. Inside. Fuck me. Do what you want with me. Please just let me come."

"Then sing for me." And he slid himself into her in one long, delicious stroke.

And she sang a melody of moans and whimpers, gasps and pants as he thrust into her again and again, his pace steady and unhurried. With every cry, he pushed a little deeper, lifted her leg higher and grew harder within. The angle rubbed the most sensitive spots inside in novel ways until she trembled against him, mini orgasms coursing through her body. Each peak of pleasure only heightened her sensitivity until she broke and crested in waves that wrung her dry. Vaguely, she glimpsed blue energy transferring from herself to him and wondered if that was him feasting on her climaxes.

"Please, please, please," she whispered, unsure if she was begging for him to stop or to never stop. The conflict only made her come again, her back arching almost violently as she buckled out of his hold.

Davin growled in response and in one swift moment, pulled out, leaving her mid-orgasm and hungering for his cock. He bound her wrists and shoved her face-first into the pillow. Next, he lifted her hips and pushed her knees further apart to ensure her ass was sticking up high, exposing her pussy in the new position.

With his grip firm enough to bruise, he rammed into her in one hard stroke. She came at once, screams muffled by the bed and for a moment, he held still for her. A guttural groan rumbled from his chest. He shifted to grab the invisible bonds that held her wrist as leverage to pull her back to him. "That's it, Paige. Come for me. How many more can you take?"

It was the last words he spoke, a rhetorical question as he pounded into her with a ferocity that caused the entire bed to shake and the headboard to bang against the wall. Her vision faded under the relentless assault as her mind detached from her body, only distantly aware that she could no longer tell when a climax ended and another one began. It was not humanly possible. Later. Later, maybe she could rationalize it. Right now she couldn't even recall her own name.

Somewhere above her, she heard a loud roar and felt her insides flooded with his seed. It was the last act that tipped her over, her body spasming almost painfully, holding his cock inside until she collapsed, darkness swallowing her whole.

When she woke, the sun had gone down and night enveloped the room. She was laying curled up against a still Davin, pinned to him so she couldn't move. As her eyes adjusted to the blackness, she noted with satisfaction that not only was he sound asleep but that his cock had softened.

Her limbs felt like Jell-O, but the sudden urge to pee drove her to remove herself from his embrace. It didn't work as he growled in his sleep and only held her tighter to him. *Not good.* Paige tried again, this time with a little more force and until she created enough of a gap to squirm and slide out of his arms.

She had just made it off the bed when she heard a growl of warning.

Paige froze.

"Where do you think you're going, Sparrow?"

She turned around, keeping every move slow and careful. Any sign of aggression could bring the incubus back out. His still glazed-over, hungry eyes told her as much.

"I need to go pee," she stammered and gestured towards the bathroom but made no other movement lest the predator decided it was an excuse to pounce.

Davin stared at her and with a more human sigh, he pushed himself up. "Fine." With more grace than she could hope to muster, he rose from the bed and stepped up behind her.

"What are you doing?"

"You're going to the bathroom. Go."

She took two paces and when he followed in step, she whipped around. "You are not watching me pee."

"Sure."

Paige wanted to stay and argue, but the urgency was too great. With a sigh, she half-ran to the washroom. When she tried to slam the door in his face, he held it open with a strength she could not beat.

"Go."

At least Davin had the decency to turn his back towards her. For now, it would do. Later there would be a reckoning. When Paige finished her business and washed her hands, he grabbed her wrist, dragging her to bed.

"Hey," she protested.

"Obey." Davin stopped short of throwing her on to the sheets but watched with possessive intensity as she climbed in and laid down. Only then did he join her, pulling her against him, body curling over hers. "Mine," he muttered with a sigh of contentment and sank back into slumber.

Guess complete control didn't return to him yet. Paige's mind struggled to process what happened, to come to terms with her decision to tangle with the demon. But soon, exhaustion overwhelmed her, and she fell back to sleep.

"Paige?"

She spun around. Rather than the familiar bedroom they shared, they were in a garden of wildflowers with an old-fashioned Victorian set of table and chairs sitting in the middle. It was set for two, a pot of steaming tea beckoning her to take a seat.

From behind a pillar encircled with vines and roses, he stepped out, amber eyes clear. In the dreamscape, he was in control.

"Shade." She breathed out his name. Here, she would always think of him as her muse.

"Are you okay?"

Paige stared at him as she struggled for honesty. She wanted to say yes, to scoff at the idea that she was also fragile, that she would not be fine after a lusty bout of sex. But what they had was more than that. The things he made her body feel were beyond human capacity.

"I'm not sure. I need time to process."

His shoulders slumped in defeat. No, she couldn't have him think that way. Her heart broke for him.

"Shade. I regret nothing." Paige wanted to be alone with her thoughts, but for his sake, she forced herself to speak her thoughts out loud. "I needed to experience, to understand all of you, not just the safe parts."

"And now you know." His tone had gone flat.

"And now I know." Her lips curved into a small smile. "And I'm still alive." She took a step closer to him. "I'm not broken. I haven't become some mindless addicted sex slave." Another step, so close that she reached for his hand, fingertips brushing his. "And you didn't hurt me." The grin turned mischievous. "At least, not in ways I don't want to be hurt."

Shade let out a breath and shook his head. "You tease. You'll be the death of me."

She laughed and felt pressure on her chest lifted.

"Paige. You saw, though. As an incubus, I..."

With a tenderness that contrasted their earlier coupling, she took his hand and raised it to hold against her cheek. "I know," she whispered. "We are different. Hell, we don't even have the same lifespans. I'm scared. But I'm more terrified of living with the regret I'll have if I didn't give this a try." Paige's voice quivered, and she swallowed hard.

When he tried to speak, she shook her head. "I wanted to be mad at you forever, but it was worse imagining you no longer a part of my life. I don't have any answers, but I know I can't lose you. And that is no less true now that I have learned about the incubus part of you."

"Paige, I..."

She never got to hear his reply. Searing pain ripped her away, slamming her back into the waking world. Consciousness rose and fell before another shot of pure agony forced her eyes to snap open as her mouth parted in a wordless scream. Her side was a mass of burning heat and she thrashed in the bed. Blood poured from her nose.

"Paige. Paige!" Beside her, Davin jolted awake. He scrambled to strong-arm her until he could roll her over, just in time to see the blistering skin forming across her thigh.

He hauled her up and carried her to the bathtub. With great care, despite her writhing body, he deposited her in there before turning on the tap. She didn't register, twisting to escape the invisible, all-consuming flames that radiated from her leg up to the rest of her.

As the tub filled, the pain receded, leaving only a jeering, high-pitched female voice echoing in her head.

"Come out, little whore. Come find me if you want to see your friend again." Then, it was gone.

CHAPTER 17
Davin

*L*ittle known fact: the effects of fae magic fade over running water, in particular with major negative workings like curses and hexes. In the past, that meant heading to the nearest river, but water moving in a bathtub would do in a pinch when combined with protective wards.

When Paige tried to rise, eyes widening with panic, Davin reached to push her shoulders until she sank back into the waters. Whatever had caused her such sudden and terrifying pain, he didn't trust that the event had ended.

"She's gone," Paige whispered with a great shudder, then turned towards him, fear dawning on every part of her face. "Davin, please, get me my cell."

What he wanted to know was how she could be sure the hex had faded, but there was such desperation in her voice, he held back his question and nodded instead. When he returned, she snatched the phone out of his hand and with the pain already forgotten, hit the dial button.

Davin wished Paige would just stop and fill him in on what was happening.

"Ains?"

He leaned closer, his preternatural hearing enabling him to pick up the words from the other end of the line.

"Paige?" A broken sob. "Oh, God, she took her. She took Lillian."

Still sitting in the bathtub, Paige shivered. If only he could take her out, wrap her in the fluffiest blanket and hold her until the panic in her eyes receded. Or at least put a warming spell on the cooling water. But he dared none of those things. Sometimes power opened the way to more power, rendering the water's protection moot. So Davin did the only thing possible and kept his hand on her shoulder, this time hoping to provide some sense of comfort.

"Ains, Ainsley, I need you calm. Where are you? Are you hurt?" A look of anguish accompanied the last question as they both held their breaths.

"At Lillian's. She came, out of nowhere, swept past every ward Lillian had as if they were nothing. She... she..." Again Ainsley's voice cracked, and she groped this time for courage to continue. "Paige. I can't get up. She... I think she broke my ankles."

Davin's grip on Paige tightened even as he paled. The last thing they expected was for this witch to come after her friends. And from the shock they heard in the other woman's voice, the strike must have happened recently, perhaps just before the attack on Paige.

This was a game of cat and mouse. She had taken one as a hostage and left another behind to tell the tale. Damaged as an example, a show of power. Intimidate, bully, and drive them into the corner where she wanted them. Paige drew in a sharp breath and Davin watched with pride as she fought against her rising horror to stay calm for her friend.

"I'm coming, Ains. I'm coming for you, you hear me? You hang on. I love you and I will be right there."

Davin stopped listening to Paige's call and turned to his own phone. This was spiraling out of control. He couldn't protect two females at the same time, in particular, if one was already injured.

He brought the device to his ear and waited until his brother picked up. "Dante, I need back-up. They hurt Ainsley and hexed Paige. We're heading over now."

There was only a moment of pause. "Text me the address. I'm on my way. I will meet you there."

When he hung up, his sparrow had assumed full warrior mode, standing in the bath, eyes blazing with fury. Only her trembling legs betrayed the pain and fatigue she must still be feeling.

"Stay here. The water's what's keeping the hex from working. I'll grab your sword and see what else I can do."

"Hurry." Paige rocked from heel to toe and back even as she gritted her teeth. "Your Oracle sucked, and I'm going to strangle the little emo wimp's neck after this is all over."

Fair. Davin returned once more with the iron dagger which he placed on the vanity counter. "Here, your clothes. But before that." He held out a necklace for her. A small strip of leather with a deep black stone, obsidian framed in silver. "I commissioned this protection charm from Marie Laveau after..." His voice cracked as he stared at the jewelry in his hand.

Memories resurfaced, images he had long suppressed, but he pushed himself to continue.

"... after I found out a hex was placed on a human friend of mine. It was slow and subtle, and we thought at first that someone was poisoning his food. But by the time I realized what it was and got to him, it was already too late."

Davin startled and met Paige's eyes as he felt her hand on his.

"I'm sorry about them." And then she gave a determined nod of permission. "But I won't die on you, Davin. Not today. Not tomorrow. Not for a long while."

That iron will in her voice soothed his anxiety. "Okay." He stepped close to fasten the necklace around Paige's neck. The nearness of her stirred his sated incubus even as every male instinct in him wanted to ensure she was okay. Instead, Davin settled to press his lips against hers in a searing kiss as he lifted her out of the bath. "I'll hold you to that."

When Paige did not collapse in pain again, Davin's fear eased a little further, enough that he felt as though he could resume breathing. Perhaps the witch had withdrawn for now, or maybe the necklace was doing its job. After all, one of the most powerful witches in history, the voodoo queen herself, had created this protection charm. Very few could rival her magics.

He studied Paige, inspecting her on where the hex may have already done physical damage. The skin on her hip remained red and puffy. The curse had traveled upwards along her side in angry lines. But even as they both looked down, they watched in amazement as the blisters healed. The speed with which she was recovering rivaled Davin's own.

Is this the awakening Seth talked about?

"Davin?" For the first time, Paige sounded hesitant. Lost. And then she shook her head. "No, later. We need to go get Ainsley."

"Later," he agreed. Satisfied that she was steady on her feet, Davin left her to dress. She had fed him well and power hummed through his body. Still, he pocketed his own weapons, just in case. When she emerged from the bathroom, lips set in a tight line, he knew they were as ready as they could ever be.

They entered the car, and he passed her several granola bars and a bottle of Gatorade he had grabbed as they left. "You haven't recovered fully, yet."

Paige opened her mouth to protest.

"Weak from me feeding on you. Eat. Please. For me."

When Paige nibbled, then took bigger and bigger bites of food, Davin exhaled. She needed more fuel. She should get more rest. Some part of him screamed at the insanity of letting her come along. Still, he reminded himself that while she would submit to him in bed, no amount of commanding would keep her away from this. One friend hurt, the other missing. Even weakened as she was, Davin suspected even if he tied her down, she would escape to save her friends.

Davin got them there in record time just as Dante pulled up next to them. His brother nodded in greeting, stoic as ever as they made their way to the house.

The violence that occurred here was devastating. The door hung on a single remaining hinge and broken glass was scattered across the floor, blown inwards by some inexplicable force. Davin's gaze moved to Paige to check on her. She had drawn the long dagger from its sheath, but her knuckles were white and she trembled with her grip. Her brows drew together, focused on putting one foot in front of the other. Davin sent a silent plea to any greater power that she wouldn't collapse from exhaustion and a thread of guilt wound around his heart. He shouldn't have fed on her. He shouldn't have made her even more vulnerable.

The house was eerie in its silence. Davin had almost expected a trap but detected nothing. Whoever had sown this chaos and destruction was long gone.

A small whimper cut through the quiet. Dante broke away from their formation and surged forward. Paige followed close behind with Davin trailing after them.

There she was. Ainsley had propped herself up against the side of a china cabinet, its contents spilled around her. Blood was still trickling down from a slash on her forehead and her legs laid stretched out in front of her, bare feet twisted at odd angles. *Yes, broken.* Bruises had not quite started forming yet, but even from a cursory look, Davin knew she would have some wicked ones by tomorrow.

Ainsley whimpered again as they approached before recognition drew a sob of relief from her. Dante kneeled down and, with a gentle tenderness that Davin had never before witnessed from his brother, brushed back the mess of curls from her eyes.

"You're safe now. You'll be okay. We'll take care of you."

If the situation wasn't so dire, Davin's jaw would have dropped in amazement at this new side of Dante that he didn't know.

"Ains. Oh, God, I'm so sorry." Paige dropped to her knees beside them and set aside the iron dagger as Dante withdrew to put down his pack. His brother was laying out first aid items, and Davin berated himself for not thinking of that.

Both girls broke into tears as Paige wrapped her arms around Ainsley, letting her friend's head rest against her chest.

"I need you to keep her calm."

Davin could anticipate what was to come. He turned away from the low murmuring of reassuring words to scan the house instead, looking for clues. They knew she was a powerful witch, but what was her motivation? Why Paige? What was it he was missing?

A high-pitched scream followed by sobs interrupted his thoughts. Another one with less intensity made him cringe. Dante had just reset Ainsley's bones. Poor woman.

And then he saw it. Amidst the chaotic destruction of the entire house, the dining table where they had tea and scones at their last visit remained bereft of debris. A single piece of paper laid upon the surface, weighed down by a hairbrush on one side and Lillian's athame, coated with red, on the other. Davin's blood ran cold as he approached until he was close enough to see the elegant cursive writing.

An address, a time set for this evening, and nothing else.

But he knew the handwriting. His hands clenched into fists as he stared with disbelieving eyes.

Anna.

He hadn't realized he said the name out loud until the others joined him, Ainsley cocooned in a blanket in Dante's arms.

"Who's Anna?" Paige asked, her quiet words echoing in the house.

Davin trembled as emotions swirled in him, choking the words in his throat. This was never about Paige. *Anna was still alive. How?*

"Davin!" This time it was Dante that barked at him.

Davin struggled to draw air into his lungs. When he spoke, visceral torment cracked his voice.

"Anna is the monster I created. And why I try to never feed on another person."

Paige looked as though she wanted to push further, but she followed his gaze, instead, to study the paper and the objects.

"So she came after me because of you."

Davin flinched at the truth of the words and nodded, numbness fogging his mind.

Paige gathered the items. "She showed up here to find something that would help her put the hex on me, and she came to hurt my friends to get to me."

Three people suffered because of him. He could wallow and self-flagellate all he wanted later, but he needed to focus on fixing this mess.

"Dante, can we use your house? If it's Anna, I don't trust my own." It pained Davin to admit that.

Dante nodded and Davin turned to Paige. "I promise you a full explanation, but right now we need to get Ainsley out of here and determine our next move, before the appointed meeting place and time."

Paige opened her mouth, then closed it again with a firm nod. Equal parts of gratitude and admiration welled up in him for her practical nature.

They left the house and Davin steeled himself for the confession of his long-lived life.

CHAPTER 18
Paige

"Anna Duffeld was a nun I met in the seventeenth century. Life was hard for women in the new world, but she was bright, curious and adventurous. I was stupid, naïve and damn awful then. They say you could get a human addicted to you, but I didn't believe that. I enjoyed corrupting innocents without thinking of the consequences. And once I introduced Anna to sex, there was no going back."

Paige sat on the edge of the loveseat, her body stiff as a board. She studied Davin as he spoke. His voice was steady, but he did not look up to face any of them in the room. With a start, she realized that this was what shame looked like.

Next to her, Ains gave her hand a squeeze in silent support. Her best friend had refused any suggestions for rest and had bullied Dante to putting her down on the other side of the loveseat. Paige was grateful, for she wasn't sure if she could get through this story without the emotional rock that was Ainsley.

Dante rounded out the audience and remained standing

behind Ainsley as if ready to help her with anything. It was endearing.

Nobody said a word. Davin took a sip of the scotch his brother had poured for him and let out a sigh. It was a bit early for a drink, but in this case, Paige felt as though she could use one herself. Maybe it would calm the storm building within.

"I was so sure that we were scratching a mutual itch, that neither of us really had feelings for each other, and when it was time to move on, I just said to her I was leaving. Thought that was all I needed to do. I was wrong. She flipped when I told her I didn't feel the same way."

The hollow expression on his face broke Paige's heart.

"I ran, like a coward."

"Davin, if Anna was a nun in the 1600s, how the hell is she still alive now?" Paige struggled to keep her tone neutral, and her words even, when what she wanted to do was take Davin by the shoulders and shake him until he showed some emotion.

Davin swallowed and looked up at Paige. "She went dark. I had introduced her to the world of the supernatural and had no qualms about sharing info with her. It seemed fun back then, corrupting her faith and her innocence. Instead, it backfired. She started delving into the occult and found she had enough power to pull off minor spells and get herself apprenticed once she left the church."

This was nothing like the Davin Paige knew today. A tiny voice whispered how much similar her own situation was to Anna. Was she addicted to the mind-blowing sex? Had he somehow ruined her in the same manner, but modernized? She opened her mouth to speak but caught a subtle shake of the head from Dante. *Dear God, there is more?*

Davin set his glass down. "She wasn't content to let me go, and she had convinced herself that I would stay if she found a way to extend her lifespan to match mine. She struck a deal with a dark entity. Eternal life and power for sacrifices she would bring it, for as long as she lived."

Would I become that psychotic if Davin told me he was leaving? No, but unease crept along the back of her neck. How would she know unless it happened? She shook her head. *No, absolutely not.* She was not some lovesick obsessive woman. She refused to be.

"Paige?" Ainsley gave her hand another squeeze, this time to jolt her from her thoughts.

Paige groaned and sagged in her seat, rubbing her temple. "You mean to tell me that all of this is coming from some stupid cliche jealous stalker ex trope?" The writer in her saw beyond all the tangled webs to the simplicity of the situation.

"She's got you there, Dav." An unfamiliar voice cut through the air as a girl of about eighteen descended from the stairs in the back of the room. Clad in a white sundress with silver hair bound in a braid, she appeared almost waif-like with her luminous indigo eyes.

She was gorgeous, delicate, like a precious doll. And yet, full pouty lips and a certain regal poise spoke of sultry experience. Somehow, the two aspects of this strange woman moved in impossible harmony. Who the hell was she?

An urge to rise and bow tugged at Paige, and she saw her confusion mirrored on Ainsley's face. Dav. Davin's siblings called him that. Was this then a succubus?

In answer, Davin rose from his seat and inclined his head even as Dante shifted to do the same.

"Ava. When did you get in?" Davin asked.

How long had she been listening to their conversation? Why didn't Dante tell them there was someone else here?

Ava threw a glance at him and shrugged. "Late last night. Now introduce us."

Her lilting voice rang with authority. This was a woman used to obedience from others.

"Paige, Ainsley, please meet our eldest sister, Avaline.

Ava, this is Ainsley and Paige." Davin gestured to each of them.

Paige wondered if she should get up out of politeness more than anything, but Avaline was already in front of her, their faces in close proximity. Paige found Ava examining her and as their eyes met, the depth of ancient wisdom in Avaline's took her breath away. This was someone that had seen the rise and fall of civilizations, that knew secrets that the human mind could not comprehend.

"So this is your chosen mate."

Wisdom my ass.

"What?" Paige and Davin stared at Avaline in shock.

"No, I'm not…"

"She's not my…" Great, now they were both tripping over each other's words.

"Right." Avaline lifted a delicate brow and shrugged. The blatant disbelief galled her, but when Ava cupped Paige's face, any further protests died in her throat. From the corner of her eye, she saw Davin's hands ball into fists.

"Hm, there's something about you." Ava murmured. Paige gaped at her. The woman was moving so fast from one vague statement to another, she was giving her whiplash. "More to you than what's on the surface. I hope you stick around, despite that brother of mine being a bit of a bonehead."

Paige wanted to purr at the warm tone of approval. Not even Davin had this kind of effect on her. Was this because she was the oldest?

There was a spark of satisfaction when she also realized that she wanted to yell at Avaline too for calling Davin names. Perhaps she had some natural resistance to incubi and succubi? *God, I hope so.*

Next, Avaline turned to Ainsley. "Oh, you poor thing. I am so sorry you got hurt because of Dav's mistakes. If there's anything I can do to help, please let me know." Her voice gentled as she touched Ainsley's hair, stroking the curls. She leaned closer and whispered to her before smiling at the stunned expression on her face. "Don't worry, it'll come in time."

Paige wanted to find out what Avaline whispered to Ainsley. Later. She hoped there was a later.

"Dante." Avaline straightened, her tone commanding once more. "You're on guard and service duty. Make sure you take care of Ainsley until she makes a full recovery. Anything she needs. Send the bill to me."

"Yes, Ava." Dante nodded once more, a man of few words.

"Please Avaline, it's unnecessary," Ainsley protested.

"Nonsense. It's the least I can do." Again a soft, almost mothering smile, so at odds with her childlike appearance.

It was the first time she saw Ainsley's protests brushed aside. Paige blinked once, twice. Avaline's dominance and command over the room was staggering.

And then Ava turned to Davin.

"You. Davin Murphy."

He winced.

"You better fix this, you hear? Time you deal with Anna once and for all. And maybe if you're lucky and grovel hard enough, your mate may forgive you for putting her through your mess."

"I'm not…" Paige made another attempt at correcting her.

"It'll be all right." Ava winked at her, though Davin looked as if he had swallowed something rotten.

There is no arguing with that woman, is there?

"Yes, Ava," Davin echoed with a sigh of exhaustion.

"I'm heading out. You all get some rest." Avaline waved and left, leaving more questions than answers.

The four of them stared at the door closing behind Ava.

"Well, that was…" Paige started.

"… a thing." Ainsley shook her head.

"Now what?" Dante asked. It was a good question and Paige turned to Davin only to see others do the same.

"I'll handle it," Davin said at last. "Dante, if you can stay here to protect Paige and Ainsley, I will meet Anna at the appointed time and get Lillian back. She won't hurt her for now."

Yeah, no.

"No way!" Paige sprang up from her seat. "You are not going alone." He was insane. *He can't walk into all of this by himself. The woman was unstable and so far, she has stayed several steps ahead of them. This is a trap.*

"Yes, I am. I am not putting you in any more danger." Davin shot back.

Paige stared at him, her temper rising until it roared in her ears. Of all the times he could have pulled a neanderthal, stupid macho stunt...

"Ainsley, would you like me to show you to a guest room to get some rest?" Dante's quiet voice cut through her thoughts. It was a tactical retreat.

"Good idea," she muttered in reply and allowed Dante to carry her away with a last glance of worry and apology. Paige understood, though. This was her battle.

Paige closed her eyes and drew a deep breath to rein in her temper. Yelling would achieve nothing. "Davin, if you think I'm letting you do this alone, you have another thing coming." Her voice hardened. "Don't turn this into some atonement shit. This Anna hurt my friends. She made this *personal.*"

"I can't stand..." He swallowed and tried again. "Already knowing that all this is because you're with me..." Some emotion, at last. His voice cracked.

"What you did to Anna was wrong. And it is a wrong that you need to right." She dared a step forward towards him.

"But that was also a long time ago, and I know that is not who you are now."

"How can you be so sure?"

His fear was palpable. That alone spoke volumes. His confession about Anna brought with it a new clarity and all of a sudden, all his previous hesitations made sense. He was his own bogeyman. But another memory resurfaced.

They laid in bed, basking in the afterglow. The sex was tender, mixed with the amount of aggressiveness that turned it to something so much hotter.

"You know, writing these little shorts, but I've been toying with an idea of a novel."

"Why not?" His eyes twinkled with excitement.

"It's an enormous commitment... I don't know if I can hold a complex enough story for a full book."

"Well, you just need to try." Shade rolled to his side and propped his head up with his arm. "I know you can do it. You're driven. You can accomplish whatever you set your mind to. Besides, bounce ideas off me and if you require a little inspiration..."

The wink he gave her made her giggle, her cheeks blushing despite their naked state. He closed the distance, pressing his lips on hers, and she forgot all her doubts.

"I'm not." She smiled at him. "But it's what I choose to believe. Because sometimes the thing you need the most is someone to believe in you. Just like how you believed in me."

Davin swept her into his arms and held her to him as if he was clinging to a life preserver. He pressed his lips on the top of her head, burying his face against her hair as he sucked in deep breaths. Her own hands rubbed his back in slow, soothing circles as she remained buried against him.

"Do you see why I can't lose you?" His whisper tickled her skin.

"And do you understand that if I'm to be a part of your life, I can't always be under your protection alone? I need to stand on my own two feet." Paige eased backward to look up at him, eyes intent. She may be only human, but damn if she was going to be the princess in the castle. "Lillian is my responsibility too, and I refuse to run away from this."

It looked as though Davin was about to protest, but he heaved a heavy sigh instead. "Did I mention you are one of the most stubborn and infuriating humans I have ever had the pleasure of meeting?"

Paige laughed then and reached up to pet the top of his head. "Yes, you've said as much before."

Davin pulled her hand down and kissed the inside of her palm, his eyes closing as if he were savoring the taste of her. She shivered. "We should talk game plan."

"Later," Davin murmured. "Let me make love to you. Not feed. Make love."

Everything in her tensed at his hushed words, even as her body responded to the request by growing damp with desire. But it was her heart that raced at an abnormal speed. He had used the L-word. *No, it was just a phrase for sex. Right?*

"No more thinking, my sparrow." Taking advantage of her momentary silence, he swept her off her feet and carried her away.

CHAPTER 19

Davin

He knew she had tangled with the demon and accepted that side of him. For her, it may be enough, but not for him. Davin needed to prove to her, but even more so to himself that he could remain in control, that he could be the lover she deserved. That he was not the same incubus he had been in the seventeenth century.

Davin set Paige down on the bed with a wink. "Stay here, I'll be right back." He chuckled as he glimpsed her puzzled expression before he left the guest room.

"Dante?" Davin counted himself lucky that he had caught his brother as he was leaving another one of the many rooms in the large suburban house.

Dante raised a finger to his lips and shook his head before leading Davin away. "Ainsley fell asleep. Let her get some rest."

"Oh?" Davin smirked.

"I won't pry if you don't." There was no hint of emotion in Dante's neutral expression. This incubus still had the best poker face Davin ever knew.

"Fine. Do you have a bottle of massage oil?"

Dante's brow knit together.

"Lotion?"

With a sigh, Dante motioned for him to follow, retrieving some from a cabinet in another washroom. As he handed it to Davin, he frowned with gravity. "You're responsible for cleaning and replacing the sheets afterwards. Detergent is on the top shelf above the dryer."

"Yeah, yeah, yeah. Thanks, bro!" Davin waved, eager to return to Paige. He had kept her waiting long enough.

She blinked as he re-entered.

Davin set the bottle aside and stripped off his t-shirt as he spoke. "Ancient Celts considered women to be equals with men in every way. They often fought alongside each other."

He grinned as he approached, his hand tugging at the tank top she had on. "May I?"

When Paige nodded her consent, he helped her out of her clothes.

"One tradition I adore is that before a battle, warriors are feted and encouraged to indulge in many vices. They believed it would raise the warrior spirit." Davin pressed a small kiss on her temple and guided her to lie down on her stomach before stripping her of her pants and panties.

"I'd like to think of it as a way to remind us what we are fighting for, what we have to live for."

He delighted in the small gasp Paige let out as his weight descended on her, settling above her buttocks. But he could still sense the wheels turning in her head.

"Davin, just how old are you?"

His movements paused and a low chuckle rumbled in his chest.

"Not so old as the ancient Celts, no. I got that from a rare copy of the *Táin Bó Cúailnge*. It's translated from the *Book of Leinster* on the famous Irish legend, *the Cattle Raid of Cooley*." His hands had resumed rubbing her back, warming her flesh with his touch, but he paused. "Enough with the history lessons. Not the sexiest pillow talk."

"Big brains are sexy."

Paige never ceased to amaze him. Any lover he had in the past would praise his skills in bed, his appearance or physique. It was perhaps the first time anyone called his intellect hot. He laughed and leaned down to kiss her shoulder. "Thanks, darling," he whispered against her skin.

His hands, slick with lotion, were soon replaced by his lips, then he continued kneading her shoulders. He focused on each muscle group with careful attention, working out each knot until she relaxed.

"Oh, dear God," she moaned into the pillow.

Paige grew silent after that, and if not for the occasional whimper and slight twitches, Davin would have thought she fell asleep. He worked his way downwards, the strength of his fingers unrelenting until she melted into the sheets beneath him.

"For the record, I'm around five hundred years old. But if you try to call me a cradle robber, there will be punishment."

He felt more than heard the sharp intake of breath but gave no reply. Worry gnawed at him about concern over whether he had overwhelmed her until he reached a particularly nasty knot at the small of her back that provoked a groan from her.

His cock twitched at the sound, but he ignored it. His libido could take a hike right now. This was about her pleasure.

"My poor sparrow." Davin's lips again replaced his hands, butterfly kisses soothing away the pain. He paused with the rubdown, giving her time to recover, and instead, refocused on attending to her in a different manner. With the tip of his tongue, he traced along the outline of her tattoo, tasting her. He so adored it, for it memorialized the moment they first met in the twilight of dreams.

His actions drew a long groan.

Davin shifted his weight to sit on top of her thighs, pinning her legs together. He drifted lower still working her muscles until he was massaging her ass, his fingers digging in, loving the feel of her soft but toned flesh in his hands. When he ventured a peek, he saw her eyes flutter closed.

"Don't fall asleep on me, Paige. I'll just do this all over again in your dreams."

Her lips curved into a smile as she turned her head to lay her cheek against the pillow. "Mmm, that doesn't sound like a deterrent to me."

Davin chuckled and nipped her where her neck joined the shoulder. "No, but I enjoy reality so much more."

For a little longer, he continued downwards, over her glutes, her calves, down to her delicate feet. When he pressed against the pressure points along her soles, she moaned in ecstasy. His cock was now straining against his pants, but again, he denied himself any relief.

Davin shifted until he kneeled over Paige and lifted his weight so that he no longer rested on her. "Roll over on to your back."

Her eyes were intent as she followed his directions, then watched as he warmed more lotion in his hands and began on her arm.

"You could have done that while I was still lying face down," she pointed out with a raised brow.

"I wanted to enjoy this view, too." His lips curved into an impish grin, but his gaze grew in intensity. So far, one purpose or another had spurred their moments together - her trying to save his life, his incubus' insistence on showing dominance. This was the first time he had the luxury to study her for real, to see her completely.

While Davin caressed her with his fingertips, his mind made comparisons between dream and reality. Here was a mole she never dreamed about. There, the skin darkened with tan lines. A light smattering of freckles spread across her chest. A small scar, faint with time, followed the curve of her elbow. He noted every imperfection and cherished them even more. This was Paige, flesh and blood, and he worked to commit everything about her to memory.

"Davin?"

He refocused on Paige's worried face and realized that his hands had ceased their task. He tried to recall the last time someone looked at him with such concern and failed.

She was the most precious thing in all his existence. And he now understood why Ava had called her his mate. Because fate had led him to her and he had long ago given her his heart.

With a free hand, Paige reached up to cup his face. He leaned into the warmth of her palm and urged himself to tell her his feelings. But fear held him back. Everything was too new, too soon. Swallowing the words, he gave her a soft smile instead and kissed her hand.

"You're beautiful," he whispered in reverence.

The blush crept from the top of her breasts up to her face like a flower blooming before him. With delicate touches, he brushed his fingers up from her neck to her cheek and rubbed his thumb against her cheekbone.

Shifting again, he leaned down, propping himself up to keep from crushing her. He kissed her and when her lips parted, he slid his tongue in to stroke hers, reveling in her taste. When she sucked, he gave a loud moan and withdrew.

Control. He had to remain in control.

"Let me, little bird." One hand traversed down her side, cupping her breast and squeezing lightly. Just like any muscle, it could grow sore, and Paige held much tension throughout her body. As she relaxed again, he resumed kissing her, from the corner of her lips, along her jaw, down to her neck. He took his time, noting the places where she would shiver or tense in reaction.

When the blush spread across her skin and her eyes half-closed with another sultry moan, he shifted his hand to trace smaller and smaller circles on her breast until he circled her nipple.

"Davin." The whimper accompanying his name let him know what she wanted and, for once, did not tease and withhold. His lips enclosed on the hardening nub, while his tongue swirled around it.

"Oh, God." She arced and almost threw him off with the sudden movement of her body. His hands moved to pin her down by her shoulders before he drew back to switch to the other side. At the sounds she kept making, his incubus stirred and clambered to take control. With a growl from his throat, he told it to go away- then, as if sensing this, Paige stopped and held herself still.

"No." The word came out hoarse, and he cleared his voice. "Don't hold back. Let me hear you." Davin would not allow the demon in him to get in the way. To underscore his point, he continued kissing down her body, following its contours until he laid between her legs and his lips reached the apex of her thighs.

She was soaked and her scent was heavenly. There was always that hint of lavender behind the musk that showed her arousal. He traced her delicate folds and watched in delight every shiver, every tremble in response.

At some point, Paige had propped herself up by her elbows to watch him and at his intense scrutiny, she tried squeeze her legs shut.

"No, little bird. Spread wide." Davin needed this, needed to remember how she looked and felt while he kept all of his rational mind.

Paige's head fell back as her legs parted for Davin, this time wider until her glistening pussy revealed itself in its full glory. Unable to resist, he leaned in and placed the flat of his tongue against her, a slow lick from her opening to the top, past her clit.

Paige's hip buckled in response and he took hold of her thighs to restrict her movements. "Keep yourself open," he commanded then continued, stroke after stroke, enough to push her closer to climax but not over the hilt.

And then with the tip of his tongue, Davin delved deeper, swirling around the hardened nub before drawing the bundle of nerves into his mouth. Her stomach tightened and when he sucked on it in earnest, she came hard against his administrations with a cry of his name. His actual name. Elation lifted his heart to soar with joy.

"Please. I need you inside me," Paige gasped, hands clenching his shoulders, trying to tug him upwards.

"Anything for you," He replied as he rose on his haunches, unbuckling and kicking off his pants, then crawled up to her. He lined himself up to her, the head of his throbbing cock nudging against her entrance. The incubus urged him to bury himself in her, to claim her with one hard stroke, to pound into her until she cried for mercy. No, that was not the point of this. He clenched his jaws, holding himself still until it quieted even as Paige squirmed and pleaded for him.

It was the hardest thing Davin had ever done in his life, but when he slid into her, inch by inch, the way her body held him tight inside thrilled him. A profound sense of rightness settled as he bottomed out and waited until she adjusted to his girth.

Paige's rocking hips were the first sign she was ready for more. With agonizing slowness, Davin withdrew, then sank back into her, his lips covering hers to drink in her moans. He set a steady pace while Paige wrapped her arms around him, fingers digging into his shoulder blades as he drove his little bird higher and higher.

When Paige crested once more, he felt his powers unfurl,

and he swelled inside her. The lights he left on flickered, pulsing to their rhythm until her orgasm reached full bloom, her head rolling backwards, her body jerking and spasming beneath him. Davin kept his eyes on her for as long as possible, desperate to hold the image of her expression frozen in ecstasy, but it became too much, her pussy clenching around him, the way she clung to him with desperation. Davin exploded, emptying his seed within, with a low growl until he fell forward to bury his face in the crook of Paige's neck.

A part of Davin triumphed. He did not feed on her. And yet the incubus remained quiet, and he sensed the beast sated. He would have to puzzle over this new situation another time.

Something wet brushed his shoulder and he looked up in alarm to see Paige weeping in silence. With infinite gentleness, Davin cupped Paige's face. "What's wrong? Did I hurt you?"

Paige shook her head and smiled through the glittering tears. "No, I am absurdly happy." A small laugh, a little broken, came through. "I don't know why I'm leaking. I'm sorry. This is silly."

Davin leaned down and kissed each tear. "Never apologize for your feelings. Just let it out, darling."

Davin withdrew and laid beside her, drawing her in his arms. The depth of Paige's emotions swept through him and he closed his eyes to steady himself. Something bigger, something he wasn't ready yet to put a name to, was growing between them and for now, that was enough.

CHAPTER 20
Paige

hirst drove her out of bed. Paige tiptoed into the kitchen and, not wanting to disturb anyone, rummaged until she found a glass and filled it at the sink.

The day had turned cloudy, but a glance at the clock told her it was late afternoon. A few more hours. She wished she could rescue Lillian now, but they had no way of knowing where she was. The address Anna had left for them was in a warehouse district, not likely where she was before the appointed time. *Cliche.*

Please be okay.

Her mind wandered, returning to the incubus still sleeping upstairs. It was easy to give reassurance when he needed them, but now that she was alone, doubts crowded her thoughts.

It was hard for Davin to hold back. She saw it in his brief pause, the way his muscles would bunch and tense, the way his jaw would clench. There was a price to being together. He would have to always restrain himself lest she become a psychotic obsessive addict like Anna. Could he do it long term? How many times could the incubus feed on her before the dependencies begin?

And was it fair to him?

Paige downed the water in one gulp and set the glass on the counter. There was also the matter of the difference in lifespan. What would happen as she aged, becoming old and gray while he remained as beautiful as he was today?

Paige's heart ached, and she rubbed her eyes.

This wasn't the time for emotions. She needed to stay strong, get Lillian back, and end this ridiculousness.

Soft steps approached, and a voice followed. "Just leave the glass in the sink. Do you want some food?" Dante opened the fridge, already pulling out some deli meat and cheese.

Paige was ravenous and nodded. Silence settled between them as they each prepared their sandwiches. There were a million questions she wanted to ask, but she did not know where to start. Her mind sorted and prioritized until she found the easiest one.

"How's Ainsley doing?"

"She's resting. The shock wore her down. But she's stubborn. Like you."

A ghost of a smile graced her lips, although guilt tinged it. She should be taking care of her best friend.

"She wanted to learn more about the incubi and whether Dav was going to hurt you."

More guilt.

"What did you say?"

Dante exhaled. "My brother made mistakes when he was young. We all did. Davin's lost, but he doesn't want to harm anyone. Perhaps together you will both find your way."

Paige's first reaction was to protest, but she stopped herself. That wasn't true, was it? With Davin, she did not know if she was coming or going.

"I'm heading out to get Ainsley a wheelchair. She's in the

third room down the hall upstairs. Check in on her in about fifteen minutes."

"Thank you." she nodded and watched the incubus leave. Was this some sense of duty or was there something else happening here? She wished she could ask, but Dante did not seem the type to divulge.

She finished her sandwich, made one more for her best friend, then headed upstairs. With slow, careful movements, she opened the door just a crack. Ainsley was a limp figure on the bed, still asleep. She was about to leave when her voice called out.

"Stop hovering and come in here."

Paige slipped inside and walked in to sit on the edge of the mattress. When Ainsley tried to pull herself up, she moved to help, propping her pillow and arranging the other shams and blankets until she was comfortable.

"Stop fussing, silly."

"I'm sorry," Paige blurted as she handed Ainsley the sandwich, head bowed in apology.

"It wasn't your fault. You can't blame yourself for your boyfriend's psycho-ex's behavior."

"He's not..." Paige trailed off.

Ains reached out, and she moved to clasp her best friend's hand. "You're going, aren't you?"

"I am. I will get Lillian back, come hell or high water." Paige was expecting protests, but Ainsley only nodded, her face serious.

"Look. Something's been bugging me about this whole thing."

"What do you mean?"

"How many times have you been with Davin?"

Paige blushed and ducked her head. "Um... three?"

"Okay. And over two years in your sleep. Correct me if I'm wrong, but you don't seem addicted to him."

"I don't think I am," Paige admitted, unsure where Ainsley was going with this.

"So why Anna and not you? Are some women more susceptible?"

"Well feeding in dreams lessens the effect."

"Yeah, but you still kept him fed. So, there should be some side effects. And it's been a long time."

Shit. She was right.

"And then there's what Ava said."

Paige leaned forward. "What did she whisper to you?"

Ainsley made a face. "Something about being asleep. Both of us. But that you're waking up soon. That it'll be my turn after and everything is as it should be."

Awakening. That's how Mr. Emo-Oracle put it, too.

Paige looked up to see her inner frustration mirrored in her best friend's features. A week ago, all Ains had to worry about was unreasonable clients and all she had to stress about was a damn YouTube interview and now look at them. Laughter bubbled up inside of her at the absurdity of the situation.

"Hey, maybe we're coming into our superpowers and this is our origin story." Paige giggled. Gallows humor.

"I'm serious!" Ainsley slapped her leg but grinned.

"Ow!" It just made her laugh harder. Soon, Ainsley joined in until they were both giggling with tears rolling down their cheeks.

"Is everything okay?" The door opened and Davin poked his head past the threshold, reminiscent of a father during a child's slumber party.

As Paige sucked in a breath in an honest attempt at calming the hysterics, she turned towards Davin. His somberness sobered her. "Is it time?"

"Not yet. But almost. We should do a little planning."

"Come in then." Ainsley waved Davin over.

Surprised, he entered the room, leaving the door ajar.

Rather than joining them, he eased into an armchair in the corner, as if to give them some space.

"Okay, what do we know?" Aisling clapped her hands together, sounding much more like herself.

"Well, she wants me dead. I think that's pretty obvious. And she'll do anything to make that happen." Paige could not help but look at Ainsley's legs.

"Anything? Does that include hurting or killing Davin?"

They stared at Ainsley. It wasn't something either of them had considered.

"You mean would she be psycho enough to do the whole 'if I can't have you, no one can' deal?" It was another cliche. How did the old adage go? Storytelling mirrors life, right? Still…

"I'm not sure. She's never attacked me before." Davin chewed over each word.

"Well, have you ever been with someone long-term since Anna?" Ainsley was pushing both of them now.

Davin paled. "No."

"But how would she know? It's not like we've been together in reality." Paige frowned as the puzzle pieces refused to fit together.

"Right, your dreams. I don't understand all the rules of this hocus pocus, but is there any way she could have spied on you there, Davin?"

The thought chilled her. Paige was not big on the idea of anyone watching her have sex. Especially the kind she and Davin had sometimes… most of the time… it was an uncomfortable topic and perhaps best left for later. Or perhaps she did not want the answer to that question at all.

"Regardless, we need to figure out how to approach this meeting."

Yups, let's switch subjects.

"Well, Anna's likely expecting both of us, and since she's a little less murderous with me, I should go in first." There was a challenge in the way Davin held himself, as if daring Paige to disagree.

"So Davin goes in, distracts the bitch somehow while Paige finds Lillian?"

"Something like that. The rest we'll have to play by ear."

Paige's stomach was sinking. It wasn't much of a plan, and there were too many unknowns. And they had no guarantees Anna would even bring Lillian.

"What if we go in together and propose a trade? Me for Lillian? That way at least we know we are getting Lillian back."

"No!" Davin stared at her, cutting her off with a single word. There was a finality to his voice that she resented, but she took a deep breath before her temper erupted again.

"Hear me out. I'm not suicidal." Paige stood up and began pacing. It was a habit she picked up a while back, and something she did every time she tried to work out a kink in one of her story plots. "I have the necklace which should keep me safe if she wants to hurl hexes at me. And since she made that deal, iron would work on her, right? She's not immune."

There was reluctance in the way Davin nodded, stone-faced.

"So if she tries to hurt me, I can defend myself." Paige paused in her pacing and clenched her fists. "Especially if you use that power of yours to subdue her."

"Pow... oh." Davin's expression faltered, and he coughed as realization dawned on him.

"Powers? Restrain? Paige, how would you..." Ainsley's cheeks turned red. "Wait, what kind of kinky stuff have you been up to? Wait, why am I asking?"

Davin cleared his throat. "Anyway. I am still against this plan." It would be too cute to see an incubus shy about sex, if she wasn't so embarrassed herself.

"It's better than anything I've heard so far." Paige sniffed, but it was the way worry creased Ainsley's forehead that made her pause.

"Are you sure about this?"

Paige only clenched her fists tighter. "She hurt you. Who knows what she's done to Lillian? I'll do whatever it takes to bring her home."

Now she turned to Davin, who held himself still. Paige needed him to agree. "Please. I promise I won't do anything reckless."

Davin paused; his expression filled with emotions she could not name. "Okay. We do this your way." He pushed his hair back to reveal glazed golden eyes. "But I'll want something in return."

"What?" Paige recognized this was the incubus talking in that sultry, silken tone.

"When we return from this, you'll know."

Paige hated mysteries and unknowns, but as of late her life seemed to be full of them. Something, though, wanted her to say "yes", and that *something* had nothing to do with wanting to rescue Lillian. Paige nodded.

"Very well, then. For now, let's see what other weapons and wards we can get you."

"Okay, but from where?"

Davin rose from the chair with feline grace. "There's a reason Dante has such a big house. Come along."

Paige's gaze traveled to Ainsley's legs once more. Part of her hoped Anna would try something just to give her an excuse for revenge for what she had done to her friend. The thought appalled another voice in her head. It wasn't Anna's fault she became what she was. She wondered if there was ever a way for Davin to right that wrong.

"Go on kids, have fun with your sharp pointy things."

Paige walked over and pulled Ainsley into a tight hug. "I'll be back. Dante's coming home soon with a wheelchair for you."

"Ah, my dark knight." Ainsley rolled her eyes with a laugh but hugged Paige in return. "And I know you'll come back. Who else will decorate my new wheelchair with me?"

When Paige leaned away, Ainsley gave her hand a light pat. "Now go."

As they were heading out, Ainsley called one more time. "And Davin. Bring her back in one piece or I'll string you up by your balls."

Paige cringed at the thought, but Davin only smirked. "Yes, ma'am. I plan on it."

CHAPTER 21
Paige

Twilight sent rays of golden orange scattered across the concrete jungle, warehouses shedding shadows over the cracked pavement.

They parked as close as they could and made the rest of the way on foot. Paige couldn't shake the feeling of being watched, her fingers brushing against her thigh where they had strapped a small iron knife to her, over her cropped leggings, and just under her long tunic. Her wandering mind wondered what Davin was thinking when he chose her outfit this morning. Thoughts like that helped stem off the abject terror of what they were about to do.

There, the designated address. They were five minutes early, but that meant little. Paige's body trembled as she stared at the door until Davin squeezed her other hand. He said nothing, but the intensity of the look he gave her took her breath away. There had been more and more of those.

"Shade, if something happens…" Her mind was a jumbled mess.

"I don't want to hear it," he cut her off. "You still have to keep your end of the deal and one does not escape a bargain with a demon that easily."

She quieted.

The warehouse Anna chose sat abandoned in a derelict state. Broken glass scattered across the floor and her Doc Martens made a crunch with each step, the sound echoing despite her best efforts. Of course, it was just her. Davin moved in silence with his feline grace.

And there was Lillian, half-conscious, tied to a single wooden chair. She bled from a cut on her forehead, pale from blood loss. *Or something else?*

"Her tank's low," Davin whispered, though the sound still bounced in the cavernous open space. At Paige's puzzled expression, he continued. "Some spells let witches drain power from others."

God. What had she done to her friend?

"Davin." His name was a breathless sigh as a slim woman emerged from the shadows. An unreasonable pang of envy stabbed at Paige. Raven hair with skin pale as snow, Anna parted her ruby lips. She reminded Paige of the princess in the fairy tale, not the evil witch that was the queen.

"That's enough, Anna. Let her go."

"Not even a 'hello' after so long, Davin?" Anna's cheeks flushed, and she bared her teeth with a hiss, but it took a moment for Paige to put a finger on what was wrong. It was Anna's eyes. The black orbs were dead, as if no emotion ever reached them. "You come here, dragging this slut you've been fucking and you still expect me to obey every command and wish of yours." She shook her head with a bitter laugh. "I don't think so. I'm not that silly naive girl you seduced all those decades ago."

"What do you want?" Paige called out.

Anna ignored her. Instead, she strolled over to the chair and trailed her fingertips from Lillian's chin up along her face. Before Paige could protest, Anna's fingers entwined in the older woman's silver hair and wrenched her head back. "You drove me to this Davin. Everything that happens is on you."

"No!" Paige's voice rang as Anna stepped in front of Davin, as if she could shield him from the cruelty Anna leveled at him. "Your actions, your choices- are your own."

A harsh laugh resounded through the air. "Oh little girl, you'll understand soon enough what lengths the lust, the thirst for this demon drives you to. Then you won't be so lofty anymore, judging me."

A chill coursed down Paige's spine. The whisper of doubt roared now in her mind. Was she staring at her future?

"What do you want?" Davin's expression had hardened, sharpening into predatory features.

"I tried to stay away Davin, to give you the freedom you wanted. But then you had to go shack up with that whore." Anna sneered in contempt. "If you needed to be with someone, then it should have been me. I gave up everything for you." She took a breath to steady herself. "So, tell you what. You come of your own volition and allow me to bind us together and I'll let them leave."

"Over my dead body!" Paige's fingers wrapped around the hilt of the long iron dagger strapped to her waist. Their plan was unraveling. They were all idiots for thinking she just wanted Paige gone. Once Davin took Paige under his protection, making it much harder to kill her, Anna must have switched the target to him instead.

"That can be arranged." Anna stepped forward.

"I'll do it." He slipped out from behind, letting go of Paige's hand to place it on her shoulder.

"What?" Paige's head jerked towards him. They could fight her for Lillian. Two against one and he had fed. Why did he agree to this?

Davin gave Paige a gentle squeeze. "You said it yourself, Paige. I have to right this wrong. Perhaps this is the way, not only for Anna but for you, Lillian and Ainsley, too. It's time I stop running."

"Davin, no," Paige whispered.

Davin smiled, the sadness echoing in his great golden eyes. He caressed her cheek as he leaned in, kissed her on her temple. "I love you, Paige."

This was goodbye. A strangled sob tore from her.

Without waiting for a reply, Davin walked away from her toward Anna, who in turn moved to meet him, her lips parting in eagerness. Her entire face lit up with new anticipation.

"Let Lillian go."

With a snap of Anna's fingers, the ropes around Lillian uncoiled themselves. With nothing holding her to the chair, she was only semi-conscious, so she slipped and fell sideways.

Paige rushed past both of them, reaching Lillian just in time to catch her. With more strength than she thought she had, she hoisted her up before casting a glance back at Davin.

They both stood in the middle of the floor now. Anna raised a hand, palm up, and when Davin took it, a runic circle, hidden before, flared to life with unnatural green light surrounding them.

"No!" Paige screamed out even as Anna began a chant in a lilting voice. Beside her, Lillian moaned in pain. Torn between getting her friend to safety and the desire to save her lover, she watched, helpless, as a tendril rose to curl along their joined hands, then grew to wind itself around Davin.

Another circle flared up, black in outline, just touching the other one such that they seemed to feed on each other. Except this time, Paige found herself and Lillian at the center. With her shaky free hand, she pulled out the iron dagger, even as from below, a multitude of small hands emerged, dark as shadows. The full duplicity of Anna's plans hit her. She never meant to let them go. Was this the entity that Anna made a deal with to extend her life? Were they to be her sacrifice to power the binding spell?

When one hand neared enough to grab Paige's ankle, she sliced at it with her blade. It worked and a bloodcurdling, inhuman scream echoed from somewhere below the concrete. A glimmer of hope sparked in her until others surged forward. Too many to count. The ground below their feet liquefied like quicksand. At this rate, even if they didn't get grabbed, the circle would suck them right in. She threw a desperate glance towards Davin, but his eyes glazed over with the lack of awareness, the gold she so loved, dulled against the encircling green.

"No," Paige cried, her heart hammering in her chest so hard it felt as if something would burst from her. Her hair rose, standing on ends as energy welled up within her, burning from the inside. She screamed again, this time in pain as she glowed. Whatever it was, it was coming, her body on fire as power threatened to explode. The black limbs retreated.

Out of nowhere, a blinding flash struck against the runes, cutting a line through half the circle. A last a howl of rage and agony reverberated through the warehouse as the shadowed hands dissipated and the ground solidified with their feet above.

When the light reached her, whatever it was inside her fell to silence, calm and sleepy again. Paige blinked away tears as her eyes tried to adjust. She could make out the outline of an Amazonian woman holding a sword blazing brightly. "Come. We must go before the witch recovers."

Struggling to keep up with everything happening, Paige stared at the woman's offered hand, dumbfounded. With a groan of frustration, the warrior came to her side and took hold of Lillian, slinging her over her shoulder. "Hurry."

A scream tore through the air as Anna whipped around, fury glittering in her eyes. *What do you know? They were not dead after all.* A split second. That was all Paige needed to decide. With a battle cry, she ran headlong into the fading green circle, equal parts desperation and love driving her every step. When Anna made a grab for her, she ducked and aimed her blade up, the tactile sense of it parting skin on top of the smell of burning flesh flooding her senses, causing bile to rise in the back of her throat.

Running on pure adrenaline, Paige grabbed Davin by his arm and yanked him towards her. He followed, stumbling like a ragdoll.

Paige dared a glance over her shoulder to see the woman holding the blazing sword up approaching Anna, who cringed from the light, in fear, while clutching her wound. That must have been where the iron dagger had caught her. Paige raised the blade once more and in return, Anna threw her a glare of pure hatred before turning and fleeing.

With that, the battle was finished.

The Amazon sheathed the sword in a scabbard strapped across her back and the light faded. Paige blinked and turned to behold her, unsure if she was a savior or a more powerful foe. Whoever she was, she was gorgeous, with ebony skin and hair, dark as the deepest shadows, held in a multitude of tiny braids. Every line of her body spoke of grace and strength.

"We shouldn't stay here," the woman said, nodding towards the door. "This human and the incubus of yours are both going to need help."

Paige glanced at Davin and shivered when she realized he had stood there, silent all the time, his eyes still glazed with no sign of recognition, or awareness, of what transpired. What had Anna done to him?

And who was she?

"Formal introductions can wait until later, Princess."

Princess? "You must be mistaken."

"Please, I will explain everything." She headed towards

the door. Left with little choice, Paige scrambled to follow, dragging Davin along, who seemed content.

"At least give me a name."

"You may call me Maeve for now."

Somehow, they made it back to Dante's place in one piece, sort of.

She drove them home and Paige found she didn't have it in her to even question how this warrior knew where she was staying. Paige had to guide Davin out of the Maeve's rental jeep . His zombie state terrified her even more than when he was near death, and she struggled for calm. Maeve followed from behind, carrying Lillian with much care.

"Paige." Dante opened the door and ushered them inside, surprise lifting his brows at Maeve's appearance.

Efficient as always, Dante busied himself checking on Lillian, cleaning and bandaging her wounds. Maeve stood in one corner, seeming to prefer to be as unobtrusive as possible. Paige sat Davin down, holding his hand as if he would respond with some recognition.

"Oh, thank God." Ainsley wheeled herself into the living room and opened her arms for Paige.

She left Davin to fall into her friend's embrace and struggled to hold back the tears now that the adrenaline of the fight was leaving her. They had succeeded in rescuing Lillian, but Davin…

"Shh. It's okay," Ainsley stroked her hair, murmuring words of comfort.

When Ainsley shifted in her wheelchair, Paige rocked to her haunches to stare at Dante towering over them. Never did she expect to see such a mix of horror and fear on that stoic face.

"Paige. What happened to Davin?"

CHAPTER 22
Paige

"An interrupted binding spell. He's half in, half out right now." Maeve pushed herself away from the wall she was leaning on as all eyes turned toward her.

"Who are you?" Dante imposed himself between her and the girls. His posture relaxed and Paige looked up in alarm, remembering practice at his dojo. This was him readying for a fight.

"Maeve." She held up both of her hands in surrender and gestured with a slight jutting of her chin at Paige "I'm her guardian."

When Dante cast a glance back at her, she only returned the look of bewildered confusion. Paige reached deep for an inner calm she did not know she possessed. With measured movements, she unfolded herself from Ainsley's side and stepped up to Dante's, facing the woman. "Please. Thank you for saving us, but no more cryptic answers. You said you would explain."

There was hesitancy as she parted her lips. "Are you sure, milady? The matter is rather... private."

First "princess", and now "milady"? At least she is consistent.

"Call me Paige. And yes, I think we need to all be working from the same information."

Maeve dipped her head in acknowledgement. "Very well. To answer your questions, it's more important to understand who you are."

"Paige is Paige," Ainsley almost sounded defensive, crossing her arms in her wheelchair.

"Paige is a fae changeling, a royalty of the Daoine Sidhe."

What?

"Paige's human! We grew up together. She looks exactly like her parents." Ainsley's voice pitched higher than normal.

"She handles iron just fine." Dante offered.

They all were so far away. Paige's heart thundered in her ear as she struggled for that earlier calm. She was mortal, as Ainsley said. There were baby pictures, photos of her pregnant mom . She grew up and aged, like anyone else did.

Awaken. Awaken. Paige couldn't stop hearing the word in her head.

Maeve stepped closer and placed both hands on her shoulders, catching her eyes with her ebony ones. "You know the truth of my words, don't you? You felt the rise of your powers when that thing tried to devour you."

She remembered. That explosive heat threatening to burst. The light that emanated from her body with fierce intensity.

Mommy, Mommy, come look at the garden.

What is it, sweetheart?

Over there, sitting on that bush, see the fairies playing?

You have a very vivid imagination, love. Never let anyone take that away from you.

She saw them as a child. Sylphs, salamanders, pixies, flower fae. She knew them all, but no one believed her. By and by, she stopped trusting herself. But why did she forget?

"Paige?" Ainsley touched her hand. In return, Paige clutched it in hers.

"As a descendant of King Nuada of the Silver Arm in the new world, your life would always be in danger. Your parents, your actual ones, sent you to live as a mortal until you matured enough to defend yourself. What we didn't expect was that you would get into trouble that had nothing to do with your heritage."

She swallowed. Once, twice. "What happened to the child?" Paige was proud that her voice held only a slight wobble.

"The poor thing was sickly, to begin with. We did our best to nurse her back to health, traveling as far as taking her to human doctors besides using our own methods. But alas, she did not survive."

How was she going to face her parents ever again?

No Paige, focus.

"And you are my guardian."

"Yes." The features on Maeve's face softened. "The royal family tasked me to monitor you, to keep you safe. I watched you grow from young but stayed away to give you the freedom of living a normal life until these circumstances forced my hand."

"It was you, talking to Seth, the Oracle."

Maeve nodded again.

"I… think I need to sit."

"Wait, wait, wait." Ainsley followed as best she could when Paige sank into the couch beside Davin, who sat immobile, staring forward with a blank expression on his face.

"I've seen Paige get hurt, cut a gazillion times, sometimes by metal that must have iron in it. So if she's fae, how come she never got affected?"

"Most iron these days are impure radiated alloys that have little effect on us," Dante replied. If the revelations surprised him, his tone betrayed none of it. "Our vulnerability to the material comes only when our powers awaken."

Maeve nodded in agreement.

Later. She couldn't afford to break down. Deal with what is before her. Everything else could wait.

"This explains Maeve for now, but we still need to figure out... with Davin." Here, her voice cracked. Already, she missed his smile, his reassuring touches.

He loved her.

No, she refused to cry.

The locks on the door jiggled before opening to show an Avaline with multiple shopping bags in tow. But her face was grim as she set each bag down and walked across the room, heels clicking against the wood.

"Dante, fill me in." It was as if none of them existed.

It was strange for Paige to hear her own story retold from another's mouth, but he was brisk in his report. As he spoke, Avaline kneeled down before Davin and stared into his eyes. Paige held her breath as she watched his sister reach up with slender fingers to touch his temple. If anyone knew what to do, she had this inexplicable feeling that it would be Avaline.

Paige's skin prickled as she rocked back on her heels and stood. A crackling energy gathered as glasses and mugs clattered on the table. With each deliberate step, the petite succubus closed the distance until she came face to face with Maeve. Despite the difference in height and stature, there was no illusion that the two were at least equal in power.

"You broke the circles with no regard for Davin."

"My priority is my charge." Maeve made no apologies.

The room shook and unbidden winds from nowhere whipped at their hair as powers unfurled. This could not continue. Dante shifted to hover over Ainsley while her best friend stared, wide-eyed, between the two ancient beings facing off.

With bravery she did not feel, Paige stepped forward on shaky legs, one hand on Maeve's arm, the other on Ava's shoulders. "Please." She kept it to an indistinct murmur until the winds died down.

The glow in Ava's eyes faded as she regarded Paige. "As the princess commands," she said through gritted teeth.

Paige tried once more. "I'm me. I'm still Paige. Ava, please."

From the corner of her eye, she saw Maeve open her mouth, about to protest, and shook her head again. "No matter what you say I am, it doesn't invalidate the last twenty-eight years of my life, nor does it take away who I worked hard to be. I am Paige Summers. I rent a basement suite from a white witch named Lillian and have a best friend, Ainsley Knight." She gave Ains a small smile and straightened when she returned it, beaming with pride.

Next to her, Avaline relaxed. "Of course Davin had to choose the most troublesome mate. But at least he chose well," she muttered beneath her breath.

There was no time to protest the title. On the list of things to wrap her brain around, the concept of mate seemed very low priority now.

Focus on the number one. "Ava, what happened to him... what can we do?"

"He's half-in, half-out." Avaline glanced at her brother, consternation drawing her brows together. "Anna, I'm guessing, has emptied him of everything that is him, and holds his essence. If the binding and a chance to complete, she would have chosen which pieces of himself, she would return and which she would keep."

"So we have to find her and make her give back all of Davin," Ainsley muttered.

"Easier said than done." Paige wanted to yank her own hair. "We have no idea where Anna went. She could have left town for all we know."

"If I may, milady. Paige." Maeve corrected herself before she had a chance to. "We can consult the Oracle."

It took thirty seconds before Paige registered who Maeve meant. It took ten more for her to rein in her temper enough to speak.

"You mean that wannabe emo goth of a money-grubbing asshole?" She did not sound outraged. She sounded reasonable.

Avaline turned to Dante. "They visited Seth?" At that, he nodded.

Okay, sure, fine. Why not? At least it was a chance to wring his scrawny neck.

"It's been a long night. We should all get some rest."

The incubus dipped his head, acknowledging Avaline's suggestion. More of a statement. "I'll go prepare a guest room."

Why wait? "But…"

"Paige." Avaline shot her a silencing look. "Anna's injured and not going anywhere. You've just been through one shock after another. A single night can make the difference between you being alert enough to save Davin or too exhausted when the time comes."

She heard the wisdom in Avaline's words, but it didn't mean she had to like it. And how did Ava even know she had hurt Anna? More mysteries. The more she learned about this other world, the more questions she had.

"Okay. Fine."

Paige had doubted she could sleep, but the morning found her opening her eyes crusted with exhaustion. Emotionally wrung out, she went through the motions of getting dressed and buckling the weapons to her, pausing only to watch the still figure of Davin laying there.

She had refused to leave his side when they all retired the previous night and insisted on staying with him in the room they last used. It was in this bed that Davin made love to her, and she was certain it wouldn't be the only time. So through the darkness to the wee hours of the morning, she laid beside him, alternating between crying and nodding off.

Their bedroom in the dreamscape felt empty without him.

"I will bring you back. I promise. And then we'll have a real heart-to-heart. You don't get to tell me you love me, then walk away." Paige leaned down and kissed his forehead before leaving the room.

When she descended the stairs, her stomach grumbled at the smell of food and, with a start, she realized she hadn't eaten since the sandwich yesterday afternoon. As she approached the kitchen table, she watched Ava and Maeve ignoring each other, then took a seat between the two. Dante came and set a plate of bacon, eggs, and toast in front of her.

Avaline slid a business card across the table. "I won't be coming with you to Seth's. However, I ask that you keep me apprised."

Despite the delicious meal, the succubus puckered her cheeks. When Paige tilted her head to one side in question, Ava breathed out her frustration.

"I promised Davin once that I would not interfere in matters concerning Anna. It was an oath I made under the bonds of our sibling-hood and I cannot risk the consequences, no matter how dire things are."

Paige accepted the card and took out her own phone, punching in the numbers.

"I'll make you a pact, Paige. Bring Davin home. I will protect yours in the meantime."

Ainsley and Lillian. Paige nodded. "Deal."

Breakfast became a fast and silent affair. Before Paige left, she climbed the stairs once more, this time to check on her landlady.

She gasped in relief when she saw Lillian sitting up, Ainsley already there with her.

"Ah, Paige." She was so pale, but here she was, smiling. Oh, thank God she was okay.

"I'm so sorry." Her eyes watered, fear of Lillian's hatred and anger keeping her from entering the bedroom until the older woman reached for her.

"Nonsense girl. You're not responsible for the actions of a deranged witch gone bad." Lillian made a tsking sound.

Paige stared at her and burst into tears. One step, then another led her to the other side of her bed, where she slipped her hand into Lillian's. Her friend was thin and frail, as if she had lost weight overnight, but she was warm and gripped her with more strength than Paige expected. It gave her hope for Lillian's recovery.

"Ainsley here caught me up to speed." Lillian chuckled as she turned her head this way and that to her surroundings.

"Well, we don't know if Maeve is lying, right?" Even as Paige spoke, she knew it was false optimism.

"Paige, dear, the fae do not lie. They may twist the truth and lead you on a merry chase, but if this Maeve did not mince words, you can trust her."

Great. Paige's face fell.

Lillian grinned. "I have to admit though, I never thought demons would be rescuing me."

A broken laugh spilled from her lips and she looked up to see Ainsley smile with sympathy.

"Then again, I never thought I was housing a changeling either," Lillian commented in a drier tone.

Paige winced. "I can move out as soon as we're back home. I understand if…"

Now the witch gave her a stern look. "And lose the best tenant I've had in years? Put that silly idea out of your head." Still holding on to Paige's hand, she shook both of theirs in the air.

"You listen to me, Paige Summers. Human or not, you stay true to who you are. And that is all we'd ever ask. And if you so much as forget a single ounce of your humanity,

Ainsley and I will be right here to remind you of it. Understood?"

Paige smiled through the tears that refused to stop falling. "Yes, Lillian."

"Now, go bring back your beau's soul. And give that witch a firm kick in the rear for me."

Paige laughed and nodded. "That I can promise."

"I'll see you out. Sorta."

As they left Lillian's room and reached the top of the stairs, Paige could not help the stupidest of questions. "How did you get up and down from here?"

Surprised by the responding blush from Ainsley, Paige lifted a brow and waited until she muttered her answer. "Dante carries me up and down and brings my wheelchair along."

"Wow."

"Hush you," Ainsley looked up but there was a sparkle in her eye and she lowered her voice. "I suppose it makes having my ankles broken more tolerable than I expected."

Paige smirked. "Hey if you want to be dating brothers together…"

"Shh!" Ainsley made a grab at Paige's hands but fell short. The two of them grinned at each other until Ainsley sobered. "Just promise me you'll be careful and you'll come back whole."

"I will." Page nodded in seriousness. "Besides, we're just going to see that damn Oracle for now. I'll call before we confront Anna for real."

"Okay," Ainsley leaned forward in the chair. "He sounds like a character."

"Yeah, well, he's about to be a blue and black one." Paige pressed a fist into an open palm.

Her best friend chuckled. "Ah, I am pleased to know this new Paige that's willing to stand up for herself. I'll be waiting for your call."

CHAPTER 23
Paige

"Woah, wait just a minute." Seth held one hand up in surrender, the other braced in front as if the gesture could ward off the knife Paige waved at him. He backed up with haste. "I'm not fae, you know. Iron doesn't work on me the same way."

"No, but a sharp edge is a sharp edge." Paige grinned as she advanced on him with Maeve bringing up the rear.

"Hey, you got your money's worth last time. Oh, hi, Maeve. Want to talk some sense into your princess here?"

"Are you shitting me? The intel you gave us before was crap. Anna went after my friends! Not me! And you sold me out after, to her!" Paige jerked her head toward her new bodyguard but kept her eyes on the little weasel.

"Hey, she attacked you and iron helped, right?"

"It helped jack shit!"

Seth continued to back up, placing the table between them and himself, then turned his palms up in the universal imploring gesture. "What about the water? It did the trick. I know it did!"

It was enough to give Paige pause, but not sufficient for her to lower her knife. "You also called me human. Multiple times. But you knew, didn't you?"

"Hey, your guardian there told me to not say anything." Maeve shrugged.

"Yeah, but you kept doing it, unprovoked. I bet you found it funny." Paige pulled out a chair and placed one foot on it, pretending to prepare to climb across the table to get to him.

"I'd wager you do that all the time, crack inside jokes like that at your clients' expense. I wonder what would happen if word got out that an Oracle lied. Especially for the right price."

Horror dawned on Seth's face, and Paige knew she had hit the nail on the head with the threat.

"Hey those were extenuating circumstances. It's not every day hidden royalty walks through that door."

Paige withdrew and even sheathed the knife. "Oh, I see, so the richer the client... come on Maeve, let's get out of here."

"Wait, wait, wait, wait, wait." Seth scuttled around the table. "You came for a reason, right? For free, just this time. And we keep all this a little secret between us."

Paige exchanged a glance with Maeve, who nodded with a subtle dip of her head. Still, she couldn't believe that worked.

"Fine. But if I find out the intel is-"

"Hey, divination is not a precise science. I'll give you as good as I've got, okay?" Seth moved to sit down at the table and gestured to the other two seats. "Please."

Paige eased herself into a folding chair and watched Maeve do the same.

"Now, how can I help you, ladies?"

"Anna Duffeld, the witch you saw, after me, last time. We need to know where she is."

Seth nodded along with her words. "Ah, she's powerful. I

remember a lot of you-don't-see-me spells. You got anything of hers?"

There was one thing. Paige took out the long dagger, unsheathed it and placed it on the table. "This blood is hers."

"Woah lady, how much weaponry do you have on you?"

At Maeve's glare, Seth quieted and studied the blade. "You want me to divine a powerful witch's presence using her blood off an iron sword?" He looked back up at Paige, incredulity widening his eyes.

In return, Paige shrugged. "You mentioned iron not working on you."

Seth opened his mouth. "I said it doesn't affect-" When they continued to stare at him, he sighed. "Fine. Just be glad I'm damn good at what I do."

He shifted in his chair and reached out, placing the tips of his forefingers, of each hand, on the blade rusting with Anna's blood.

Paige leaned forward, fascinated by the twitches and twists of Seth's pasty features. It was obvious he was hard at work as his eyes moved back and forth behind closed eyelids and sweat beaded on his forehead.

Without warning, his eyes snapped open with a loud gasp. He held his hand up to command for a pause, then scrambled towards another smaller table to the left of him. Seth grabbed a half-empty bottle of tequila with trembling hands, unscrewed the top and downed a good healthy amount before he pulled it away and wiped his mouth with the back of his forearm.

Well, that was new.

He stared hard at the two of them. "Are you sure you want to do this, Princess?"

Paige hated the title but gave up on correcting him for now. "Just tell us what you saw."

With more reluctance than before, Seth sat again. She didn't think he could get any paler but, she was wrong.

"Blood magic. Loads of it. Out in one of those rental fancy schmancy vacation homes by a lake forty miles out. She's hiding there, trying to deal with iron poisoning. This witch is nasty, Paige. She has been sucking up all life energy around her. The land surrounding the cabin is pretty much dead. So, whatever you are confronting her for, I hope it's worth it."

Seth's use of her name startled Paige. She hadn't expected him to recall it. An unreasonable sense of gratitude welled up in her. Seth may be a money-grubbing opportunist, but he wasn't evil by nature.

"It is."

And then he had to go spoil it.

"Well then, this concludes our deal, and you have what you came for. Remember, our little secret."

"Sure, Seth."

When they returned outside, Paige let out a slow exhale. Despite it being early morning, the sweltering heat was already beating down hard.

"Paige, we should return to Dante's home to plan the assault. We also need to retrieve Davin if we want this to work."

Paige stared at the sky above, weariness creeping into her bones. Her mind rewound to the beginning, and she tried to remember when it had all started. Had it only been a week ago?

Maeve cleared her throat, drawing Paige's attention to the now.

"Yeah, let's go."

An awkward silence hung between them during the drive back to Dante's. At first, Paige focused on the information Seth gave them, but her mind returned to wrestling with the idea that she was not human. What did it mean? What was she? Did she have an extended lifespan too? Who were her actual parents?

"Maeve?"

"Yes?"

"You said I was royalty of the Sidhe. Descended from... King Nuada?"

The woman nodded as she drove. "The Daoine Sidhe are featured in Irish mythology. When this is over, there are several books I can recommend, but on the basic level, we are the original faery. King Nuada was a strong ruler when we first arrived in Ireland and fought against the Fir Blog." She paused as she made a turn. "The weapon I carry is one of our people's greatest treasures, his sword named the Claíomh Solais."

Was Maeve boasting? Paige allowed herself a slip of a smile. "So we're Irish fairies."

"In a manner of speaking, yes. We are a long-lived race with an affinity for magic, including a certain resistance to it. But no wings. Do some reading later. The humans have documented it well despite thinking it's only folklore."

Right, they recorded it. Or human imagination shaped faerie in the first place. Chicken or the egg. Her head hurt.

"So are my parents in Ireland?"

"No, many of us immigrated here, same as the mortals."

"Oh."

Another pause.

"You don't have to do this." Paige stole a glance at Maeve. "I know your job is to protect me, but I am deliberately putting myself in danger. You don't have to follow me into the fire."

A ghost of a smile tugged at Maeve's lips. "I'm glad you at least realize what you are about to do. But it's clear to me that this incubus means a lot to you. So yes, you are taking a big risk, but it does also mean I will be there to protect you."

"Why?"

"Because—" her expression turned wistful— "your parents would have done the same for me." She paused as she made another turn. "When your parents had to give you up for your own safety, it almost broke your mother. The only thing keeping her from going insane with grief is the fact that you're alive and well. So I will make sure you stay that way, for her sake."

Paige wondered what her faery parents were like to garner such loyalty.

They lapsed back into silence until they pulled up to Dante's house. Eager to check on Davin, it took all of Paige's willpower not to leap out of the vehicle. As is, she kept her pace brisk as the door opened for her.

"She's up in a cabin by the lake. One of those luxury vacation rentals." Even as the words tumbled out of her mouth, she had to stifle a giggle. Could this become any more cliché? A cabin. In the woods. Perhaps it was hysteria setting in.

"We just came to get Davin. Is he upstairs?"

"Slow down, Paige."

As Dante stepped back, she saw Lillian sitting on the couch. "Fools rush in where angels fear treading, my dear. Now sit."

There was no disobeying Lillian. She entered and sat down in the armchair. Maeve stood behind her and Paige let out an impatient sigh. "Maeve, you're not some servant of mine, so please stop acting like you are."

"I'm fine standing."

Paige resisted the urge to facepalm.

"Now," Lillian stated, "Dante here was kind enough to set me up with a computer and I could access my library as well as some others. I've sent a message out to the coven and got some responses."

Paige blinked once, then twice. Her mind struggled to comprehend the words coming out of Lillian's mouth.

"Oh, my dear. Just because I'm old and the craft is older doesn't mean we haven't caught up to the twentieth century. We've digitized most of our, and our predecessors', *Books of*

Shadow. It's the modern great work we undertake." Lillian squared her shoulders with pride.

"Wow…"

"Never mind that, though. Let's talk about that botched binding spell. Now, most rituals and spells rely on three things: power, will, and focus. Anna's will is strong, and Davin's own willingness to go through with it was also essential. Don't look so shocked. Avaline saw it through Davin's eyes."

Paige wondered if she was the most clueless one in the room, but Lillian spoke on as if she didn't notice.

"We know her source of energy comes from that foul creature beyond the portal. Keep that in mind as she'll call upon the creature's help."

"The whole thing reminded me of an Elder god straight out from Lovecraft's stories," Paige interjected, glad she had something to contribute for once.

"Knows nothing about the Sidhe, well versed in Lovecraftian lore," Maeve muttered beneath her breath.

"Hey! I played a lot of board games, okay? Arkham Horror was one of my favorites," Paige protested as she looked back. Her hearing must be improving.

Maeve only shook her head with a sigh.

"Children." Lillian sighed.

"Sorry." Chastised, Paige turned to face her landlady to pay closer attention.

"Now, as for focus, for greater spells like this, most witches rely on symbols. I remember when Anna was making preparations, she kept fiddling with an empty vial on a silver chain. My guess is that she has bottled Davin's essence in there."

"So we just have to get near enough to break the thing?"

"No!" Lillian looked up in alarm. "There is no telling if those parts of his spirit will come back to his body, once freed. And with that creature present, it may gobble up Davin."

A shudder coursed through Paige. She was a fool for thinking she could rush in.

"Leave the incubus here. Retrieve the vial, bring it back here, and we can design a ritual to return Davin's essence to where it belongs."

"I'll be going with you and Maeve." Dante stepped forward.

"But what about-?"

"That's what I'm here for." Finn strolled down the stairs, hands in his pocket. "You didn't think I was just sitting this one out, did you?"

Paige's jaw dropped.

"I promise I'll behave and guard the house. Ava will be coming home soon, too. So you guys go get Davin back." Rather than the mischievous grin she always associated with Finn, his countenance had turned both serious and grim.

"Only you and Maeve are free to act against Anna, but there are no geas keeping me from defending you."

"But-"

"No buts." Ainsley wheeled herself out from another room to position herself next to Paige. "Besides, I asked him to."

"I was lucky last time and had the element of surprise, but I am unsure if the same trick would work twice."

Maeve nodded towards Dante. "I would appreciate the help."

Paige glared at all of them. They were ganging up on her. With a groan, she rubbed her face. "Fine. Me, Dante and Maeve."

Ainsley patted her shoulder, sympathy in her eyes. "So, when will you leave?"

At that, Paige dropped her hand and looked around the room with solemnity. "Now. We go now."

CHAPTER 24

Paige

here was one more thing Paige had to do. It was self-indulgent, but no one had protested and she couldn't resist. No, deep down in the darkest part of her, she had to admit that she wasn't sure if she was going to make it back.

"Hello, Davin." She kneeled down by the bed, knees falling on the soft rug. With one hand, she brushed his hair back, then stroked his curls. His eyes remained closed, and she yearned for that golden gaze one more time.

"I miss you." Nothing she said seemed sufficient, but she tried anyway. "I know you can't hear me, but I'm going to get you back from Anna now, okay?" She shook her head again, unsure what she was trying to say. "I don't know what will happen, but I'll make sure Dante comes back with you even if I can't." Her voice broke with the last two words and she rubbed her eyes. "If... if I don't make it, don't blame yourself, okay? Everything I'm doing, I'm doing because I want to... because... because I love you, too."

Paige rubbed at her cheeks with the heel of her palm and

gave a small broken laugh. "I guess it's easier to admit when no one's listening. I'll be going now. It's my turn to save you. Wish me luck, Shade, like you always do."

Only Dante and Maeve waited for her downstairs. She had already said her words to Ainsley and Lillian, and no one wanted lingering goodbyes. Unlike Paige, they had convinced themselves that she was coming back. Paige appreciated the vote of confidence, because she didn't share it.

Dante placed a hand on Paige's shoulder. "We'll see them again. Come on."

"Yeah."

They took the one jeep, with Dante providing directions to Maeve. It was the longest drive in Paige's life as she watched the suburbs thin out to farmland, which ceded to denser forests. By the time the vehicle hit the service roads, the anxiety building up in Paige threatened to explode.

"How do we know... oh." Dante's eyes widened and Paige swallowed hard.

Seth wasn't kidding about the land being sucked dry of life energies. As they arrived at a break along the tree line, they left the jeep to scan along the shores of the lake. Properties dotted along the water, spaced far apart but on the other side, one in particular stood out, surrounded by dead grass and trees that looked as though they would topple over any minute. Paige regarded the devastation with a sinking feeling in her stomach.

They got back in the car, grim silence hanging in the heavy air. Maeve parked a ways from the property and as they clambered out, each of them adjusted their own personal arsenal.

"Seth mentioned wards, and I doubt Anna would leave her base unprotected. Follow me and keep about ten paces behind." Maeve kept her hand on the hilt of the sword but did not draw. Instead, she tugged a crystal pendant that hung from a long chain out from beneath her top and held it up. A soft light emanated from the rock.

They moved ahead as a unit, stopping several times as soon as the light from the crystal flared up. Then they would tread with care sideways until the brightness died down again.

Paige's skin prickled as a breeze picked up. Her eyes scanned the property, back and forth, as Maeve called for another stop. The fog gathered.

Beside her, Dante drew a blade, widened his stance, and lowered his body. "Get ready," he murmured under his breath.

She drew the long iron dagger that had served her well thus far.

The first one came just as the breeze transitioned to wind. The air whipped into a frenzy but did naught to clear visibility. A disembodied head with long stringy hair, burning eyes and wings on either side in place of ears came at them, jaws opened wide exposing rows of sharp-pointed teeth. It stopped low in its flight path, aiming for Paige. She ducked and Dante sliced into the air.

It shrieked as the blade cut through its hair, but it took off and disappeared into the mist again.

"What the…"

"Flying heads," Maeve called out from the front. In the fog that blanketed them, the illumination from Maeve's sword of light remained muted but still served as a beacon. With a nod to Dante, they ran to join her, and soon they were standing back-to-back.

"They mean to eat us. Undead spirits of humans that indulged in cannibalism. Don't let them latch on to you." Maeve eyed the mist.

"I think it's safe to say we don't have to worry about tripping a ward anymore."

"Here they come." Dante shifted the grip on his sword.

That one must have been a scout. Now the entire flock came screeching through the air. They were nearly impossible to see, as Paige lost count of how many tried to attack them. All thoughts fled as she focused on hacking at their attackers, mindless with hunger. They reminded her of the inugami. *Great, a flying inugami. Herds of them.*

"There're too many of them," Maeve called out.

"Get Paige to safety. I'll hold them off."

"Wait, Dante, no!" Paige screamed, even as Maeve's strong arm wrapped around her midsection.

Dante spared a glance back at her. "I'll be fine. Eyes on the goal. Get my brother back."

Still, with misgivings on her mind, Paige nodded up towards Maeve who let her go. With Dante drawing the flock's attention to him, they sprinted until they entered the cabin, slamming the back door as it shut behind them.

The sudden eerie quiet chilled Paige's bones as they stood there panting, catching their breath. But as they remained still, she grew aware of the ticking of an antique clock somewhere. It did not help with the creepy atmosphere.

"Dante..." Paige looked in the direction they had come.

"He'll be okay. He hasn't even started using his powers yet."

That was right. She recalled the way Davin's features would sharpen, how the air would crackle when his incubus rose to the surface and his powers unfurled. Dante remained as cool as a cucumber, fighting with his martial skills alone just now. If... when... she gets back, Paige decided to sign up for his classes.

Dante was buying them time. They had better not waste it. "Let's see if we can figure out what's going on here first."

Maeve nodded at that and together they snuck through the house with care, weapons sheathed for stealth. Every time a floorboard creaked, Paige winced and awaited discovery.

Turned out, she didn't need to worry. As they came to the

basement, descending the stairs to what must be a storage area, they found Anna resting in a nest of those black shadowy hands. But rather than pulling her into the portal, they seemed only to be holding and caressing her, leaving curling wisps of shadows wrapped around her body.

At least she's clothed. I don't know how much more of this I can take.

With Anna's eyes closed, and seeming to not notice them, they crept along the wall until they could hide behind a large shelf holding various tools. Maeve nudged and nodded towards the other end of the room where something glittered from a small table in the corner.

"Protection ward." Maeve mouthed without a sound, drawing a circle on her palm with one finger.

Realization dawned on Paige. Anna must have been absorbing more energy from the eldritch creature and, not wanting to risk it getting greedy and devouring Davin's essence, had set the necklace aside. Or, she hoped that's what it was.

Paige tapped Maeve at the shoulder and made a pointing motion from her eyes to Anna and the portal. And then, she pointed to herself, to the table, and walked her fingers. Doubt clouded Maeve's face, but she nodded, albeit with reluctance. Paige let out a sigh of relief. There was no time to debate strategies here.

Paige hugged the wall, grateful for the shadows the various furniture and even piping casted. At least she felt less exposed this way. Almost. Her heart pounded in her ears and she wished she believed in some greater deity so she could pray to someone for good luck. *Shit. Do gods exist?* She scolded herself. *Not now! Focus!*

And then she was there.

The thing looked like a miniature version of a test tube completed with a cork stopper, with silver wiring twisted around it to hold and attach it to a fine chain. Amber and gold shimmered and swirled within the glass. This was Davin, and his essence was beautiful.

The circle appeared to lie dormant. With shaky hands, Paige crouched down to pull out the iron knife tucked in her boot. A small thing, it would do for this purpose. But when she held her blade up, her hand wouldn't stop shaking.

Brave. She had to find her courage. *Ugh.* After this, she would not have any qualms writing about werewolves, vampires and witches. That genre made way more money, anyway.

Paige drew deep gulps of air into her lungs to steady herself. There was nothing, only the task ahead. She would do this. There was no other choice.

As ready as she could ever be, she switched her grip to hold the knife, the tip pointing downwards. In one swift stroke, she cut the protection circle. Her flesh burned with the heat of its last flare of light before it died. *It worked!*

So focused she was on the task, she missed seeing Anna's eyes snap open on the opposite side of the room. But no one could miss the scream of fury that tore from the witch's throat.

The hands from the creature set Anna down, gentle like a loving partner, then parted, though did not retreat to the portal. Anna took a step towards Paige and the table, her appearance a far cry from the well-manicured doll she had seen last time. Hair matted and stuck to her clammy, pale skin. Black veins were crawling up from her bare shoulder, up along her neck, drawing odd, and unflattering patterns across her cheek. Anna's sleeveless shift was dirty and clung to her thin body. The iron poisoning was doing a number on her.

Without missing a beat, Paige snatched the necklace with her free hand, dropped the knife and drew her long dagger out. It didn't fail her last time. The only way Anna was going to get the vial back, was if Paige was dead.

Maeve emerged from her hiding place; the blazing sword

already drawn. But before she could approach, Anna muttered a quick incantation, flicked her hand and sent Maeve flying. Paige's guardian slammed against the shelf and crumpled to the floor. Paige watched in horror as one of the black shadow hands braved the light and wrapped its fingers around Maeve's ankle.

But Maeve was made of tougher stuff than this. She maintained her consciousness and sliced her sword at the hand, and the creature screamed in rage and agony. Yet, only more limbs surged forward, as if determined this time to exact revenge on the one that deprived it of its prey earlier.

The throbbing on Paige's right knee drew her attention back to herself. A pressure pressed against her, but there was little else. The obsidian necklace, however, grew warmer and warmer until Paige yanked it out from underneath her shirt. Davin's gift was protecting her, even now.

With a snarl, Anna ripped apart the ragged puppet in her hand. There was a flash of pain at her midsection and the stone burned hot for a moment before both sensations faded. *Voodoo doll? Really?*

"I've had enough of you, bitch. Where. Is. Davin?" Anna stalked towards her. Paige had no illusions that she was any less dangerous. Too late, she berated herself for not clarifying what powers witches had besides spells, wards and hexes.

As she drew closer, their eyes met. There was a new madness dancing in the witch's, her lips twisted into a permanent rictus of pain.

And in those glowing orbs of sickly green, Paige saw her own death.

CHAPTER 25
Paige

tairs! If she could grab Maeve and get up the steps, at least they may dodge the abomination's efforts. She spared a quick glance towards her guardian but could discern the other woman within the mass of limbs. Only the sword's glowing light let her know the creature had not yet pulled the other Sidhe into the portal.

The momentary lapse in attention cost Paige. Her only warning came as a murmured incantation when ghostly fingers brushed by her neck. Anna must have an arsenal of spells ready. Choking by ghost hands was not high on her list of ways to die. She brought the blade up to cut in the air. By sheer luck, the touch dissipated.

When in a fight, a moving target is much harder to hit.

Dante's advice surfaced in her mind. This would be the same whether it was a strike or a spell, and she hoped Anna's worked the same way. Paige scrambled, choosing to zig zag rather than run in a straight line.

A whiff of wind brushed by her face and she changed directions. But by then Anna must have learned her pattern.

The forces batted at her like a cat playing with a mouse until she neared Maeve. An invisible force slammed into her body, striking true this time, to send her spinning in the air. Paige's eyes widened in terror. With no control of her trajectory, she traveled in an arc right into the center of the portal.

Time slowed. The hands withdrew from Maeve to embrace their new prey. Anna crowed in triumph. Paige knew with a certain clarity what she had to do. "Maeve, catch!"

With all the strength she could muster, she flung the precious necklace to Maeve just as the hands closed in on every part of her limbs, restraining her.

"No!" Anna's scream tore through the air as she extended a hand towards the vial with Davin's essence glittering within. The cry tapered off into another incantation, the words too soft for Paige's ears to hear.

The slender glass wobbled, struggling against an invisible opposing force that tampered with its natural path even as Maeve reached out in a desperate attempt to catch it. All three women watched in horror as the necklace brushed by Maeve's outstretched fingertips, then fell to the floor, shattering open.

The golden essence swirled in the air and another shadowy hand shot toward it. Anna threw herself in the same direction, trying to intercept. Paige strained and fought against the hands as more and more enveloped her, screaming in wordless rage and grief.

Helpless in her restraints, something broke inside of her and scorching heat surged from the pit of her belly up to fill her entire body. Some part of her registered she glowed with an aquamarine light that grew with intensity. But her mind blanked as an inferno raged cross her body, inexplicable flames consuming her until her grief became blinding pain.

Then that something burst from her and she squeezed her eyes shut with a shout. Stillness descended.

Paige squinted as she adjusted to the soft light. She stood, fluffy puffs of cloud floating by her ankles, blanketing the ground beneath her feet. *The dreamscape.*

"Sparrow?"

Tears threatened to fall, as she heard the familiar voice. Paige pivoted on foot, spinning around to behold the great golden orbs that looked on her with equal parts warmth and confusion.

Was this her dream? Did she conjure him out of her own desires to see him?

"Davin!" They both turned to watch Anna struggle to make her way towards them.

Nopes. Paige would not be conjuring that witch if this was some wishful imagination of hers.

Paige's hand dropped to her side, seeking the blade she relied on, then startled in surprise when she realized it was not here. In fact, she had none of her weapons with her. She shivered, hating how vulnerable she felt without her blades. When had she become that attached to them?

As Anna reached them, both women glared at each other. But when the witch raised her hand to prepare for an attack spell, Davin moved to stand before Paige, shielding her from any harm Anna may intend to inflict on her.

"That's enough." Tendrils of dream stuff bounded Anna's hands together. When she parted her lips, Davin shot her a look full of threat. They all knew that in dreams, the incubus held the most power.

Only when Anna snapped her mouth shut did Davin resumed speaking. With a heavy sigh, he pushed his hair back. "I know I did you wrong. I thought the binding would be a way to make it up to you, but if we're here, it means it didn't work."

Paige could sense the frustration in Davin's voice as he searched for the right words.

"The spell failed because that bitch had help," Anna hissed.

Davin cast a glance back at Paige, a question in his eyes, but she shook her head. He needed to focus on this, to find closure, for all three of them. Questions about herself could wait.

"Would you have been happy with me as your mindless slave?" Davin asked, his voice quieter now. "Would you have been satisfied knowing I was there because I was obligated to, because it was what I had to do to protect Paige?"

Anna opened her mouth to protest but fell silent before she could muster any words.

"Do you still love me, Anna?"

To Paige's surprise, tears began streaming down Anna's face.

"That's not a fair question, Davin." Her voice was small. In that moment, Paige saw her for what she was, a woman imprisoned by a desire she had no control over, a passion that drove her to make one mistake after another. That she tried so hard to let him have his freedom all this time was a testament to her sheer will.

Davin took a step closer but made no move to touch the witch. "You loathe me, don't you? For ruining your life. There may have been infatuation, even love at some point, but that has long turned into hatred."

Anna gritted her teeth, hands clenching into fists as she sucked in a breath, attempting mastery over her crying. "Yes. Yes, I hate you, Davin. I hate you for making me want you. For this hunger that I can never sate no matter what I do."

"Then let me try to fix it. Allow me to do the one thing I should have done all those decades ago instead of running. Give me a chance to find a cure for you."

Was that possible?

A harsh laugh. Anna shook her head. "You think I haven't tried? I've searched through the entire occult world."

For the first time, Paige spoke. "What about other forms? Like Sidhe magic?"

Anna's eyes widened in surprise.

"There are other avenues. Let's not give up, okay?" Now Davin offered a weak grin. "Let us all help you. You don't have to do this alone. Not anymore." Without waiting for a reply, he released the bonds on her wrists.

"You've changed." Anna looked up at Davin with soft, sad eyes and a bittersweet smile. "I'll take what you give and hold you to it, Davin Murphy." And with that, as if she willed it on her own, she faded from their dream.

Davin let out a long exhale as he turned to meet Paige. "I missed you." Now he took a step forward and opened his arms.

The offer was all she needed as she tumbled into them. His scent surrounded her, and she buried her face against his chest, allowing herself a good cry at last. This was what she wanted, what she fought for, no matter if he was human or demon. She loved him.

"Ah, Paige, I'm so sorry. I hurt you, didn't I?" Davin brushed his lips against the top of her head.

She smiled up at him through the curtain of her own tears and in return, he took slow care in wiping them away. Time passed unnoticed as they stared at each other, reunited once more, albeit temporary, hearts too full for words.

By and by, she came to herself and turned to look around the dreamscape. It had shifted back to their bedroom.

"Did you bring us here?" she kicked herself in her mind for the question. It was the last thing she should say. She wanted to tell him she loved him, that she forgave him and chose to be with him. But the words wouldn't come, not right now when she knew what awaited her once she left the twilight of dreams.

Davin tilted his head to one side and closed his eyes, then

straightened to face her. "No, not entirely. I sense Sidhe magic blended with mine."

The fire that exploded from her. Was this her doing?

A sheepish smile tugged at his lips. "I talked big in front of Anna, but fill me in on what happened? The last I remember, Anna's binding ritual held me immobile and then that dark entity had you." As he spoke, horror morphed his expression as the realization hit him. His arms tightened around her. "You are real, right? You escaped somehow."

Laughter bubbled at the irony of his words. Paige reached up and stroked his face with fondness. "Yes, I am real. I survived. I had some help from a fae named Maeve. She cut the circle that powered Anna's binding spell, which is how your essence got completely dissociated from your body." It was the best condensed, Reader's Digest version she could give, unwilling yet to go into details, in particular, the part about her being some royalty changeling. He had enough shock for the day.

"Maeve," Davin repeated the name with a blink as if still trying to come to terms with her explanation.

"Yeah, she's a Daoine Sidhe. If you need help with Anna, ask her. Tell her it's a request from me." She hoped he wouldn't notice the finality in her phrasing.

About to speak again, Davin paused when everything in their bedroom wavered and grew more translucent. Whatever time their combined powers bought them was running low.

"Davin, listen to me." She reached up, cupping his face with both hands, urgency now driving her next words. "Your body is at Dante's. Use the dreamscape to return to it."

"What about you?"

Paige shook her head. "I'll be okay. Maeve and Dante are both with me. What's most important is that we get you back to your body." She was lying through her teeth, remembering she had been captured by that thing in the real world. Paige was afraid of where she would wake. But Dante must have survived the flying heads, and if she could distract the eldritch monster long enough, Maeve should be able to escape. Maybe Anna would even help.

"Paige."

She saw his unwillingness to part with her in the way he narrowed his eyes and how his arms only tightened around her. That wasn't good. He had to leave. Her magic rose in response to her needs. With a small smile, she kissed him and tasted his lips. It was a desperate smooch, full of wants and words unsaid. Davin responded in kind, moving against her with an urgency that spoke of promises and desires, promises that she wished with all her heart she could make him keep. With tears welling up again, she shifted her hands to place both palms on his chest, and with her own powers unfurling, she gave him a hard shove, pushing him out of their dream and on his way back to his body.

Around her, the dreamscape shimmered and faded. Paige closed her eyes and readied herself. It was time to face the end.

CHAPTER 26
Paige

Time had been standing still.

Once more, the multitude of hands surrounded her, pulling and tugging. Paige's eyes snapped open as motion resumed, scanning the chaos unfolding in front of her. Anna stumbled to stop herself, turning towards Paige with a new understanding dawning on her. It was proof enough that what happened in the twilight of dreams did, in fact, happen.

"No, she isn't for you!" Anna held out her hand, palm forward. There was a hint of power in her command. No one was under any illusion that the witch controlled the thing that had kept her alive all these years. But what Paige didn't expect was for the creature to hesitate, as if confused. Anna must have never before tried to deprive it of its prey.

It was enough as the hands holding her slackened, just a smidgen. Not sufficient to escape, but at least to free an arm. But it was too little, too late. It had already pulled the lower half of her body into the opening.

"Paige!" Maeve cried out in desperation.

She turned to behold the grim face of her guardian. Maeve

nodded, then swung back to throw the Claíomh Solais towards her. Paige reached out, hope flaring within her as her hand closed upon its hilt. And then the creature pulled the rest of her through the portal.

Madness. That was the only way to describe what she saw. There was no up or down, no sky or land to orient herself. Even space had planets and stars as references, but here, there was nothing. The light emanating from her sword was her only source of comfort. And consternation for the creature.

In some ways, Paige almost wished she didn't see anything at all. Here, the full extent of the eldritch horror threatened to overwhelm her mind, to drive her to the brink of insanity. A multitude of slitted red eyes dotted along the top, all trained on her with hungering intent. Its maw opened, rows upon rows of sharp-pointed teeth dripping with venom, waited to tear apart her flesh.

The terror manifested not only in appearance but mentally as well. A pressure pushed at Paige's mind like tentacles slithering and probing to seek entrance to her deeper psyche. There was a reason that pop culture had later added to the Lovecraft mythos that the Elder Gods drove people insane. Or was that how these creatures gained that power?

Whatever it was, the light she held seemed to anger it. Although it was unwilling to let go of her, the thing ceased pulling her in further. Instead, it shook her, as if trying to dislodge the sword from her grip. Paige was never a fan of rollercoaster rides in the first place, but this was a thousand times worse. With both hands, she clung to her weapon, squeezing her eyes shut as she tried her best not to hurl.

"Keep your eyes open. Stare at a fixed spot. Imagine a barrier shielding you." A voice startled Paige, and she looked up. Another sentient being was the last she expected in this space. Rather than trying to seek the source of the words, she followed the instructions, imagining a steel wall encircling herself.

A new song resonated in her head, one that coursed through the recesses of her mind, cleansing the small stains and footholds the creature left behind. It called to something within her and on pure instinct, Paige summoned that heat that burned through her. The magic came gentler this time, a soothing warmth that raced through her. With conscious effort, she directed it to the sword when her eyes snapped open, glittering in the strength of her newly awakened power.

The Claíomh Solais flared to life brighter than even when Maeve wielded it. Paige understood, without knowing how, that it was reacting to her direct descendancy from its original owner. Not missing a heartbeat, she plunged the sword toward the nest of limbs that held her.

The creature's screech was enough to drive any human to insanity. But at the height of her powers, she only hacked and cut until she freed herself. It wasn't sufficient. Using the mass of arms she had just finished detaching from the monster, she launched herself straight towards its gaping maw. One stroke upwards, another down, she felt slime, the thing's blood oozing out from the cuts she made. Splashes landed on her skin and burned and ate at her like acid, but she was beyond pain by now.

"You need to aim for the heart. There!" A ghostly finger pointed below the mouth and it took her seconds before she spied it. There! A tiny orb, pulsing red. She plunged her sword straight into it and felt the jeweled center shatter under the impact.

The creature let out the most blood-curdling scream yet. But Paige grinned in triumph as it thrashed in its death throes.

"The portal. Go. Now."

She cast a glance over her shoulder to see the exit beginning to close. Her eyes swept across, sighting the source of guidance at last. A figure of a lanky man with a mop of light brown hair and rimmed glasses gestured towards the only way home.

"Come with me," She called out, refusing to leave someone here, especially when they helped her survive. Without waiting for a reply, she grabbed his hand with her just freed one, relieved that she found a solid wrist to grasp. Again, using the creature's own body as a launchpad, she pushed off until she threw herself through the portal, tumbling and rolling over, in the most ungraceful landing of all time until she came to rest on the flat of her back.

She had returned. She was alive.

Every part of her hurt.

"Paige!" Maeve and Dante's faces hovered into her vision as she blinked, readjusting to the dimness of the basement.

"Ow."

Wonder and awe highlighted her guardian's features. Funny how she never quite noticed that though Maeve had as neutral a face as Dante did, her eyes were the most expressive thing. Paige gave a weak smile, then tilted her head to study Dante. From him, she sensed worry and newfound respect. *Weird.* She never before could read Dante. Was this heightened empathy another new ability of hers?

From the corner of her eye, she spotted the one that she had pulled through with her. He was staring at himself, his lips parted in awe. She didn't blame him, for he was translucent. Was he some kind of spirit? Wait, everyone was reacting as if she was the only person that fell out of the portal. Did no one see him?

"Paige?" Dante passed a hand over her face.

Maybe she was just hallucinating. Did concussions cause hallucinations? She refocused her gaze. "Davin's okay. He should be awake at your place by now."

The incubus nodded, but the concern did not leave his features. Oh, he was worried about her.

When she tried to move, she groaned. "I think I may have

knocked my head a little." She made another attempt to lift the hand that still held onto the blade, but winced. "Okay, maybe I knocked my entire body around a little."

Maeve chuckled, the sound awash with relief. She leaned down and took the sword from her, sheathing it in its scabbard. "Can you walk?"

The floor was nice and cool against her clammy skin. It tempted Paige to say "no". Moving meant more aches. But she also knew she couldn't stay here forever. "I think so."

Dante kneeled beside her and wrapped an arm around her waist while looping her arm over his neck. He hoisted her up, making sure to balance her against him enough to hold her weight.

Less than twenty paces away, Anna laid in a crumpled heap. Paige jerked her head towards her. "Help me over there."

The three of them hobbled over to where she lay. Anna stared up at them with a soft laugh.

"Hello, Godslayer."

"Hello, witch." The title didn't sit well with Paige, but she was too damn tired to correct her. "Come on, get up. Davin made you a promise and I will help him keep it."

Another chuckle, even weaker than the first. Anna shook her head. "It's too late for me. I've lived way past my time." She turned and nodded towards the space where the portal had been. "That was the only thing keeping me alive."

"I'm sorry." When Paige was hellbent on slaying the monster, she thought little of the consequences. It was just instinct. Hers or the sword's. She didn't know which.

Anna shook her head. "Don't be. This was inevitable. And now I'm free." She smiled and Paige saw the expression that would have attracted Davin all those years ago. A mix of innocence, and certain joie de vivre. "Davin's a changed man. Take care of him. Love well."

And with that, she fell apart until there was nothing left but ashes.

They stood there, staring at the woman who had caused such destruction.

"Rest in peace," Paige murmured.

"You know, she's right."

Paige and Dante turned their gazes toward Maeve. A new sinking feeling settled in Paige's stomach. "What do you mean?"

"*Claímh Solais* is a weapon of our people capable of ending an immortal. Using it to slay one from a different race..." Maeve glanced back at where the portal was. "That'll have consequences. Your reputation as a god slayer will spread." She nodded at that space. "And they'll come for you."

Behind Maeve, the spirit bobbed his head in agreement.

Great. Paige groaned.

"Problem for another day. We need to get home." Dante dug into his pocket with his free hand and fished out his phone. "I have twenty missed calls from Davin."

It worked. Davin got back to his body. Despite the pain pulsing through her, Paige's lips spread into the most idiotic grin. Hallucination temporarily forgotten, she nodded again. "Yeah, let's go."

The spirit followed. Paige opened her mouth to speak, then closed it again when he shook his head. As soon as they made their way out of the house, he floated off in the opposite direction without so much as a goodbye. Everything in him spoke of an urgency she didn't understand, but there was no way to ask. He didn't even give her a name.

It wasn't until she was sitting in the car with Maeve, driving through the night, that Paige dared to examine her wounds. The monster's blood had left patches of blackened skin ringed with red, angry blisters. Bruises, blue and yellow, blossomed around her limbs and her midsection where the hands had held her tight in their grips. Her fingers found a bump on the back of her head where she must have banged it when she rolled out of the portal. She pushed her vision away to breathe through the pain, then shuddered as the image of the glowing ruby eyes flashed in her mind like an afterimage.

"Home."

The single word from Dante was enough to jolt her out of the developing nightmare. It wasn't hers, but Paige looked up and thought she had never seen a place so welcoming. They would be okay. She was going to be *okay*.

The door flung open as Dante and Maeve helped Paige out of the car. Davin paused, eyes widening as he regarded the sorry state of them all. Paige flashed him a weak smile and watched as he rushed down the steps in long strides that carried him within a split second to her side. Both brother and guardian stepped back.

"Davin," Paige began, emotions making her voice hoarse.

With no chance for more words, in one swift motion, Davin swept her off her feet. Over his shoulder, she glimpsed Ainsley and Lillian peering out from the door. Ainsley's tears flowed freely and Lillian patted her on her back.

Her family. She made it back to them after all.

"Thank all the powers above and below." Davin choked with his own relief as he buried his face in her hair. With great care, he carried her inside.

"Wait." As soon as they entered the house, Paige tugged at Davin's shirt until he paused. She reached out to Ainsley and Lillian. "I'm home."

Lillian patted her shoulder. "Well done, Paige."

Ainsley took her extended hand and squeezed it. The long-time friends needed no words between the two of them. Later, they would exchange stories, but for now, it was enough to know they were alive, and they all survived.

Davin cleared his throat. "If you'll excuse us, I need to tend to our warrior here."

Paige ducked her head and blushed. Both women, young and old, gave a small laugh and waved at them to go.

Davin carried Paige to the bedroom she had left him in, taking the stairs two at a time, though he was careful not to jostle her. By the time he laid Paige down on the bed, her eyes drooped with weariness, despite the pain being too insistent to let her sleep.

As Davin peeled off her clothes, she reached up to stay his hand. "It doesn't look pretty."

His gaze traveled up to meet hers and brushed the skin above her arm with one finger. "I figured."

"Wait."

When Davin made no move, Paige swallowed. "Anna…" This was harder than she expected.

"Anna didn't make it. I wasn't thinking when I killed the thing." There was so much more to say, but her thoughts were choppy, bordering on incoherence.

Something akin to grief flickered in his face, and his sad smile was full of regret.

"She saved me. She tried to keep that monster from dragging me through the portal, and it gave me enough room to catch and bring the sword with me to kill it." Now Paige closed her eyes, knowing she was making little sense. "She said to me in the end, that she's now free. I think Anna's at peace."

Davin nodded once in acknowledgement and bowed his head in silence.

A knock interrupted them. Davin rose to open the door and returned with a tray full of first aid supplies.

When she tried to move, Davin shook his head. "Let me take care of you, please."

Paige was too tired to protest, but she dared not close her eyes lest she saw the creature again.

Davin didn't bother to tug her clothes off. Instead, he took a pair of scissors and cut each piece off. They were too ragged and torn anyway to keep. As the material parted to reveal the extent of the damage, Davin sucked in a breath.

"Let's agree to never do that again, okay?"

"Do…?" Paige blinked at him.

"Me getting dissociated from my body. You slaying an elder god."

The absurdity of his statement made her laugh. Oh, God, it hurt even to giggle. Why did she sound so broken?

Davin brushed her hair back and kissed her forehead. "Let's get you patched up."

His touch was gentle as he maneuvered her to scout out all the burns, dabbing a cooling ointment on each before wrapping them in bandages. In time, she would heal, but for now, this would do. Of the bruises, there was naught to do, but Davin held up some painkillers and a glass of water. Soon, the pain dulled to a distant ache and her eyes closed.

Once done, Davin put everything away and scooted into bed with her, gingerly wrapping his arm around her. His warmth was a soothing balm to a psyche that was almost torn asunder, and she shifted to snuggle closer.

"Sleep, Sparrow. My turn to take care of you."

"Mmm," she mumbled, vaguely registering what he said. As slumber enveloped her, she exhaled. Sleepiness blurred her mind and the next words rolled off her tongue more easily than if her full consciousness had any say. She was in no position to speak them but practicality had long left the room. "I love you."

"I love you too, darling."

A smile tinged lingered on her lips as she fell asleep, hiding the fears and doubts deep in her heart.

CHAPTER 27
Davin

*D*avin brushed stray strands of hair back from Paige's sleeping face, studying her with awe. He was still trying to wrap his mind around how his little sparrow had become a god slaying warrior. But more so, how she had risked everything to save him, even after he thought she would run from both what he was, and what he had done in the past.

And she loved him.

Davin's lips curved into a bemused smile. He wasn't sure if she was aware what she had let slip before sleep overtook her, but he would take the words to heart. It gave him the courage to imagine a future with her, regardless of their differences in lifespan. A future together as mate, if she would have him.

Not yet, though. She had been through too much and it would not be right of him to push for more at the moment. But when things settle… For now, he would focus on taking care of her, on proving to her that a long life with him would be a happy one.

When Paige shifted to cuddle closer to his warmth, she whimpered and Davin resisted the urge to tighten his arms around her. The incubus in him wanted to run his hands over her, to cling and never let her go again, but he reminded himself that she was fragile and any force would only exacerbate her wounds.

Another whimper drew Davin's attention. She laid still, her brows furrowing, but it wasn't until her hand resting on his chest balled into a fist that he muttered a curse and pushed himself to slip into his trance.

The darkness that greeted him in the twilight of dreams was nothing like he had expected. A distinct lack of solid ground to stand upon, at first surprised him, and he had to will it into existence. At the sound of anguish and fear, he ran, heart pounding, until a scene straight from his worst nightmare rose before him.

A behemoth creature with a multitude of red slitted eyes and angry black hands, more than he could count, hovered over a crumpled figure of Paige. That was when realization hit him.

This was what she fought.

The horror of it almost overwhelmed him, but with great effort, he shook it off and moved. The monstrosity had no dominion here. His preternatural speed took him to Paige's side where he scooped her up without ado and brought her to their bedroom. With a flick of his wrist, the curtains on the balcony doors closed, and a fire started in the fireplace.

Paige trembled in his arms; her eyes squeezed shut. He leaned in closer, trying to capture the words tumbling in whispers from her lips. "Not again, please, not again. Can't do it again," she said repeatedly.

Davin attempted to lay Paige in bed, but she clung to him with a heartbreaking whimper.

"Paige, darling, look at me. It's okay. You're safe. The thing is gone. I'm here."

He recalled the hero's welcome she receives when she came back. Davin kicked himself. He had taken care of her physical wounds and thought that was that. Did any of them have any idea how damaged her psyche was?

"Davin?" Her voice croaked.

"Yes, my sparrow, I'm here. It was just a nightmare."

She swallowed hard and shook her head. "Was it? Or was it like the inugami?"

Shit. He didn't have an answer for her. It could be night terrors, but there was so little information out there about the capabilities of an elder god that not even he could be certain. Davin cursed himself for the promise to always be honest with Paige. And that meant no misleading words.

"We don't know, but you don't have to fight it alone. I'll always be here."

Paige let out a broken sob. He wished he had better answers.

"We'll figure this out, okay? Ava can help."

She nodded, and he spied with relief a glimmer of hope in her eyes.

"Now rest, love. I will guard you tonight." *And forever.*

Davin woke alone, her side of the bed already cold. Panic hammered in his chest and the incubus in him drove him to his feet. Without bothering to change his clothes, he rushed downstairs with preternatural speed. *No, not the kitchen, not the living room. Where is she?*

And then he saw her, facing away from the patio doors, sitting on a swinging chair out in Dante's Zen garden. The early morning light created a halo effect around her and he rubbed his eyes before opening the sliding door, approaching barefoot over the cool slabs of rock. She sat still, with a mug of hot steaming tea in hand, making no acknowledgement of his approach, but the sight of her unwounded the coils of tension in his stomach.

Davin stood beside her but remained silent, letting her

lead. After last night, she looked almost fragile as she huddled in a blanket, bandages and bruises peeking out from beneath an oversized t-shirt.

A bittersweet smile graced Paige's lips. "I keep trying to figure out how we got here. A week ago, I was just like any other ordinary human. And now I find out I'm not even that, and I have something out of a Lovecraft book haunting my dreams."

There was a lot to unpack there. Pieces fell in place. The healing, the awakening, the power she exuded when she pushed him out of the dreamscape. It would explain why she was less susceptible to his incubus' influence. But just what was she?

Paige turned to look up at him, her eyes haunted. "Am I broken, Davin? Did the elder god break my mind?"

Paige's question stabbed at his heart. Davin sat down, wrapping an arm around her. When she relaxed again him, he kissed her forehead. "No, darling. You are made of stronger stuff that that. This is trauma you're dealing with. You don't fight and kill a thing like that without some lingering effects. Time will help. Your friends will help. I'll help."

"I don't know if I can, if I'm ready…"

"There's nothing you need to do, Paige."

"But feeding…"

Davin smiled at that. "You know, just being around you seems to fill me. As long as I can hold you, I'm satisfied, both sides of me."

Paige opened her mouth, then closed it, then sighed.

He needed to take her mind off the nightmare creature. "Tell me about Maeve?"

He hadn't expected Paige to wince, but he waited for her words to come.

"Maeve was the only reason the elder god didn't devour me when Anna was binding you. She was who Seth was talking to over the phone, and she explained that she was my guardian, assigned by my birth parents to watch over me." Paige shook her head as if still in disbelief. "I'm not human. She said I'm a changeling. My fae parents left me with my mortal one to protect me. Because being a descendant of King Nuada meant my life would be in danger otherwise." Paige muttered beneath her breath. "The weasel called me 'princess'."

His little sparrow was Daoine Sidhe royalty? If he wasn't so stunned, he would have laughed at her disgruntlement.

"Davin?" She looked up at him and in her eyes, he saw a glimmer of aquamarine. Power.

When he didn't reply, she withdrew from him, her body curling into itself as if to ward off the sting of rejection. He shook his head and pulled her back to him, his palm cupping her face to tilt it towards him.

"Don't even think about it. No matter what you are, you will always be Paige Summers. Nobody can take that away from you unless you allow them." He leaned forward to rest his forehead against hers. "And Paige Summers is the woman I fell in love with and the one I want to be with, if she'll have me."

It had the desired effect. She blushed. "I'm not sure…"

So she wasn't aware of what she had let slip last night. Davin understood. The feelings were there, but her life had just grown so much more complex and she needed the space to sort all that out before she was ready for the commitment those three words would bring. He could wait. They had time. "You don't have to give me an answer right now, Paige. You've been through a lot and the last thing I want is for you to feel pressured. I only need you to know that I'm here."

There was weariness in her smile, but he glimpsed a bit of the woman from before all this. Like her physical wounds, she would heal, eventually. He'd see to that.

"Davin?"

"Yes?"

"I think I can handle a kiss."

He chuckled, trailing his hand down to trace the contours of her face before tilting her chin up. "I believe that can be arranged." As he leaned forward, he brushed his lips against hers with a feather-light touch and when she didn't withdraw, he pressed a little harder, deepening the kiss with leashed desires.

In return, she parted hers with eagerness. Davin took it as an invitation, and darted his tongue into her mouth, dancing and enticing hers until she delighted him with a moan.

With an abundance of reluctance and regret, he eased back and rubbed the pad of his thumb against her lower pouty lips. He could see the sexual haze that began clouding her face. "No, my little bird, I don't want to hurt you."

"I'll be fine. Please," she whispered, so full of wanting. "I need to know it's still the same between us."

The plea was his undoing. He rose from the swing and offered a hand. As she slid hers into his, he pulled her up and led her back to their bedroom.

She reached for his shirt as soon as the door closed behind them, but he stayed her hands.

"Let me." With as much gentleness as he could summon, Davin undressed her and laid her to bed. Everything was slow, deliberate. It would crush him right now if he hurt her.

Davin started with a kiss on the corner of her mouth, keeping himself braced above her, ensuring he didn't press down on her. Davin trailed butterfly kisses down along her jaw, until he reached her neck, changing tactics to nibble and suckle across her flesh. For the first time he consciously released his aura, allowing the pheromones to heighten her arousal, helping her focus on it rather than the pain in her body. For this, he would use every skill he had honed as an incubus to give her what she asked.

Paige gasped at the heightened sensitivity he provided. Davin drifted his hands lower, preceding his lips as he caressed her body, scratching at all her most sensitive spots. Where there were bruises, he touched with his fingertips, careful to not apply any pressure. "Try to stay still, Sparrow."

Davin moved lower still until he reached the apex of her thighs. He smiled as she parted her legs for him, her hips thrusting upwards with an eagerness that surprised him. It was a heady feeling to see her body craving his touch as much as he craved hers. He took his time, drawing lazy circles across her skin to prolong the anticipation. He lowered his head to press kisses around her breasts, closer and closer until his breath was upon her hardening nipple.

"Davin, please."

A smirk tugged at his lips, but this morning he would give what she needed rather than tease. Later, when her wounds had healed, he could play with her the way he wanted. He paused then with exaggerated slowness, licked one stiff nub. At her moan of encouragement, he lowered his mouth to it and sucked hard.

She buckled against him and Davin drew on his powers to restrain her hips, lest the sharp movements in moments of passion aggravate her wounds. He eased back, then blew a chilly breath, delighting in the way her body shivered in reaction, the dusky pink around her skin darkening.

Certain that he had secured her, he repeated his administrations on the other side. As she jerked beneath him again, he parted her folds, his fingers zeroing in right away on her clit. With no build up, he circled the sensitive area surrounding the bundle of pleasure, sweeping his tongue over her nipple in the same motion but with an inverse direction.

"Oh, God." Paige gasped before her head rolled back and she came shuddering, flooding his hand with her wetness. It was a gentler climax than the more explosive ones she'd had in the past, but the last thing he wanted was for sex to be painful. At least not the non-pleasurable kind of pain.

There was something he couldn't resist, though.

Just as her orgasm tapered off, he slid himself down to rest between her legs, keeping them apart. Voice hoarse with desire, he inched closer. "Paige, I need to taste you." He spared a glance to see her gaze down at him with eyes as round as saucers, but soon he was staring at her pussy instead, studying the feast before him.

Remembering that she was likely oversensitive by now, he swept across her slit with the flat of his tongue, lapping up her juices. He heard her exhale with a sigh of contentment and felt her body shift to lie back. When she relaxed, he switched to using the tip to explore her folds, dipping and scoping her nectar to sate the hunger within him. Soon, her breathing quickened and her moans filled the air again.

"That's it, my love. I need you to come for me." She was about to crest again, and the Neanderthal in him crowed with triumph. He redoubled his efforts. His tongue pressed tight against her clit before he drew it past his lips. Two fingers delved into her entrance and curved upwards, pressing against her g-spot. She came undone with a scream of pleasure by his hands, and he continued until he sensed her tipping to oversensitivity. He slowed his movements, gazing up at her as she smiled, softening her face and smoothing over the lines of fatigue and fears.

Despite his own throbbing needs, a deep satisfaction settled in him and even his incubus quieted as if sated. He slid up along the bed and drew her to tuck her body against him.

"Davin."

"Yes, love?"

"I'm not in a place where I know where I'm at emotionally yet. There's too much about my own life I don't understand." Paige swallowed and shifted until she was laying face to face with him.

"I get that, Paige. I'm not asking..." Davin's brows drew

together in confusion. Hadn't he made his lack of expectations clear?

"Let me finish." She shook her head. "What I'm sure about is that whatever happens, wherever this weird new life takes me, I want you to be a part of it. It may lead to some not-so-cheerful places. It may mean a whole different set of dangers, but I'd like for you to walk this path with me, if you'll have me, and not just in our dreams."

This was more than Davin could expect at the moment, more than he even hoped. With solemnity in his eyes, he nodded. The answer came easily and resonated with every fiber of his soul. For her, he would do anything. But for now, the words he would give her would be enough.

"There's nowhere else I'd rather be. At your side. Always."

EPILOGUE
Paige

*It was a game of dominance and she was too much of a
sore loser to give in, no matter the dark promises that
danced in his eyes. In her fierceness, she refused to submit and so, as
soon as they reached his bedroom, she pushed him onto the bed. She
followed without missing a beat, straddling his waist, surprised by
how easily he submitted.*

*Then she discovered his trap. They wrestled, but his much larger
size gave him the advantage and despite her being on top, he
regained full control once more. She strained against his tight grip
as he held her hands behind her, her breasts mashed against his
chest. Trapped against him, she could not help but moan as he rolled
his hips, ensuring she felt every single inch of his hardened cock
grinding against her.*

Paige Summers, Daoine Sidhe, stretched in satisfaction,
staring at her laptop screen. Three months later and she got
back on track with her writing at last. It had taken weeks to
get even the first paragraph right, but once the words came,
they poured out of her. It helped that things between her and
Davin had stabilized enough that her muse could give little

pieces of encouragement and inspiration again. Small tastes since she was still healing.

With a yawn, she rubbed her eyes and glanced at the sleeping body lying in repose on her bed. Despite the penthouse he owned, Davin had been spending so many nights here, he might as well have been living here on a permanent basis. His love for Lillian's baking alone had kept him coming back, never mind Paige's presence.

Maeve had suggested she invest in property, to move to a house of her own, given that as a Sidhe princess, she was also rich. Like richer than even Davin. But she had refused, preferring the rental suite now that it was all repaired. This was her home and Lillian was family.

Her family had grown larger. Her guardian had rented an apartment a block away. Dante had become her teacher but was still hovering over Ainsley. And there was the spirit that had guided her in that other dimension. Somehow, she knew with an inexplicable certainty that their survival in the other realm had bounded them to each other and that he would return when he finished what he had left her to do.

Her thoughts turned back to her lover. The last few days, she had gotten used to the idea of being his mate, though she never said the word out loud yet.

Paige pushed her chair backward and crossed the space to the bed. She slipped between the covers and curled up against Davin as his body shifted to accommodate her presence. Even as sleep overtook her, she marveled at how they fitted together.

When she opened her eyes in the dreamscape, she found herself in their shared bedroom alone, the only sound an antique clock ticking somewhere. That damn noise only meant one thing. She spun around to face the large balcony windows and summoned the imaginary version of the *Claíomh Solais.*

The hands came first, reaching for her again, slithering

through the cracks even as a multitude of red eyes peered through the glass panes.

Logic told Paige that this was a dream but to this day, she still wasn't sure if her own sick memories had conjured it or if this thing was a separate entity, terrorizing her dreams like the inugami had. No, she had killed it with the real version of a god slaying sword. This monster can no longer get to her when she was awake, or so she kept telling herself.

All she knew was that she was damn tired of fighting it and the fears it brought.

The windows faded without warning until that entire side was a solid wall and with that, the eldritch horror dissipated from the dream.

Strong arms wrapped around her waist and she jumped, instinct driving her to bring her elbow back to ready for a swing. The body behind her shifted in a well-practiced move to avoid the strike.

"It's all right, Sparrow, I've got you. I've got you." Davin's comforting voice soothed her frayed nerves and her muscles relaxed. The conjured sword of light faded away.

"Sorry," she mumbled, unsure if she was apologizing for the attempted blow to his gut or for the nightmare she kept producing, night after night. Even after three months, her fight had left her traumatized. Every time she closed her eyes, all she saw were those malevolent red orbs and the maw with terrifying sharp teeth.

"You have nothing to be sorry for." He kissed the top of her head then repeated the gesture on her shoulder. "I wish I could take this pain from you."

At that, Paige smiled and turned in his arms to wrap hers around him. "You do. You keep my fears at bay." She tossed a look back towards the now blank wall. "I don't understand why I can't manipulate the dreams like you do." Frustration crept into her tone.

"Patience. You've only been practicing for a little while,

and I suspect you're still replenishing your powers from the battle all those months ago. Besides, your body had been focusing on healing."

With a soft sigh, Paige tucked her head under his chin and pressed the side of her face against his chest. So much for super regeneration. The wounds derived from the Elder God's blood seemed to heal a lot slower than others, despite everyone's attempts at speeding it up. The last week had been the first time she had her full range of motion again, although parts of her skin still puckered with scars.

"Come on, let's see if we can get you a few hours of rest before we have to wake up." Davin climbed into their bed and patted the space next to him. It was too tempting an offer to refuse and Paige followed, slipping under the covers in a mirror of real life to settle against him.

He trailed his fingers up and down along her bare arm, the motion almost hypnotic enough for her eyelids to droop. In her occult research, she had figured out that sleeping here meant leaving the dreamscape and sliding into a deeper, dreamless sleep. She would return to this room before she woke for real, but comforted by Davin's presence, she relaxed until she could let her consciousness slip away.

When Paige opened her eyes, the skies were still dark. Anxiety drove her to shift in the bed. Today was the day. They would meet her biological fae mother and father for the first time. Not that she was ready to call them Mom and Dad yet, but she needed to understand what she was, including her powers' nature and limits. When she last talked to her human parents, her real ones as far as she was concerned, on the phone, the waterworks had broken out and she had to make some quick excuse about having a cold. That led to them fussing more, which made her crying worse.

"Sparrow." A hint of warning as she found Davin watching her.

Her fidgeting must have woken him up.

"It's too early to worry." Rough with slumber, he shifted to prop himself up and look down on her with glazed golden eyes.

Paige swallowed. She may have awakened the incubus more than the man.

"You sleep. I'll do some writing," she murmured, keeping her movements slow as she slipped out of bed.

He grumbled and reached out, hand wrapping around her wrist. "I don't think so. I think someone needs a distraction."

As she obeyed his lead to lie back down, he leaned over to whisper in her ear. "And we haven't celebrated your recovery yet."

A shiver ran down her body and she pressed her legs together. That's right. He had not fed on her in the last three months, insisting she needed all of her energy to heal. "Ah." That was the only reply she managed.

Davin chuckled and skimmed his fingers across her, down her arm, then skipped to her stomach, toying with the hem of her shirt. "I will take that as a yes." His breath tickled her ear and his lips nibbled the ridge of it.

She tilted her head to expose more of her skin to him, baring her neck in an age-old sign of submission.

It drew a growl from him and he slid his hand under her clothing to cup a breast, his fingers gripping it with firm possessiveness. "You know what that does to me, little bird. Are you sure you're ready to dance with the demon?"

For the first time, knowing that being a fae protected her from becoming addicted to him, fears no longer held her back. There was always a possibility that she could still die from the incubus overfeeding, but her reserves were now much deeper and he had proven already time and time again that he could restrain himself. She licked her lips, a challenge in her grin as she released a small flick of her power, her body shimmering with a faint blue before fading.

"Bring it on."

His answering smirk hovered in her vision as he didn't shred her top with one powerful tug. When she opened her mouth to protest, he covered it with his own, swallowing her words with a searing kiss. Around them, the scent of sandalwood and citrus intensified until she groaned with desire. Every brush of fabric, every touch of his body against hers only heightened her arousal further until all she craved at the moment was him.

"You better strip the rest of your clothes off or you'll lose them the same way." Davin traced a finger in lazy circles around her exposed nipple, dragging his fingernail even as they hardened into pebbles, aching for more.

No, he would not distract her! He wanted an excuse to rip her clothing to shreds. With herculean effort, she pulled her head out of the sexual fog clouding her mind and reached for her shorts and panties, sliding them off in one swift motion.

"So eager," he murmured, his eyes skimming down her naked body in admiration. Her skin flushed red at his gaze. As he lowered his lips to replace his finger, she forgot any protest she had against the verbal trap he had set. He drew her nipple in, feasting on the sounds she made in response.

Her stomach tightened as he alternated between the two sides, swirling his tongue around. Paige's eyes rolled backwards. She had heard of women climaxing from simulation on their breasts alone. Never would she have thought that would apply to her.

"Shade," she gasped, buckling against him. Her hands reached for his drawstring pants, the urge to free his straining member was strong.

"No." Davin snarled and the now familiar invisible ropes snapped around her wrists, drawing them high above head. Other bonds wrenched her legs apart, keeping them restrained for his pleasure.

Davin sat back on his haunches, watching like a predator studying his prey. A finger trailed down, dipping into her wetness to trail it up along her slit. Another shudder passed through her body as she strained against his power's hold, wanting to close her legs, conscious of his scrutiny. Yet, somehow, she only grew wetter, her juices dripping down to the sheets.

The smug smirk on his face made her whimper. He could read her thoughts. Still, he didn't move and only stared at each of her trembles with hunger. Her chest rose and fell in the drawn-out anticipation.

"Fuck me." It came out more of a whine than she wanted. Provoking the incubus may have been stupid, but she needed it, needed him. "Fuck me or let me fuck myself."

He snarled at her. "I told you before, your pleasure is what I give you." Without another word, he got up and left.

What. The? Hell?

Minutes passed as he kept her stewing. It was worse than she had imagined as the arousal did not fade. Instead, with each second of waiting, she only grew more sensitive until every slight stirring of air sent tremors throughout her body.

When he returned, she was ready to beg. And then he blindfolded her, the silken material caressing her face.

"The wait can make you taste so much sweeter. I've never made you wait before, have I, Paige?" His voice, full of dark warmth, slid across her skin and she felt him close. She shook her head. There was a savage gentleness to his words. Dear God, what had she done?

The whimper turned into a sharp yelp when something cold pressed against her stomach. She sucked in a breath as the thing trailed down and nudged against her folds until it contacted her clit. Without giving her time to adjust, the object started vibrating.

Paige screamed and buckled in a swift orgasm. But there was no relenting, no mercy. His warm mouth closed over her pussy and he thrusted his tongue into her opening to devour her. At some point he switched and pushed the still cold toy into her with long hard strokes, while he flicked his hot tongue over her clit repeatedly. Her climax spiraled onwards, colors exploding in her vision as she spasmed and contorted against the bonds. He varied the movements and poked and prodded the swollen nub but never allowed her body to acclimatize. Oversensitivity threatened to overwhelm her.

And then he withdrew, giving her some temporary respite. Paige panted, blinking several times. When he slipped off the blindfold, his face, illuminated by his golden aura and her shimmering blue one, filled her sight.

His features had sharpened in his feral hunger. He kept his eyes on her as inch by slow, agonizing inch, he pushed himself into her, his bonds still keeping her open for his pleasure.

It was all she could do to keep from coming again.

"So tight and wet." His harsh groan resonated in her ear as he moved, each stroke methodical and controlled. Paige had thought he would take her in a frenzy, but this slow ruthlessness was beyond anything she ever imagined.

He adjusted the angle of her hips as he fucked her until she gasped at the sudden shot of intense pleasure, different from the one that radiated from her clit. With a nod of satisfaction to himself, he began thrusting at a faster pace, hammering at her g-spot until she crested, clamping down to hold his cock deep within her. He held himself still, bearing down as until she came down from her orgasm. The bonds released her legs.

For a fleeting moment, she thought him done. But he proved her wrong when he flipped her over. The binding to her hands provided no resistance, rotating her such that they remained tied high above her head. Davin lifted her higher and leaned forward.

"Mine." With an animalistic growl, he thrust all the way to

the hilt into her with one savage stroke, burying himself deep in her.

Paige's lips parted into a wordless scream as her body arched almost violently. With a grunt, he moved a hand to the back of her neck and pinned her to the spot with inhuman strength. Satisfied with his control, he began pounding into her with relentless ferocity, pushing her to come harder and harder with each successive orgasm until they all bled into each other, her world comprising nothing but sheer mindless pleasure. Somewhere in the remote parts of her mind, she grew aware of the incubus feeding on her, but she cared not what he took.

With a roar, Davin gave one last thrust, pushing as deep as possible, and emptied his seed in a torrent into her. It drove her to the most violent orgasm yet until darkness consumed her overloaded brain. With that, Paige passed out.

When she came to again, she groaned, reaching with gentle fingers to prod her sore, achy core. She was clean, though. He must have seen to it.

"If you want another round…" Davin winked as he laid on one side of her, head propped up by his hand.

She had no energy to chuck a pillow at him so only moaned and closed her eyes.

"Ah, the sound of a well-fucked woman."

Damn that smugness in his voice. But she could not deny his statement. So she let out a soft sigh instead and drew on the last of her strength to curl up against him. A small smile graced her lips as he leaned down to kiss her temple.

"As much as I enjoy our post-coitus cuddles, we have to get up soon, love."

Paige groaned. "Fifteen more minutes."

Davin chuckled and tightened his arms around her. "All right, fifteen more minutes."

Fifteen more until the next step of their journey together.

THE END

The Wayward Shadows will continue with Ainsley and Dante in
THE GUARDIAN'S WAY

THE TRIALS OF
The Summer Changeling

A PAIGE SUMMERS SHORT STORY

Paige stared at the archway created by the foliage of two large oak trees. Sunlight filtered through the canopy of the forest and patches of brightness highlighted the uneven trail.

"It's this way," Maeve pointed ahead. She had explained a thousand times beforehand, but Paige still had trouble wrapping her head around the concept. Not another world but small dimensions carved out and sustained by the magic of her people, attached to this reality to emulate the Faery homeland they could no longer return to. Each dun was a pocket, and this one was owned by her birth parents.

Pocket worlds.

Not that different from the dreamscape, or so Davin kept trying to convince her.

She rubbed her temple.

"Are you okay?" The incubus beside her placed a hand on her back, concern deepening his voice.

No. "Yeah."

Maeve frowned as she turned to face them. "You shouldn't be feeling any ill effects until after you cross."

Great. Who knew traveling across dimensions, even when it wasn't the elder gods' realm, would induce motion sickness? No, she needed to stop whining and just do what they came to do.

As if sensing her resolve, Maeve gave a firm nod of approval. "I will pass first." And with that, she walked through the space between the trees. The air shimmered before stilling, this time without her guardian on the other side.

She sucked in a breath. *I have fought against a decades-old witch. I am dating an incubus. Even slew an elder god. And the idea of stepping into this fairy fort terrifies me way more.*

"You ready?" Davin asked, the heat of his palm a reassuring comfort.

She swallowed hard and took a step forward. He matched her pace, but she halted in her tracks and pulled Davin back with her hand. "Wait. Wait. Wait. Wait. Wait."

He paused and cocked his head to one side in question. To her, he seemed no different from usual, poised yet relaxed.

"What if they hate me? What if I hate them?" It wasn't the first time she asked those questions in the days leading up to this, but doubts assailed her mind once more, now so close to meeting her bio parents, parents from what she understood, had no choice but to give her up at birth.

"Paige, love. Listen." Davin moved his hands to hold her shoulders and spun her around to face him. "You are here to learn about your past and the implications of coming into your powers. You have no obligations to whatever is required of the daughter of fae royalty. These were the rules you negotiated yourself when you agreed to meet with them."

Davin was right. She didn't have to call them mom or dad. Her mother and father were the ones she spoke to over the phone a couple days ago. The guilt of not telling them about what happened to their birth child stabbed at her, but she pushed it aside for now.

"Let's get this over with so we can go back to our regular lives." She squared her shoulders and readied herself.

He took a step backwards and made a small flourish. "After my princess."

Paige rolled her eyes and chuckled before she walked past him and into the portal.

Vertigo hit her as she stepped into the land of Faery, and she struggled not to vomit. Meanwhile, Davin appeared beside her, unfazed, and frustration welled up within as she wondered why the transition impacted only her so much. But she swallowed hard and waited for nausea to subside instead

"It'll get easier," Maeve murmured.

"Daughter!"

She looked up and deja vu hit her. Long silver hair done up in various braids held up by a circlet crowned the slender man, composed and regal, as expected of the Faery ruler. And though he uttered the title softly, his voice carried through and echoed down the tunnel.

A tunnel! Of all the environments she imagined she'd stepped into, this was not one of them. But the walls shimmered with pinpricks reminiscent of starlight.

"Paige,"

Pulled out of her wonder, she flushed at being caught like a gaping tourist and cleared her throat. "Lord Midhir" She bowed first, bending at the waist with her arm across her chest.

Maeve repeated the gesture. "My lord."

"Lord Consort," Davin murmured, dipping his head low in greeting. Maeve had drilled the exact etiquette in both beforehand.

When her biological father nodded in acknowledgement, Paige straightened, as did the others. But she widened her eyes in surprise when he crossed the distance between them and took her by the shoulders.

"You are well? Maeve recounted to us your battle."

Her first instinct was to say she was fine. It was the answer she gave everyone these days. But that would be a lie, and Maeve had also informed her just how bad falsehoods were in the faery realm, so she said what she had told no one except Davin. "I am struggling. My physical wounds have healed but…"

Worry created shadows on his face. "You fought a powerful foe. Healing would not be easy, even for our kind. We can only imagine what consequences there may be."

It was what she had tried to avoid thinking about. But before she could ask him what he imagined, he held out an arm for her. "Come, let us get you to Court before your mother grows too impatient."

Paige glanced back at Davin, who gave her a smile of acknowledgment. As she stuffed her trepidation down into a deep hole, she took his arm and nodded.

She had pictured this scene a thousand times, but nothing could prepare her for the way the tunnel opened to an old forest with trees towering over the path. Globes of lights floated and twinkled amongst the leaves while the trunks curved to create archways over them. As they walked, Paige thought she glimpsed faces peering from the foliage all around.

The Lord Consort lowered his head towards her. "Pay them no heed, daughter, We are a curious folk."

Daughter. Again. Paige wondered if she should correct him, for she was not quite ready to call them her parents yet. But she held her tongue as they arrived at a glade. The thick green ceiling of the forest gave way to an open sky, all purple and oranges. She recalled a theory that it was always twilight here, but seeing it still took her breath away. As Davin stepped up to the other side of her, she tore her gaze from the distance to study what was before her.

Tall, lithe fae, all looking human save for the odd clothing and sharp features, mingled amongst themselves, the soft murmurs of conversation falling and rising. They didn't stop but turned ever to eye them with curiosity. But as the crowd parted to reveal the center of attention, a woman stared at them. She was youthful and almost too beautiful, as if crossing the uncanny valley. With a wreath of flowers as a crown on top of a waterfall of light blond hair and a tanned complexion, she was an avatar of the sun. Queen Aoife. The Queen of the Summer Court.

Well, I've gone from romance to straight up fantasy. Or would this still be paranormal? This was so not the time to dwell on that question.

With a wave and a kind smile to her subjects, the crowd dispersed to take up their positions around the glade. Meanwhile, she hiked up her dress and glided across to settle in the higher of the two thrones made of trees, branches twisting and weaving with each other into a regal seat, leaves fanning out from behind.

The Lord Consort patted her arm and flashed her an encouraging smile before leaving her side to sit upon the lower throne.

Paige bowed even deeper than before. "Your Majesty." *I look nothing like her. Like them.* She held her position and felt more than saw the fae queen study her. Perhaps she was coming to the same conclusion. Maybe this was all a mistake and Maeve had gotten her mixed up with someone else.

"Welcome to the Summer Court." Her lyrical voice,

though soft, had no problems carrying across the open space. "This is her then?"

Paige tilted her head up just enough to catch the queen addressing Maeve directly.

"Yes, Milady." Maeve also held her position bent at the waist. "And this is her consort."

"Ah, the incubus."

"Well, shall we get started then?"

What? This time, Paige snapped up before she could remember protocol dictated that she should have remained still. The confusion must have shown on her face as a peal of laughter spilled from her biological mother's lips.

"You can't expect that I declare you my heir without some kind of test," she exclaimed, amusement dancing in those cerulean eyes, too vivid to pass for a human.

Heir? "I think there's been a mistake," Paige stammered and added, "Your Majesty" Protocol be damned. This was happening too fast.

"Milady, she wielded the Claíomh Solais," Maeve spoke at the same time.

Queen Aoife gestured for silence. "The Court has been too long without a successor to secure its stability." Her expression softened. "And I have been too long without my daughter. Afford me this courtesy and—" she swept her hand across the air — "the knowledge of our people will be yours."

That wasn't part of the conditions they had negotiated for her visit, but the hint of hope in her face weakened her resolve.

"Your Majesty," Davin spoke before she could, "this isn't why we came. Paige visited to understand the powers waking within her."

And to see if their magic can help me figure out whether the Elder God in my dreams is just PTSD or something else. But Paige didn't give voice to that thought.

Aoife lifted a brow as she regarded Davin as if she was

appraising him for the first time. "Why wouldn't you want to know if the one you bed is the Fae princess of the Summer Court? It would make you a lord consort and elevate your status much."

Paige flushed at both her bluntness on their relationship and the implied insult toward Davin. If Avaline was here, she would be livid from such insinuation.

"With all due respect, Queen Aoife," Davin replied, his posture relaxed, his tone lazy. "I don't give a damn about status, only that the woman I love gets what she needs."

"Then you will have no problem with her taking the test."

What? Irritated now, Paige bit back a growl but spoke up, anyway. "He might not, but I do."

The crowd muttered, but Paige was past the point of caring. "I have the right to know what I am without being your... your..." She waved at the surrounding fae. "Without being turned into your court jester!"

"And it is well within my rights to determine if you are indeed who you say you are before I impart the knowledge of our people." Aoife straightened and tilted her chin up. "In fact, it is my duty to do so."

There! Her in. "Fine. For the information, then. Not for succession." There was no way in hell she was going to let someone she didn't know make her into some fairy princess.

Aoife looked as though she was ready to protest when Midhir placed a hand on Aoife's arm. Paige couldn't figure out what the glance Midhir gave Aoife was, but she sighed.

"Very well. We can discuss matters of succession later."

It wasn't good enough, but Maeve shot her a dark look of warning and it was so unusual of her, Paige snapped her mouth shut.

"So, what form do these tests take, Your Majesty?" Davin remained polite, but Paige detected a note of irritation.

The Queen, however, only laughed as if she could sense his frustration and found it amusing. "It's all very simple, I assure you." She nodded at a group of three fae standing off to one side, and they bowed in return before stepping away.

Curiosity piqued now, Paige watched as they returned with two items. Another held something long, wrapped in red silk, while the others lifted a heavy cauldron between them.

"I have taken the liberty of sending for our treasures from the other courts. Just as you can wield Claimh Solias, the way these sacred treasures react to your touch will determine the legitimacy of your claim." Aoife remained composed, but her eyes gleamed with anticipation.

It seemed simple enough. But what was the catch?

The summer court queen motioned the fae with a come-hither motion, and two of them lifted the large bowl-like cookware to set it before her. Dadga's cauldron of plenty. Paige sucked in a breath as they regarded her with stoic expressions that gave no hint to what their expectations were.

"Maeve informed us that Claimh Solias burns brighter and harder with you as it's wielder. As it had reacted to you because of your heritage, so should these other treasures."

Queen Aoife could be explaining the weather with that casual tone, but Paige did not miss her and everyone else leaning closer. She turned her gaze back to the archaic kitchen cookware her subjects presented before her.

"Go ahead."

Fuck it. Paige grabbed the rim with both hands. For a moment, nothing happened. An immense wave of vertigo washed over her as the strange metal grew hotter to touch and glowed. White light intensified until it swallowed her whole.

The sound of gulls from a distance made her open eyes she hadn't known she closed. Paige stared at the cauldron that seemed to have journeyed with her and beyond that, an endless ocean, water lapping at the sand at her feet. But instead of heat beating down on her, a gentle breeze ruffled her hair and brought gold and orange leaves dancing through the air. Her sight adjusted quick enough as the light dimmed toward the late evening.

"The Summer heir." Whispers surrounded her, and she turned around to locate the source, to no avail. "The changeling." More voices took the title up. "The changeling. The changeling."

Who were they? Where was she? What was going on?

"You know, this trial is fixed. The cauldron's broken."

Paige spun on the balls of her feet to look at the new speaker. She stood with deep auburn curls framing her face and a wreath of fall leaves crowning her head. Younger than Aoife with sharp pixie features, the girl could be a sister of the Queen of the Summer Court.

"Who…?"

"Aurnia of the Autumn Court."

Oh.

"Not that this is the Autumn Court. Just…" Aurnia waved her hand in the air.

"Are you related to Aoife?" Paige blurted out.

A peal of laughter greeted her, and amusement danced in the golden eyes of the fae queen. "You're a bold one for using her name so casually, even if you are supposedly her daughter."

No, Paige would not let Aurnia bait her. Instead, she returned her attention to the famed treasure, running her fingers along the side of now the inert object. She paced herself as she walked around, studying the intricate scenes etched in the metal until she came upon a gash she hadn't noticed before.

This cauldron was not in the shape to hold anything.

"See?" Aurnia spoke right beside her, so close to her ear.

Paige yelped in surprise and jumped.

Aurnia laughed once more, as if delighted by how she

startled Paige. But she ignored the tall, graceful woman in favor of bending down again to study the flaw.

"What happened?" Paige asked without looking up. She brushed one fingertip along to trace the crack.

"Not something you have to concern yourself about."

Paige glared up at her in response, and Aurnia rolled her eyes with a theatrical sigh. She reminded Paige more of a petulant teenager than the capricious queen Aoife appeared to be.

"Spring was careless with it when they loaned it out to a mortal who tried to use it in a way it wasn't intended to be used. This was the result, and everyone agreed that Autumn Court would become its new caretaker."

That was more of an explanation than she expected. She blinked at Aurnia, who gave her a nonchalant shrug.

"So now what?" Paige muttered under her breath. Touching this treasure had brought her here, so theoretically, it already reacted, proving her claim. It was strange that Claimh Solias never took her anywhere. Was it because the cauldron was damaged?

"Tsk. So many questions, but still not asking the right one." Aurnia reached out and hopped her nose.

She was growing tired of these games, and it took a lot of effort to suppress her resentment. If the cauldron hadn't transported sure to the Autumn Court, then this could be a dreamscape.

Which meant all she had to do was wake up to leave

But no. There must be a reason that she was here. Was it part of the test?

"The prodigal daughter figures it out at last!" Aurnia clapped her hands together.

Can she read my mind? Paige studied the fae, but her golden eyes only gleamed with anticipation.

"Fine. I'll bite. What do I have to do?"

Aurnia grinned. "Fix it."

Of course it'd be fixing the damn cauldron. "I don't suppose you have any idea how." Paige tried not to let hope grow within her but if Aurnia was in a more forthcoming mood…

Those inhumane eyes softened in something Maeve had drilled into her to not expect from the Sidhe. Sympathy. "Poor niece of mine. Think. Have Maeve not taught you the lore of our people? What does the cauldron symbolize?"

A clue. "Plentifulness."

"Good. A start. What else?"

She could do this. Words flitted through her head. "Feast. Giving." Paige spitballed words along to Aurnia's growing enthusiastic nods. She peered at the images depicted, the ones of a man offering a platter to two women. "An act of giving," she murmured again.

"Yes. To exemplify selflessness."

"You're talking sacrifice," Paige whispered, a shiver running down her spine.

"Feed it your humanity."

"What?" she stared at Aurnia wide-eyed.

"You must give up something you value. Your ties to mortals will be what holds you back from becoming fae, so it makes the most sense to let that go." Aurnia tilted her head to one side as if puzzled by Paige's reaction. "It's an easy trial. Touch it again and bring your memories of your human life to the surface of your mind."

That was insane. Paige snatched her hand away as if the cauldron had burned her. About to open her mouth to protest, she snapped it shut when she found Aurnia's face inches from hers.

"You're awakening. If you don't get to embrace your powers, they will turn on you and eat you alive."

There was no concern on the Autumn Queen's expression, just a grin now became malicious. It must be true for the fae do not lie but how come Maeve never told her. Did Davin know?

A fog enveloped her mind as she closed her eyes, the shimmering blue of her magic laying under her skin. She recalled the warmth turned painful. And remembered feeling more alive than ever.

Touch the cauldron. Feed it the memories of her life as a human. Do it or implode. Paige touched the treasure of her people with her fingertips. What would it feel like to tame the wilderness inside her?

"You listen to me, Paige Summers. Human or not, you stay true to who you are. And that is all we'd ever ask. And if you so much as to forget a single ounce of your humanity, Ainsley and I will be right here to remind you of it. Got it?"

Lillian's words surfaced in her mind. The edges of the memory faded, and Paige backed away, breaking the contact.

Her humanity or her life.

There was only one answer.

The fog in Paige's head lifted, and she glared at Aurnia. "No."

The Queen blinked at her in surprise. "Excuse me?"

"Send me back," Paige replied instead. "I will not sacrifice a key part of who I am, just to mend something that is not my responsibility." With her resolve hardened, she leveled Aurnia with a firm glare.

"You'll die," Aurnia warned.

"Then I die as a human." Paige lifted her chin and straightened.

Aurnia rolled her eyes and waved her hand. "Fine. Whatever."

Then she was back in a blink.

Paige stumbled and almost toppled over but righted herself in time. Her head spun, and she wondered if she even left at all. She looked around the room to the emotionless visage of Queen Aoife and to Maeve's face, twisted with concern. Where was Davin?

"The spear."

Wait. Why continue this farce? She had already failed her first test. But before she could protest, someone pressed a long pole to her hand. Another immense wave of vertigo washed over her as the weapon glowed like the cauldron. From somewhere next to her, she heard Davin cry out her name and his fingertips brush against her arm. Oh. There he was. And that was her last thought as the weapon swept her away once more.

For a second, her entire world was white silence until sharp laughter rang through the air. Paige spun around even as color bled back into her vision until she could see her new surroundings.

It was still twilight, but this time, night had crept deeper in and dark clouds blotted out the brilliant colors of the Summer Court, fading out into blackness in the horizon. And in the middle of it all, another woman who could be the identical twin to Aoife and Aurnia. Except she had cropped her jet-black hair into a pixie cut and she wore something closer to the modern world with expensive designer jeans torn at the knee and a deep red blouse with the top buttons popped open.

"She would set the trials upon her own daughter. And they call me cruel."

There was only one person this could be. "You're the Winter Queen." Paige had faced an elder god. She refused to be daunted by this woman, no matter how capricious her reputation was.

She dipped acknowledgement. "Queen Ailbhe."

Something pressed harder and harder inside Paige's mind, and she rubbed her temple as she looked around. Ailbhe's violet eyes bore into hers. Oh no, she would not let them influence her mind twice. Paige growl and shook her head clear. In return, the faery laughed again and spun on her heels. "This way."

The pressure eased right away, leaving Paige breathless and disoriented. She called out for Aibhe to wait, but stopped herself before she vocalized the plea. A show of weakness may not be the smartest thing. With an inward groan, she scrambled after the fae queen.

Snow covered the landscape they traveled through, but there was life and growth everywhere she looked. Jack rabbits darted around the underbrush. They passed by a cave and she glimpsed a family of bears deep within hibernating. Winterberries hung from the foliage, bright spots of red amidst evergreens. But always in the distance, the sound of metal clashing and roars a full thunder away.

"What's going on?" Paige asked at last.

"Did you think we do naught but frolic and indulge in our vices all day?"

There was no sting in her words, but Paige wondered if caused offense all the same. "Just—"

Aibhe held a slender hand up, cutting her off. "We train. We prepare."

"For what?" Paige whispered.

"For the day's other races attack. For the days when others seek to steal or take what is ours." She stopped and turned to face Paige in full. "You slayed an elder god. Even you must realize there are consequences."

It was condescending, but a lot of fae were. Paige focused on the underlying message. "You would come to my aid?"

Aibhe shrugged. "It depends." Then she resumed her walk.

Between the lines again. The Sidhe never lied, but she would have to always guess their meaning. Was she offering her the Winter Court's large army in return for passing the test?

"Ah. Here we are."

They stopped in front of a twisted dead tree and Paige stared up in horror. Davin hung in the middle, unconscious, with branches wrapped around his wrists and ankles, holding him up.

"Get him down!" Paige shouted, fear hammering in her chest. Was this what they wanted her to sacrifice now? They were insane.

The Winter Queen nodded in the direction next to her, and she looked down to find Lugh's spear jutting from the ground.

No, no, no, no, no, no, no.

Paige shook her head

"Kill him. Shed your mortal connections."

"Davin's not even human!" Paige screamed.

"He is using you as one." Aibhe's voice, on the other hand, remained indifferent.

"He's my mate." She yelled out without thinking, but the truth of it sank deep into her soul. They didn't just love each other. An untouchable bond joined them forever.

"Is that your answer?" Aibhe asked.

Did she anger Winter? Not that it mattered. Paige braced herself for any consequences that would follow. "Yes."

"Very well."

That was it? No entreating? No threats? Nothing like Aurnia trying to persuade her to go through with the test?

"Wait. What about Da—"

Queen Aibhe waved her hand and this time, the nightmare in front of her faded until she found herself back amongst the trees and faeries of the Summer Court.

"Davin!"

"I'm here." In three strides, he closed the distance between them and pulled her into his arms, hugging him with such ferocity that took her breath away.

"You're okay. You're okay." Paige clung to him, afraid that if she let go, they would whisk him off to their sick twisted games again. She should have come alone. She should have not come at all.

"Paige." He shook her with gentleness that belied the desperation he emanated. "Paige. Look at me."

As she wrangled her fear, she pulled back and stared up at his great golden eyes, so different from Aurnia's.

"They kept me under, but I heard everything. They would not catch me so unaware now that I am guarded. I promise you."

Wait. What? Paige flushed. He picked up everything? Then—

Aoife cleared her throat. "If you are all quite done..."

She would have to deal with the consequences of what happened later. She stepped out of Davin's embrace and he let her go, although his hand lingered on the small of her back.

Aoife stood, regarding them both. "Come walk with us, daughter."

From behind, Maeve stepped up and so did the Lord Consort. Somehow, that reassured her more than before, but she still glanced at Davin, worry turning the corner of her lips downward.

He kissed her on her forehead instead. "Finish this. I'll wait here. Remember, we are mates, which means they cannot break us apart."

Fuck. He heard her. She was certain her cheeks were red as tomatoes right now.

"Go on, my sparrow."

She glanced at her bio parents, then turned to give Davin a searing kiss. He responded, holding her closer, but she stepped back with a teasing grin. "Fine." Before he could reply, she danced away and followed her parents. Sometimes it was fun to be a brat with him and to hold her fears at bay. Laughing in the dark.

"How much of this may we be expecting when we have

those two visiting?" Aoife asked Maeve as they excited the glade, following a trail that Paige hadn't spotted before.

"All the time, I'm afraid, my Queen." Maeve replied with wry humor in her voice

Aoife let out a small sigh of resignation as she waved her hand. There had always been a background of whispers, murmurs and giggles, but all that fell silent.

"Ah, privacy at last," Midhir breathed out.

"There is one more trial, daughter. We go to it now."

"Wait." Paige stopped in her tracks and set her hands on her hips. No more mysteries. She would get her answers. "I failed the other ones, so what's the point?"

Aoife turned and a slow smile spread across her lips and she appeared warmer. Next to her, Midhir let out a laugh.

"If it helps, your mother did not pass those tests either."

"What?" Paige stared at them, her mouth opening. The two seemed like different people, closer to the ones she pictured in her head, the ones that inspired Maeve's loyalty and the ones that would do anything to protect their daughters.

"You must go through the trials in this order, but only this last is certain. There is no pass or fail, only a measure of the type of ruler you may become in the future."

Oh no, not this again. "What if I don't want to be a ruler? I can't just walk away from my life, from my friends and the family I have."

Aoife walked back toward her and held her by the shoulders. They were the same height and for the first time, Paige found little small similarities in the way their eyes pointed, how their hair parted. "And we can talk through what that looks like on another day. But come, this last part, you must face on your own. Have courage, daughter of mine."

The three of them parted for her to reveal a stone arch, a monolith similar to the ones found at the famous Stonehenge.

The Lia Fáil. Legends dictated it would scream when the right sovereign of the Tuatha dé Danann passed under it.

Paige stepped back, hesitation and wariness making her stiffen. "I thought you said this wasn't a heritage test," she stammered.

"It isn't. The Lia Fáil has many functions, not just in determining the rightful ruler. Go on."

She glanced at the three of them, but at Maeve's nod, she sighed. "Okay, okay." She walked forward but paused as Midhir grabbed her arm and pulled her into a hug.

"Be strong, my daughter. And stay true to yourself like you already have," he whispered and let her go.

Still puzzled by how he would even know, she turned to glimpse the space between the stones fill with light. Well, fuck it.

She steeled herself and walked through it.

And found herself home once more. Except, she wasn't, for she saw Ainsley and herself as well as another woman their age, vaguely familiar, sitting around Lillian's large wooden dining table.

"So, what do we do?" the stranger asked with a sign of resignation as she looked at the two of them, rocking the chair on its back legs. Why was grief etched on all their faces including her own?

"We have no choice. We have to defend ourselves," Ainsley replied.

"But what do we have to fight with? You realize these are the elder gods. Immortal beings that have been alive since the dawn of time. The kind that could drive a person mad just by their appearance alone, right?" The woman remained seated, feet on the table and gestured.

"We have the Winter and Summer Courts' forces with us," the other Paige spoke. She almost didn't recognize herself in those words. Calm, confident, glowing with power.

Was this her future she was seeing? Or is that what would

have happened had she passed her tests? But it wasn't just her. Ainsley glowed with magic too. A different kind, Paige's senses told her, but still, something all the same.

"Paige!"

She recognized Davin's voice and watched as he rushed into the house, Dante and Finn behind him. Dante held a sword, dripping with blood, the same weapon he fought with when they faced the monsters outside of Anna's place before. A loud crash and a horrible screech followed them from somewhere outside.

Then they all faded away.

"Wait!" Paige reached out. She needed to watch more. To know more.

"It'll break you if you see more. Why do you think Seth drinks so much?"

She was becoming quite annoyed by the disembodied voices trying to surprise her. "That was one possibility of all the futures?"

"I was always a clever one."

I. Paige turned to stare at herself. Or another version of herself that had pointed ears and silver hair. Her eyes glowed the ocean blue of her power. This was her had she stayed in the dun. Had she survived growing up with her parents.

"Hello Paige."

"Hello…" Of all events that she had lived through the last few months, this trial took the cake.

"Cadhla Ní Argatliam. That is my true name. Our true name."

Paige blinked at her. She did not know even how to spell what she just said, much less call it her own.

"I thought you were the Lia Fáil," Paige offered, feeling rather lame.

"Hmm. yes I am that too," her double started then shook her head. "It's too complicated to explain but let's get back to you."

With a snap of her fingers, Paige found herself laying on a couch and her other self sitting on a wheely chair with glasses perched on her nose. *Like a therapist's office.*

"So, tell me, Cadhla, or Paige as you prefer. If you want to remain human, why are you here?"

Paige pushed herself up but about to protest, she cut herself off. There was a seriousness the way her double studied her with and it hit her. This was all a metaphor. An important one. *Okay, I'll play along.* "Because... of my powers. I need to understand what I am," she replied.

"Very valid." Cadhla scribbled something in her notebook. "And what have you figured out so far?"

Paige glanced around the office and noticed so much of her own life represented. The books on a shelf nearby comprised ones she authored and some of her all-time favorites. The desk was a replica of the one she wrote at home, her laptop perched on top. A photo frame hung on the walls, in it, a snapshot of her Christmas with her parents.

"That I failed the trials so I won't be able to control my powers and I'll explode. Or implode. Not sure which yet." She couldn't help the bitterness in her voice.

"Aurnia said you would die if you..."

Paige scrunched up her nose to recall the exact words. "If you don't get help to embrace your fae powers, they will turn on you and eat you alive," she quoted. Oh. Get help. Not pass the trials.

Cadhla grinned. "Mmhmm."

Paige formed an O with her mouth. "So..."

"Our parents love us. They knew what could happen when they sent you to the human world. But they are also Queen of the Summer Court and Lord Consort. They have to act the way their positions dictate them. They would never have been able to get you here to me without putting you through all the trials."

The implications threatened to overwhelm her. "So, who am I? What am I?" Paige whispered.

Cadhla jumped up from her chair and spread her arms out the room. "Look around you. You are who you are. Nobody could ever change that. The *what* could never change that." She hopped over to sit down next to her. "Our experiences shape us, just like this one will set you on the path to discovering what is possible for you since you've seen what the extent of the queens' abilities." She leaned and rested her head against Paige's shoulders. "And I can't wait to see what we can do."

She felt their powers. The truth of Cadhla's words settled within her in a way she couldn't explain. She hadn't realized that until Cadhla explained it. "I can't wait either." She wrapped an arm around her other self and closed her eyes.

When she opened them again, she stood in front of the inert stone, staring at her family, Blue caressed her skin before the power faded back to a sort of sleepy contentment.

"Well done," Midhir's tone warmed with approval.

But Aoife didn't wait. She hiked her dress up, ran up and flung herself on Paige. "Welcome home, daughter."

***

So now she had two sets of parents. Paige curled up against Davin on the couch, her head resting against his shoulder, his arm around her shoulders as she reviewed the trials with a fresh perspective.

"What are you going to tell your human parents," he asked.

She considered for a moment then let out a soft sigh. "Nothing. I played it out in my mind a thousand times. Why bring them the grief." She closed her eyes. "This decision will haunt me for the rest of my life. Maybe they deserve the truth. Maybe I'm being selfish. But I don't know what telling them would accomplish other than hurt them."

Davin's arm tightened around him. "I think there's no right or wrong answer here."

"No. No there isn't."

They fell to silence but not long after, Davin spoke again. "So Cadhla…"

"She's in me. Or I'm in her. But whatever it is, I am content. My powers, I'll figure out but they don't feel… scary anymore. And my psychological wounds…" Paige shrugged. "I suspect it'll get better once I use my magic more actively."

Davin squeezed her shoulder. "I'm glad." The pride in that single word made her grin, but that faded at his next words, replaced by heat crawling up her cheeks. "So… mate…"

She could deny it but if The Lia Fáil had taught her anything, it was the truth of things important. Besides, she was fae. Lying would bring dire consequences. "Yes. Mate."

Paige felt more than saw Davin's smile. "Good."

ACKNOWLEDGMENTS

Often a writer's life is depicted as this lonely road one travels on with only their characters as companions but that is often far from the case. Instead, I have been fortunate enough to travel on this journey with friends that help me battle foes such as self-doubt and other fears.

So, I want to take this opportunity to thank AJ, my alpha reader who always embraces my story with an unbound enthusiasm, Lori, my PA who believes my abilities far more than myself, Tracy, my editor who brings a certain discipline to my words that make them sing and my tireless street team out there getting my stories heard.

My appreciate goes out to my husband, who makes the space for me to write and tells me to never quit and my two kids without whom I would be writing significantly faster, or not writing at all.

To my readers of the early version of this story on Inkitt and Wattpad, I don't think Davin and Paige would have made it to full book format without you. Your support means the world to me. And to you, the reader who holds this book in your hand, thank you for coming along for this ride.

If you've enjoyed the story, please consider leaving a review where you can. It goes a long way to helping spread the word on the story.

Go raibh maith agat!

ABOUT THE AUTHOR

P. Stormcrow grew up with a love for love and somehow that turned into authoring contemporary and paranormal BDSM romances. Fierce women and sensitive men fill her stories while she examines social norms and challenges conventional tropes of the genre through her craft. Born in Hong Kong and raised in Canada, she enjoys writing about both cultures.

She's also a techie, a graphic designer, a mother, a lover, a fighter and a little bit of everything else in between. When she's not typing away madly on her phone and running into poles, she enjoys copious amounts of tea, way too many sugary treats and all the sci-fi / fantasy / paranormal shows TV has to offer.

Find out more on her website at https://pstormcrow.com

AN EXCERPT FROM BOUND BY RED

Want more stories featuring fierce women like Paige in paranormal romance? Here's an excerpt from P. Stormcrow's most popular novella, Bound by Red.

BOUND BY RED

Scarlet stared at the empty seat before her, wondering why the fuck she agreed to this. Oh yeah, one of her friends had insisted on having someone to share her foray into online hook-ups. At first, Scarlet was horrified, then curious, and when she matched with a six-foot-two, made-of-abs, flannel-clad Adonis who worked at the local sawmill, she had to admit the ego boost was nice. Plus, he was a first-class skilled flirt. At least online. Scarlet wondered what G-ma, who was forever trying to match make for her, would say if she knew she was now meeting boys from a phone app.

If only Mr. Lumberjack would show up and prove that he wasn't catfishing.

Right now, him ghosting seemed a more likely possibility. Her date was late, and he wasn't replying to any of her messages. Scarlet glanced at the clock, then at the door, before taking a sip of her all-too-expensive chai latte. At least she had the foresight to treat herself.

The jingle of bells by the door announced another customer and when Scarlet turned, her heart skipped a beat.

If her date was the sun with his fair coloring of blonde hair and baby blues, then this man was of the night. Disheveled jet-black hair accompanied even darker eyes set in a face chiseled with high cheekbones and tanned skin. He wore a black t-shirt despite the cooling weather, one that only accentuated the rippling muscles beneath though he was far from a bulky build. Every movement spoke of a predator's grace but rather than fear, it evoked something else within her.

She grew warmer between her legs and wished that he was her Tinder date instead.

He turned and she caught the full impact of his focus. She stiffened, her cheeks warming with embarrassment as she realized he had caught her checking him out. But the intensity of his gaze held hers, making it impossible to look away. Something else tugged at her from the inside, something beyond the lust he first inspired when he walked in the door.

"Scarlet?"

Her real date, fifteen minutes late, walked right into her line of sight, forcing her to look up instead.

Oh, fuck. He was the real deal. Her eyes widened and her lips parted in a small O.

When he returned her stare with an amused quick of his lips, she swallowed to rehydrate her suddenly dry throat and stood up too fast, jostling the table, almost spilling her drink. She made a grab to steady it only to brush her hand against his as he had reached out with the same idea. With an awkward laugh and a mumbled thanks, Scarlet withdrew her hand quick enough. "Yeah. Derrick, right?"

The smile he gave her was every bit as charming as she discerned from the photos, a mix of warmth with a hint of charm tugging at the corners. She forced herself to relax a smidge and tried to remind herself that if he was here, the attraction was mutual. Scarlet dug deep for confidence and reassured herself that she had outgrown that awkward gangly nerd persona that had plagued her when she was younger.

"I'm glad we finally get to meet in person." Without waiting for a response, he stepped closer to her and drew her in for a hug.

Scarlet stiffened, enveloped with sudden warmth. She could hear his heartbeat and reddened, confusion clouding her mind. It was a level of intimacy she had not expected and her breathing shortened in response.

"And you're even more adorable in person." His lips brushed by the tip of her ear as he whispered.

Her own heart pounded like thunder in her ears. Part of her melted into a little puddle. Another part wondered if he was being too presumptuous with his invasion of her personal space and whether she should be protesting.

Before she could decide, however, he stepped back. "I'm going to go grab a drink. Be right back."

"Sure." She wasn't sure if he heard her as he stepped away without waiting for her reply. Was this confidence on his part or arrogance?

Scarlet's mind wandered from the question, leaving it unanswered. Instead, she found herself scanning the rest of the coffee shop for the dark-haired man she saw earlier. No luck. He had disappeared as if he was no more than a figment of her imagination. And maybe he was? An unsettling pang of regret settled in the pit of her stomach. Perhaps it was for the best. She sat once more, returning to the drink in front of her more for lack of anything better to do.

www.ingramcontent.com/pod-product-compliance
Lightning Source LLC
Chambersburg PA
CBHW061608100726
47898CB00002B/571